GARY SEVEN'S UNCONSCIOUS BODY WAS THROWN TO THE FLOOR . . .

. . . while Isis's claws scratched futilely at the polished steel surface of the control panel as the cat tried to keep from sliding from its perch. A shrill siren started blaring as, all around the engineering sections, circuits began to pop and explode.

"God help us all, lads," Scotty said softly.

STAR TREK®

ASSIGNMENT: ETERNITY

GREG COX

POCKET BOOKS

New York   London   Toronto   Sydney   Tokyo   Singapore

An *Original* Publication of POCKET BOOKS

POCKET BOOKS, a division of Simon & Schuster Inc.
1230 Avenue of the Americas, New York, NY 10020

STAR TREK is a Registered Trademark of Paramount Pictures.

A VIACOM COMPANY

This book is published by Pocket Books, a division of Simon & Schuster Inc., under exclusive license from Paramount Pictures.

ISBN: 0-671-00117-5

First Pocket Books printing January 1998

10 9 8 7 6 5 4 3 2 1

POCKET and colophon are registered trademarks of Simon & Schuster Inc.

Printed in the U.S.A.

Acknowledgements

Thanks to Art Wallace and Gene Roddenberry for making "Assignment: Earth" one of my favorite episodes of the original *Star Trek* series, not to mention Robert Lansing and Teri Garr and, of course, Isis.

Thanks also to John Ordover, for letting me bring all these characters back; to Sumi Lee, for Russian profanities; to Patrick Nielsen Hayden, for going to amazing lengths to install a balky ditto drive; to Howard Weinstein for beating me to the punch with a Gary Seven comic book; to Tor Books, for letting me make a graceful exit (of a sort); and, most of all, to Karen, for hours of careful reading and contemplation.

ASSIGNMENT: ETERNITY

Prologue

Camp Khitomer, Khitomer Outpost
United Federation of Planets
Stardate 9521.6
A.D. 2293

THE TRAITOR'S BLOOD still pooled on the tile floor. Excitement, and a nearly palpable sense of relief at the disaster so narrowly averted, suffused the assembly hall. Ambassadors, ministers, and delegates from a dozen different worlds looked on in shock and amazement.

"It's about the future, Madame Chancellor," Captain James T. Kirk declared as he helped the President of the Federation back onto his feet. The President held his hand over his heart, shaken by his close brush with death only moments before. "Some people think the future means the end of history. Well, we haven't run out of history quite yet."

Kirk stepped away from the podium and the President, addressing his explanation to a regal-looking Klingon woman standing nearby. Chancellor Azetbur, daughter of the martyred Klingon leader Gorkon, listened gravely.

Near the back of the spacious chamber, amidst the stunned onlookers, a lone Romulan went completely unnoticed. All eyes were on Kirk and Azetbur. *Good,* Commander Dellas thought, savoring her apparent anonymity. It was just as she'd planned.

"Your father called the future 'the undiscovered country,'" Kirk continued. "Some people can be very frightened of change."

Only a few meters away from Kirk, Commander Spock stood guard over his prisoner, the disgraced Starfleet officer Valeris. Slowly, cautiously, Dellas began to work her way through the crowd towards the elevated stage where Spock and his comrades-in-arms now stood. Her eyes zeroed in on the unsuspecting Vulcan.

Azetbur weighed Kirk's words, then nodded somberly. "You've restored my father's faith," she said.

High above the heads of the delegates, a shattered glass skylight testified to the location of the failed sniper's former perch. *A difficult shot,* Dellas decided, coolly evaluating the traitor's attempt to shoot the Federation President. *I will not make the same mistake.* Easing and elbowing her way through the throng of spectators, keeping to the left to avoid the sizable Klingon delegation, she drew ever nearer to Spock and his crewmates. The Vulcan remained unaware of her approach, intent on the historic drama unfolding before him.

"And you've restored my son's," Kirk replied to Azetbur. Throughout the assembly hall, ministers and ambassadors from many different worlds rose to applaud Kirk and his companions. Dellas clapped as well, the better to blend with the crowd. She quickened her step, a determined look upon her face, until only a single row of applauding delegates stood between her and the platform occupied by honored Starfleet heroes. Ironically, she found herself standing directly behind Sarek of Vulcan, her target's legendary father, and a young Romulan delegate. *Pardek,* Dellas thought grimly, recognizing his face from her preliminary research for this mission. Was it just her imagination, or was the future senator already eyeing Spock with a thoughtful, scheming expression on his face?

She glanced about quickly to see if anyone was watching her, but all eyes remained on Kirk and Spock and the others as they accepted the gratitude of the entire assembly. *Excellent,* she thought. There would never be a better opportunity. Ceasing to clap, she slipped her hand beneath her grey civilian robes and drew out a compact, palm-sized disruptor. The metallic weapon felt cool in her hand.

Spock stood less than seven meters away from Dellas, a few steps to the left of his captain. His calm, impassive face offered no clue to his feelings at this moment. Dellas considered his poise and dignity. *Just like my father's.* She experienced a twinge of regret at what she had come to do.

Then she raised her weapon, took aim, and fired.

A coruscating beam of hot, blue energy flashed through the gap between Sarek's and Pardek's heads. Kirk gasped in horror as the beam zipped past him to strike Spock. The Vulcan's stoic expression betrayed only momentary surprise before the disruptor beam dissolved his molecular cohesion. The destructive energies suffused his body, consuming it entirely. For an instant, there was a glowing blue silhouette where Spock had stood, then nothingness. "No!" Kirk cried out as he watched his friend disintegrate before his eyes.

The assembly erupted into pandemonium. Dozens of delegates, humanoid and otherwise, shouted and cried out as they fought each other to reach the exits. Dellas heard Spock's father emit a single, strangled sob before letting the crowd's desperate flight carry her away. She deftly slipped her weapon back into her robes. *Done,* she thought. She felt calm, relaxed, almost Vulcan in her serenity. *It doesn't matter if they catch me or not. I've done what I had to do.*

Spock was dead, and the future had been changed forever.

Chapter One

811 East 68th Street, Apt. 12-B
New York City, United States of America
Planet Earth
A.D. 19 July 1969

As USUAL, she felt lost in the fog. The glowing azure mist, swirling and luminescent, enveloped her completely. She could see nothing but blue all around her, hear nothing but her own rapid heartbeat. No matter that she had entered this unnatural fog dozens of times before and emerged safely each time; part of her always worried that *this* time she would disappear into the mist forever.

Don't be ridiculous, she told herself. *You use elevators, don't you? You don't worry about crashing down twenty-five floors every time you step into an elevator, right?*

Yeah, another part of her psyche replied, *but elevators are normal. Traveling by radioactive smoke is just too freaking out-of-this-world!*

She stepped forward, deeper into the mist, which did not feel cold or moist like real fog; it was a seething cloud of energy that tingled like static electricity and seemed to pass beneath her skin and between each individual molecule of her body. For a

5

heart-stopping second, she felt as if she was dissolving into the fog, as if there was no longer any difference between her and the swirling mist, and she hastily frisked herself to make sure she was all still there. She ran her fingers over the rough denim of her jeans, her soft, cotton, tie-dyed T-shirt, the bangs of tinted, honey-blond hair just above her eyes. Still solid. Still intact. Thank God.

Was this trip taking longer than usual? Although she had only entered the fog moments ago, it felt like centuries. "Hello?" she called out. "Are we there yet?"

As if in response, the fog grew thinner before her eyes. Through the churning blue haze, she glimpsed a darkness beyond—and a blinking green light somewhat further on. She rushed forward and suddenly the fog was gone. She stumbled onto a carpeted floor, tripping slightly as if she had encountered an unexpected step, but managing to keep her balance. She shook her head, torn between exasperation and relief. After the fog, coming back to reality—any reality— was always a bit of a jolt.

At first, all she could see was a translucent green cube, about three inches wide, floating in the darkness a few feet away. A chartreuse glow lit the cube from within, flashing even more brightly for an instant just as the cube emitted a curiously feminine "beep."

Then, as if summoned by the beep, the overhead lights came on, revealing a neat and tidy office decorated with contemporary furniture. The green cube sat atop a large black desk, next to a silver pen and pencil set. The carpet turned out to be a pale orange color, matching a couch and plush chair across the room from the desk. Framed paintings, landscapes mostly, hung on the walls, except where cedar bookshelves occupied one entire wall of the office. Encyclopedias, atlases, and other hardcover reference books filled the bookshelves.

The room's ordinary-looking furnishings were reassuringly familiar. "Home sweet home," she murmured, then turned around to look back the way she'd came.

What she beheld provided a jarring contrast to the mundane appearance of the rest of the office. A shining steel door, more suitable to an airlock or a bank vault, stood wide open, exposing a darkened chamber in which the luminescent fog continued to swirl and billow, seeming to come from nowhere yet never spreading beyond the rectangular boundaries of the doorway. No matter how hard she strained her eyes, she could not see beyond the fog; for all she could tell, the shadowy tunnel behind the fog could have stretched to infinity—and probably did. *I am never going to get used to this,* she thought.

Her sneakers, a new pair of P.F. Flyers, tapped impatiently against the carpet as she peered into the fog. "C'mon," she muttered. "What's taking you so long?"

The mist refused to answer her. She glanced over at the flashing green cube on the desk, wondering if she should risk interrupting the process by consulting the cube. "I'll give them five more seconds," she decided. *Four, three, two . . .*

Just as she was about to give up, a figure appeared in the mist, hazily at first, but quickly gaining form and definition. Unlike her, he emerged from the fog with the calm and confidence of one completely at ease with the procedure. He was a tall, slender man dressed in a conservative gray suit. His neatly trimmed brown hair was edged with gray at the temples, while his light brown eyebrows faded, almost to invisibility, against his craggy features. The man's face wore a grim, sober expression, lightened somewhat by a hint of ironic amusement. His right hand gently stroked the head of a sleek, black cat he held securely against his chest.

Always the cat, she thought. *So how come kitty can't come through on her own? I did.*

7

The cat let out an inquisitive mew. A collar of silvery fabric glittered around its neck. Its eyes were brilliant yellow ovals pierced by thin slits of black.

"Yes, Isis, we made it," he murmured to the cat. Behind him, the fog faded into nonexistence, leaving not even a stray wisp to linger in the office. The empty space beyond the doorway now looked merely dark and featureless, like an unlit closet. The green cube beeped again, and the heavy steel door began to close automatically. Wooden panels slid out from hidden recesses in front of the doorway, concealing the gleaming metal door behind three shelves of cocktail glasses. Within seconds, all traces of the enigmatic fog chamber had vanished from sight.

The blond woman was no longer surprised by the office's transformation; she'd witnessed the change too many times before. "About time," she protested, crossing her arms as she leaned back against the sturdy desk. "What kept you?"

"A few last-minute details," he replied, "but I think I can now safely guarantee that Col. Armstrong will take a very remarkable walk tomorrow."

"Really?" She let out a long sigh of relief. Her eyes widened as the full enormity of the man's statement sunk in. "Wow. Man on the moon. Even after all I've seen in the past year, I can still barely believe it."

"Welcome to the Space Age, Miss Lincoln," said the man who called himself Gary Seven. He placed the cat gently onto the carpet. "Trust me, this is only the beginning."

Roberta Lincoln, age twenty, walked across the office and dropped onto the orange couch. Isis, her furry black nemesis, hopped onto the couch as well, and Roberta scooted down to the other end of the couch, putting at least one full cushion between them. "The beginning," she repeated. "That's what that spaceman from the future, Kirk, said, too." She sunk deeper into the couch, her gaze drifting heavenward as if she could probe the depths of interstellar space right through the ceiling of the office. "Good thing me and you got to help out a bit."

Isis made an indignant squawk.

"Oh yeah, you, too," Roberta conceded. *Sheesh, now even I'm talking to the cat! Bad enough that the boss keeps Kitty better informed than me. . . .*

Seven, also known as Supervisor 194, allowed a bit of a smile to curl his lips, apparently amused by the byplay between Roberta and Isis. He removed his jacket and hung it neatly over the black metallic chair behind his desk. "All part of the job," he said, loosening his necktie. "The human race has enormous potential, but it still needs a little help now and then."

Some job, Roberta thought. Tearing her gaze away from the ceiling, she glanced around Seven's unassuming office. When she'd first started working here, for Seven's immediate predecessors, she'd had no trouble accepting that "encyclopedia research" was all that was going on. *Boy, was I in for a surprise. If I told anyone else half of what goes on in here, they'd think I was pulling their leg—or that I'd lost my mind.*

"You know," she said, "the way you talk, sometimes I think you forget that you're part of the human race, too."

The wry smile disappeared from Seven's face, replaced by a more pensive expression. "Very perceptive, Miss Lincoln," he said, a touch of melancholy deepening his voice. "You may have a point there. Knowing what I do, having been where I've been, there is a bit of a . . . distancing effect." He gave her a serious look from across the room. "I'll have to count on you to keep me in touch with the rest of my species."

"Uh, sure," Roberta said, uncertain how to respond. How do you relate to a guy whose ancestors have been trained by aliens for six thousand years? "Say, that *2001* film is still playing a few blocks away. I haven't seen it yet." Had Seven (she could never think of him as Gary) ever gone to the movies? She had no idea. "Maybe we can hit a matinee some-time?"

Isis hissed and gave Roberta a dirty look. She scratched her claws on the arm of the couch.

"Hey, don't blame me," Roberta said. "It's not my fault they don't let cats into the movies." Of course, Isis wasn't always a cat, but Roberta tried not to think about that. It was just too weird. "So, what do you say?" she asked Seven. "I'll even spring for popcorn. Dutch treat."

Seven opened his mouth to respond, but was interrupted by a piercing, high-pitched whistle from the cube on his desk. The glowing cube flashed urgently, and Seven reacted as if jolted by a live electrical wire. Movies and moon landings were instantly forgotten as Seven snapped to attention. He was out from behind the desk in an instant, striding across the floor toward the bookshelves. "Computer on," he said sharply.

"What is it?" Roberta asked, quickly catching Seven's mood. Isis sprung from the couch, landing on all four paws only a few inches away from the bookshelves. The fur along the cat's neck lifted itself in alarm.

"Emergency beacon," Seven explained, his gaze glued to the wall containing the bookshelves, which now began to swing outward, rotating a concealed computer bank into view. Flashing horizontal and vertical lines, in various combinations of colors, formed changing patterns on the surface of a gleaming, high-tech computer that was the size of a large refrigerator. Seven called it a "Beta-5" computer, although Roberta had no idea what exactly distinguished it from, say, a Beta-4 or a Beta-6. She only knew that Seven's computer, based on an ancient alien technology, was smarter than any other machine on Earth, circa 1969. She wondered if the rest of the world's computers would ever catch up with the Beta-5. *Not in my lifetime,* she thought.

A circular viewscreen, smaller than the average television, occupied one section of the apparatus. "Computer, identify distress signal," Seven instructed.

The Beta-5 responded to his vocal command. "Executing," the machine reported. Its voice, although identifiably feminine, had a distinctly inhuman echo. "Signal is fragmented due to transtemporal interference."

"Transtemporal?" Seven said. Judging from the tone of his voice, Roberta decided that was not good news. *Transtemporal,* she thought, *as in time travel?* She hopped off the couch and hurried to join Seven and Isis by the computer.

"Confirmed," the Beta-5 stated. "Tracking source of transmission. Location: Romulan Star Empire, coordinates 83-62-171. Date, by current Earth chronology: 2269 A.D."

Roberta's jaw dropped. *2269? Three hundred years from now?*

Seven merely nodded grimly in response to the computer's startling revelation. "Can you reconstruct the content of the transmission?"

Illuminated lines flashed in sequence. "Attempting to integrate signal." Visual static appeared on the view screen. Roberta looked over Seven's shoulder, trying to discern some sort of recognizable image from blurry electronic snow. She wished she knew what she was looking for.

A pattern began to take shape upon the screen. Soon she could make out a scratchy picture of a man's face, accompanied by snatches of a desperate voice interrupted by bursts of static:

"146 to 194 . . . exposed . . . capture imminent . . . technology beyond . . . at risk . . . future history . . . recommend . . . urgent . . . self-destruct . . . emergency . . . no escape . . ."

Roberta thought she heard a harsh, sizzling noise in the background, followed by a loud, metallic crash.

Then the static cleared for an instant and she got a better look at the speaker. To her surprise, she saw that he had the same sort of strange, pointed ears as that Martian guy, Mr. Spock. He looked in bad shape, like he'd been in a fight. His lip was swollen and a trickle of green fluid ran down the man's face from a nasty-looking gash on his forehead. *Green blood?* she thought. This was too weird.

The sizzling noise grew louder. The face on the screen screamed once, a ghastly sound that tore at Roberta's heart, and the screen went blank. "146," Seven barked, "please respond. This is 194. Repeat: respond immediately!"

The screen remained blank. "Transmission halted at origin," the Beta-5 announced. Seven's head drooped below his shoulders. He clenched his fists in frustration. For a second, he looked incredibly tired.

"Mr. Seven?" Roberta asked hesitantly. "Are you okay?"

He lifted his head and stepped away from the computer. He took a deep breath. "I'm fine," he answered, "but I'm afraid the future is not."

"The future?" Roberta echoed.

"Precisely, Miss Lincoln, but which future? That's the real question." All business now, he addressed the Beta-5. "Computer, analyze future history for divergence from standard time line."

Lights blinked upon the face of the futuristic apparatus. A loud hum emerged from the machine as it processed Seven's request for at least five minutes. Roberta was taken aback by the delay. She had never known the Beta-5 to take more than ten seconds to answer any query, no matter how complicated. "Is something wrong?" she asked.

Isis seconded Roberta with an inquisitive meow. Seven shushed them both as the Beta-5 spoke at last. "Alternate time line established. New future deviates significantly from established parameters."

"Point of divergence?" Seven demanded.

"2293 A.D. Khitomer Peace Conference. Assassination of Spock of Vulcan by anomalous temporal element prior to initial meeting with Pardek of Romulus. Result: elimination of Vulcan-Romulan reunification efforts in latter half of the twenty-fourth century."

The twenty-fourth century? Roberta wondered, struggling to keep up with the computer's revelations. *When did we get on to the twenty-fourth century? What happened to 2269?*

"I see," Seven said thoughtfully. "Source of anomaly?"

"2269 A.D. Romulan Star Empire. Coordinates 83-62-171."

Okay, Roberta thought. *That's more like it.* She still had no idea what was going on, except that someone was going to kill Mr. Spock—who hadn't even been born yet! Never mind the Age of Aquarius, her mind wasn't expanding fast enough to keep up with all these bizarro concepts. She still had trouble believing that she had actually met an intelligent being from outer space; now she had to worry about his assassination, almost a hundred and twenty-five years from today? *Help,* she thought. *I need an Excedrin.*

On the rug, Isis meowed and rubbed her head against Seven's trousers until he picked her up. Roberta wondered grumpily if the cat had figured out any more than she had.

Seven walked briskly across the office and retrieved his jacket from the back of his chair. "I'm afraid I have to postpone any movie plans," he stated. "We have to leave again, immediately."

"For 2269 or 2293?" Roberta asked, hoping that it was a blatantly ridiculous question. *Please tell me he's not saying what I think he's saying.*

Seven answered quite matter-of-factly. "2269. That's the root of the trouble." He placed Isis on the top of the desk and put on his jacket, then pushed down the pen attached to his pen and pencil set.

Roberta heard a familiar clicking sound, and watched as, across from the desk, the shelves of decorative glassware receded into their hidden crevices, exposing the massive steel door guarding the fog chamber. A circular handle on the door spun automatically, and the doorway swung open once more. Roberta gulped as Seven hurriedly manipulated a control panel on the inner face of the door. She didn't like the looks of this.

"Time travel?" she asked. "You're not joking, are you?"

"As you may have noted, Miss Lincoln," Seven replied, "I seldom joke."

Isis sprung off the desktop and padded over to Seven's side. To her dismay, Roberta saw an unnatural blue fog began to form inside the interior of the hidden chamber. "Why the big hurry?" she objected. Things were moving far too fast for her. "The future's not going anywhere, is it?"

"The longer we delay, the further it may go off-track," Seven explained curtly. Seeing the bewildered look on Roberta's face, he paused to elaborate. "Future events can sometimes threaten the past, Miss Lincoln. Indeed, our own continuing knowledge that the future has been changed may have the effect of ensuring that change unless we take action to reverse it; even the primitive quantum theory of this era concedes that the act of observing reality can actually change the reality being observed."

Roberta's head was inclined to take Seven's word for it. "This is one of those step-on-a-butterfly, change-the-whole-world kind of things, right?"

"Basically," Seven confirmed, "but in reverse. It's not common, and it's certainly not reasonable, but it is possible, take my word for it. We have to act now, before any temporal backwash robs us of the opportunity."

"Oh," Roberta said, trying to come to terms with the concept. "Do I need to pack?"

Seven cracked a smile. "You'll find the twenty-third

century extraordinarily well-stocked." He checked his suit's inside pocket, drawing out a slim silver device the size and shape of a fountain pen, then replacing the device in his pocket. "I believe I have everything we need. Except——" A new thought seemed to occur to him. He rushed back to the desk and picked up the green cube. "Here," he said, tossing the cube toward Roberta. "Take this."

The cube chirped when she caught it. She snatched a psychedelic handbag off the plush orange chair by the couch, and stuck the cube into the bag.

The luminescent fog swirled within the confines of the chamber. It looked to Roberta like a glowing blue whirlpool, a vaporous vortex from which she might never return. Gary Seven stood to one side of the doorway, holding Isis against his chest. "After you," he said.

Roberta swallowed hard. *2269*. How long would it take to travel forward three hundred years? What would the world possibly be like then? She glanced back over her shoulder at the wooden doorframe on the other side of the office. Beyond that door, she thought, lay her world as she knew it: Manhattan, movies, and moon landings. "Here goes nothing," she whispered.

Taking one last look at the twentieth century, she stepped back into the fog.

Chapter Two

Captain's log, stardate 6021.4.

The Enterprise *is on an emergency mission to the planet* Duwamish. *Massive flooding has endangered the Federation colony there, and Starfleet has directed us to deliver desperately needed food and medical supplies, as well as to assist any necessary evacuation efforts. As the* Enterprise *is the only Starfleet vessel in this sector, I can only pray that we get to Duwamish before too many lives are lost.*

"YOU SHOULD GET some sleep, Jim," Dr. Leonard McCoy groused. "You look like hell."

Captain James T. Kirk sat up in his chair upon the bridge of the *Enterprise*, strenuously resisting an urge to yawn. The ship's chief medical officer hovered beside him like an anxious mother hen. "That's a harsh diagnosis, Bones," he protested. "Whatever happened to your bedside manner?"

"I'm a doctor, not a diplomat," McCoy said. "I'm serious, Jim. It's been less than a week since that nasty

business with Dr. Lester, and here you are, pushin.
yourself as if nothing at all had happened to you. Foi
heaven's sake, Jim, your entire mind was transferred
out of your body and back again. That's not exactly
like getting over the flu."

Thanks for reminding me, Kirk thought. It wasn't
one of his happier memories, although the experience
of living within a woman's body had been . . .
educational, to say the least. He was glad to be back in
his own flesh and bones, though. For a while there, it
had looked like his five-year exploratory mission was
going to come to an abrupt and singularly frustrating
halt. "You said there were no side effects," he reminded the doctor.

"I said I couldn't *find* any side effects," McCoy
said. He shrugged his shoulders beneath his blue
medical uniform. "I also prescribed plenty of rest,
just to be safe."

I don't need rest, Kirk thought defiantly, *I need
action and a chance to get back to work.* The last
thing he wanted was to spend more wasted hours in
his quarters, "recuperating." Emergency quarters
had to be prepared for refugees from Duwamish.
Food rations and medical supplies had to be cata-
logued and prepped for immediate usage. Emotional
counseling would need to be provided for those who
had lost their loved ones and their homes. Kirk made
a mental note to himself to make sure all the ship's
transporters were capable of functioning at maximum capacity, just in case they'd need to relocate
large quantities of settlers in a hurry. He reached for
the command intercom panel on the port console.
Better check with Scotty, he thought. *Get an update
on the status of the primary energizing coils and
pattern buffers . . .*

"I'm serious, Jim," McCoy persisted, placing a
restraining hand on Kirk's arm. "You have a good
crew. Trust them to do their jobs without you for a
few hours."

"Spock, help me out here," Kirk said, attempting a light, breezy tone. "Dr. McCoy is trying to drive me from the bridge."

Spock stepped away from the bridge's science station, where myriad lighted panels and controls glowed against the polished black surface of the science console. He descended into the sunken command module to stand near Dr. McCoy. "As unusual as it may seem," he said, "I must concur with the doctor in this instance."

"What?" Kirk exclaimed. "Spock, not you, too?"

The Vulcan first officer displayed no reaction to his captain's look of betrayal. "Even at maximum speed," he explained, "we will not reach the Duwamish system for 9.4 hours. It is only logical to conserve your strength until it is needed."

"Hah!" A broad grin broke out on McCoy's weathered face. "I never thought I'd have to fall back on Vulcan logic, but our pointy-eared friend here has the right idea. Save your pigheaded stubbornness for some time when it might actually do some good."

"I guess I'm outnumbered," Kirk said, deciding to concede defeat gracefully. He scanned the bridge, reassuring himself that all was in order. Sulu was at the helm, while Chekov and Uhura held down their usual posts at the navigation console and the communications station, respectively. On the main viewer at the front of the bridge, the stars zipped by at warp speed. One of the astronomical prints mounted above the duty stations caught his eye: a full-color reproduction of a swirling nebula, now forever frozen in space and time. The bridge of the *Enterprise* struck him at this moment as just as durable and unchanging as that two-dimensional nebula. *Maybe Bones is on target after all,* he thought, *and the ship can get by without me for a few hours.* He rose from his chair and stretched, no longer bothering to suppress a weary yawn. A nap was sounding better and better. "Mr. Spock," he announced, "you have the bridge."

He was just turning toward the bright red doors of the lift entrance when, without any warning, a tremendous vibration shook the bridge. The floor beneath his feet rocked from one side to another. Kirk seized the armrest of his chair to keep from being thrown to the floor. On the opposite side of the chair, McCoy was not so fortunate. The ship's doctor staggered back and forth, then began to pitch forward. He fell toward the hard duranium floor, only to be rescued at the last second by Spock, who somehow managed to take hold of McCoy's arm while simultaneously maintaining his own balance. *Good work,* Kirk thought as he struggled to keep standing. "Red alert!" he called out to his crew. Uhura, holding tightly onto the communications console, responded at once to his command. Red warning lights began flashing all around the bridge, accompanied by a high-pitched siren that drowned out the gasps of the other crewmen.

The vibration lasted several seconds, during which he could feel the throbbing of the floor through the soles of his boots. Then the shaking began to subside, and the bridge gradually righted itself as the *Enterprise* stabilized its course. Kirk dropped back into his chair, all thought of rest forgotten. "All stations report, what the devil was that?"

"Captain," Ensign Chekov called out. "Sensors report a transporter beam of *astounding* power, a hundred times stronger than anything we've got!"

A transporter? Kirk thought. He had never felt a transporter beam like that before, except for—his brain resisted the notion that occurred to him—but that was three centuries ago!

Spock's mind seemed to be racing down the same channels. "As I recall, Captain," he said, releasing his grip on McCoy, who had regained his balance, "we have experienced this phenomenon before. . . ."

"Captain, look!" Chekov interrupted as two blurry blue outlines suddenly materialized at the front of the bridge, only a couple of meters away from Sulu's station at the helm. The figures were blurry at first, seemingly composed of a swirling blue energy, then quickly defined themselves. Alerted by his memory, Kirk recognized the intruders even before they fully solidified.

It was Gary Seven and his attractive young sidekick from the twentieth century. What was her name again? Kirk quickly retrieved the data from year-old memories. *Roberta Lincoln, that was it.*

But what were they doing aboard the *Enterprise* in this day and age? Kirk had never expected to encounter the pair again, let alone in his own time and on his own ship. Even their clothing, he noted, belonged on Earth a few centuries ago. Seven wore an antiquated suit and tie, while his female companion had dressed more casually in a loose-fitting, multicolored shirt and a pair of faded denim pants. They both looked like they had stepped out of some sort of historical costume drama.

Chekov leaped from his seat and drew his phaser. Sulu looked ready to do the same. Even McCoy instinctively placed his hand on the medical tricorder hanging from a strap over his shoulder. "Don't move," Chekov ordered the newcomers, "or I will fire."

Seven ignored both the young ensign's weapon and the blaring alarms. "Hello again, Captain Kirk, Mr. Spock," he said calmly. As usual, Kirk noticed Seven had his cat with him. The sleek black animal nestled against Seven's chest, seemingly unruffled and undisturbed by its journey through time and space. By contrast, Roberta Lincoln looked around with wide-eyed astonishment; Kirk guessed she'd never seen the interior of a starship before. "Forgive the intrusion," Seven stated, "but I need your assistance."

"Captain?" Chekov asked, sounding confused. He kept his phaser aimed at the intruders. "Do you know these people?"

"You can stand down, Ensign," Kirk replied, rising from his own chair. Flicking a switch on the command functions panel on the starboard armrest of the chair, he deactivated the siren and blinking red lights. "Cancel red alert status." It occurred to him that few of the crew had actually met either Seven or Roberta; only he and Spock had actually beamed down to Earth during that mission. "I don't think you'll need that phaser, at least I hope not. Meet Gary Seven and Roberta Lincoln. They're time travellers from twentieth century Earth, or so I assume."

Cradled in Seven's arms, the cat squawked noisily, as if angry at being overlooked. Kirk didn't even try to remember what Seven's pet was named, although he found it slightly odd that Seven never seemed to go anywhere without the cat. *At least it's not a tribble,* he thought.

"Good Lord," McCoy said, staring in amazement at the strangers on the bridge. Kirk wondered if the doctor was remembering his own harrowing trip to Earth's Depression era, McCoy's only firsthand encounter with the twentieth century. "Kind of a long way from home, aren't they?" the doctor said. "In time *and* space."

That was certainly true, Kirk thought. Earth was hundreds of light-years away from their present location, not to mention a century or three removed from Seven's own time. *This must be serious,* he thought. Seven wouldn't have come all this way without a strong reason.

"Excuse me, Captain," Lieutenant Uhura spoke up from her post at the communications station. She pressed a compact silver receiver firmly against her ear. "Chief Engineer Scott is hailing you from engineering. He wants to know what's happening."

"Tell Scotty the situation is under control," Kirk instructed.

"I'm glad you think so," McCoy grumbled. The doctor gave his captain a dubious look.

Kirk shrugged, then turned his attention to their unexpected guests. "All right, Seven, what's so important that you had to shake up my ship to get here?" His fists clenched at his sides. *That damn beam almost shook my ship apart,* he thought. Last time around, the *Enterprise* had intercepted Seven's transporter beam by accident. *Don't tell me that this was just another coincidence. I won't buy it.*

"I'm here on an urgent mission, Captain, the nature of which I can't fully disclose. Unfortunately, in this century, I don't have access to all the resources I had in your past, so I need the *Enterprise* to help me complete my mission."

"You'll have to tell me more than that," Kirk challenged Seven. He walked across the bridge, stepping up from the command module and circling around the navigation console until he was less than a meter away from Seven and his companions. "I suppose you are still working on behalf of some mysterious alien benefactors—"

Seven nodded.

"—whose nature and location you're still unwilling to divulge?"

"Exactly," Seven confirmed. "I trust you appreciate the delicacy of my position, Captain. As a visitor to your era, I don't wish to disturb future history any more than absolutely necessary. At present, your Federation remains unaware of my sponsors, thus it is imperative that I do nothing to change that situation."

Kirk shook his head, scowling. "That may have been good enough back in the twentieth century, but not anymore. Your activities in the past are a matter of history; there's nothing I can do about them. But this is my era now—my present—and you're the one who doesn't belong here. And I don't like the idea of you, or the aliens you represent, meddling with our affairs. Humanity's grown a lot since the twentieth century. We don't need any cosmic baby-sitters these days."

"Actually, Captain," Seven replied, "that's exactly why I need your help. In this century, the human race has indeed graduated to a higher level of civilization, and no longer requires the intervention of my superiors."

"Well, bravo for us," McCoy said. He had remained within the circular command module, keeping one hand on the red guardrail just in case the ship lurched again. "Hear that, Spock? Modern-day *homo sapiens* isn't nearly as primitive as you think."

"No matter what level of advancement, Doctor," Spock answered, not far from McCoy's side, "there is always room for improvement. Especially with regard to humanity's frequently unrestrained emotions."

"What's wrong with emotions?" Roberta blurted out. Her gaze, Kirk noted, kept drifting back to the points of Spock's ears. *Just wait till she sees an Andorian,* he thought. *Blue skin and antennae are even more eye-catching.*

"Please, gentlemen," Kirk asked Spock and McCoy. "Not now." He turned back to face Seven. "What are you saying? That the Federation is outside your jurisdiction now?"

"More or less," Seven said in a noncommittal manner. "That's why there is no organization or infrastructure in place to assist me in this era. My superiors, and my successors, are occupied elsewhere in the galaxy, safeguarding the development of sentient races that your civilization will not encounter for generations to come." Seven calmly stroked his cat's head as he spoke. "Given time, I could certainly acquire a starship of my own, and whatever equipment and personnel may be required to complete my mission, but time is exactly what is at stake."

"Meaning what?" Kirk demanded, growing annoyed by Seven's cryptic remarks. He was exhausted, the ship was facing a difficult rescue mission, and the last thing he needed now was a meddlesome time traveler with a secret agenda. True, Seven had proved trustworthy the last time they met him, but that didn't mean Kirk was ready to turn over the *Enterprise* just at Seven's insistence. *I need more than that,* he thought. *A lot more.*

Seven paused, weighing his words carefully. "I can tell you that I'm here to untangle a temporal paradox that threatens both our futures."

Kirk didn't like the sound of that. He knew, from painful experience, just how fragile the time line could be. Memories of Edith Keeler came unbidden to his mind. "What sort of paradox?" he demanded. "Is something going to happen to change the past?"

"No," Seven said. "But your own future could be changed—has been changed—unless action is taken immediately. I have reason to believe that an event damaging the proper procession of history will originate several hours from now, at a specific location within this quadrant. Trust me, that's all you need to know, except for the coordinates of our destination."

"I need to know a good deal more than that," Kirk protested. "This ship is not going anywhere, except on its current course, unless I hear something better than a couple of ominous hints and warnings."

Seven refused to give in. "Think about it, Captain Kirk. Do you really want to know your own future?"

Now there's a question to give one pause, Kirk thought. There was a reason that time travel into the future, although theoretically possible, was expressly forbidden by every responsible scientific and civil authority. Not even a Klingon really wanted to know the day of his own death. Certainly, he thought, Edith Keeler had been better off not knowing her ultimate destiny. Kirk glanced at McCoy and wondered if the doctor was thinking of Edith, too. It had been nearly three years since they'd both watched her die, but the very thought of time travel still brought up too many painful memories.

"As far as I'm concerned," Kirk answered finally, "the future is not set in stone. I'm planning to get there the old-fashioned way, one day at a time."

"Unfortunately," Seven said, "your enemies may not share your patience. It may interest you to know that the source of the temporal anomaly lies within the current boundaries of the Romulan Empire."

"Good Lord," McCoy exclaimed.

"Fascinating," Spock commented.

"The Romulans?" Kirk said, momentarily surprised that Seven had even heard of them. Seven obviously knew a lot more about the universe than the average twentieth century human, but just how familiar was he with present interstellar politics? *Are the Romulans really up to something,* Kirk wondered, *or is Seven just playing on my justifiable paranoia where the Romulan Empire is concerned?* He frowned; it had been less than one standard year since the Romulans had formed an alliance with the Klingon Empire, and the situation remained tense. The *Enterprise* had nearly been captured by Romulan forces the last time Kirk crossed the Neutral Zone.

"Please, Captain," Roberta spoke up. "I don't know who or what a Romulan is, but I know you can trust Mr. Seven. I've been working with him for months now, and he's definitely one of the good guys."

"It's not necessarily a matter of trust, Miss Lincoln," Kirk replied, deciding to direct his attention to Seven's youthful secretary. Perhaps she would be more forthcoming than her tight-lipped employer. "This is a Starfleet vessel. I'm responsible for the safety of my crew and the security of the United Federation of Planets, including the planet Earth. I can't just take off on some sort of wild-goose chase because of something that might happen in the future." He gave Roberta his most charming smile. "I don't suppose you know what this is all about, do you?"

The cat in Seven's arms hissed angrily. Roberta flinched, then gave the feline a dirty look. "I wasn't going to say anything!"

Seven stepped between Kirk and Roberta. "If you have any more questions, Captain, you can direct them to me. Although I can't promise you all the answers you'd like."

"This is my ship, Mr. Seven, and I'll interrogate anyone I have to," Kirk said. He looked Seven squarely in the eye as he quite deliberately stepped around the other man to speak to Roberta again. "We may have been born in different centuries, Miss Lincoln, but we're both from Earth. I'm from Iowa, actually. I know we both have Earth's best interests at heart, but, to be honest, I'm not entirely sure where Mr. Seven's true loyalties lie. What do you know about these mysterious aliens he works for?"

The cat hissed once more, but Roberta ignored the animal's warning. She cast a quick glance at Spock, then looked away nervously. "Er, well," she hesitated, clutching a brightly colored handbag to her chest. "I'd like to help you, Captain. I really would. But Mr. Seven . . . he works on a strictly need-to-know basis, you know? James-Bond style. For your eyes only, and all that. This tape will self-destruct in five seconds. . . ." She shrugged her shoulders. "I'm just along for the ride."

James who? Kirk wondered. He didn't buy Roberta's dumb act for a minute. He knew she knew more than she was letting on. *With a little more time,* he thought, *it might be possible to win her trust, maybe coax more of the truth out of her.*

"Captain," Seven said, "I can assure you that I am not working on behalf of the Romulans, the Klingons, the Tholians, the Gorn, or any of your present antagonists. My sponsors are far beyond the petty power struggles of this era. But time is of the essence. We must embark for Romulan space immediately."

At the helm, Sulu looked back at Kirk, ready to make the course correction if necessary. "Sir?"

"The Romulan Empire," Kirk said to Seven, "in case you've forgotten, is off-limits to all Starfleet vessels. Crossing the Neutral Zone could be seen as an act of war. I'm going to have to think long and hard about your request," Kirk said honestly. He strode past Seven, back to the captain's chair. Taking his seat, he gestured towards the main viewer. "In any event, there's nothing I can do for you right away. As it happens, the *Enterprise* is already on a vital mission that cannot possibly be delayed."

Seven glanced at the stars streaking past on the viewer. He seemed unimpressed. "I'm sure your mission is very important, Captain, but the danger I've detected has to take priority. All of future history is at stake."

"Listen, Seven," Kirk said, anger coloring his voice. "I've had quite enough of your high-and-mighty, all-knowing pronouncements. I'll give your warning serious consideration; you've earned that much for your benevolent efforts in the past. But right now there are thousands of lives at risk on a planet several light-years away. Real flesh-and-blood lives, not vague, unspecified time paradoxes, and the *Enterprise* is the only hope those people have."

"Amen," McCoy muttered, his hand on the back of the captain's chair. "We're on a mission of mercy, damnit."

"Spock," Kirk asked, "how far are we from the Duwamish system?"

The Vulcan did not need to consult any monitors to provide an answer. "Approximately 8.23 hours, Captain, assuming no further interruptions."

"Thank you, Mr. Spock," Kirk said. He looked

across the bridge at Gary Seven. "There you have it, Mr. Seven. In a little over eight hours, we will arrive at our current destination and commence relief operations. By then, hopefully, you'll have decided to share a little more of your information with me, so I can make an intelligent decision regarding your proposal."

The furrows on Seven's brow deepened, and, for a moment or two, Kirk was convinced that Seven was going to argue the matter further. Instead, Seven sighed deeply and stroked his cat's head. "Very well, Captain, if that's your decision. I only hope the future will survive your doubts."

"That's a risk I'll just have to take," Kirk said. "In the meantime, consider yourselves guests aboard the *Enterprise*. Mr. Chekov, escort Mr. Seven, Miss Lincoln, and, er, their pet to the visitor's quarters on Level Three."

"Aye, sir," Chekov responded briskly. He kept one hand poised above his phaser, just in case. Seated at the helm, a few centimeters away, Sulu studiously examined the images on the main viewer. He looked relieved that Kirk's confrontation with Seven had been defused so easily.

"Actually, Captain," McCoy spoke up. He walked over to join Chekov and his charges. "I wouldn't mind giving our guests a quick once-over in sickbay. Twentieth-century Earth was a cauldron of virulent and contagious diseases. I want to make sure no nasty bugs travelled through time with them."

"That's not necessary, Doctor," Seven said. Kirk wondered if Seven had merely guessed McCoy's profession, which wouldn't be too difficult given the doctor's reference to sickbay, or if he could actually spot a Starfleet medical officer by his uniform. Just how much did Seven know anyway? "The transporter mechanism screens for viruses and bacteria."

"Indulge me," McCoy said with a grin. "When was

the last time I got to observe real-life products of ancient medicine close-up." He peered at Roberta's own friendly smile. "Good God, are those actual metal fillings in your teeth? You poor child!"

The cat in Seven's arms flashed her own ivory fangs at the doctor.

Chapter Three

So this is the future, Roberta thought as their two escorts guided she and Seven through the corridors of the *Enterprise.* So far she liked what she saw. A bit sterile and antiseptic, perhaps, but remarkably clean and civilized-looking. If she hadn't known better, she would have never guessed that she was actually aboard a spaceship. Compared to the cramped capsules that the Apollo astronauts had been squeezed into, these roomy hallways were positively spacious. Her brain automatically compared her present surroundings to the NASA space footage she'd seen on television. "Hey," she asked as an idea occurred to her, "how come we're not all floating around weightlessly?"

"Artificial gravity," the younger crewman said with a unmistakably Russian accent. His name was Chekov, Roberta recalled, thinking that he reminded her of one of the Beatles. Paul maybe, or George. "It's revolutionized space travel, ever since it was invented by some very brilliant scientists at the University of Moscow."

The older man—Dr. McCoy, Roberta remembered—snorted at Chekov's remarks. "I think the Vulcan Science Academy might have a bone to pick with you."

"The first *Terran* prototypes were tested in Moscow," Chekov insisted patriotically. Roberta just shook her head in amazement; she was still flabbergasted to see Russians and Americans working together in space. What had happened to the space race, not to mention the Cold War? She was old enough to have vivid memories of the Cuban Missile Crisis. The situation aboard the *Enterprise* seemed so far away from those nerve-wracking days of fear and suspicion that it was almost impossible to believe that they were *merely* three hundred years in the future.

And that wasn't the half of it. Just looking around the bridge where they'd first arrived, Roberta had seen a black woman, a Japanese man, a couple of Americans, a Russian—and an honest-to-goodness *alien,* for pete's sake—all cooperating together peacefully. Compared to 1969, it was like some sort of wild, utopian fantasy. *Wow,* Roberta thought, feeling deeply moved all of sudden. It seemed like the late Martin Luther King's dream had actually come true after all: a world where no one was judged by their race or nationality. "This is fantastic," she said.

"This old place?" the doctor said with a grin. Roberta caught a trace of a southern accent. "It's nice of you to say so, but you should see Earth these days."

"I'd like to," Roberta replied. Her eyes widened as a Chinese woman in a bright red uniform hurried past them in the hall. "Gee," she exclaimed, "who would have ever guessed that miniskirts and go-go boots would still be popular in the twenty-third century?"

"Excuse me?" asked the mop-topped young Russian. "What do you mean?" *On second thought,* Roberta mused, *maybe he reminds me more of one of the Monkees.*

"Everything old is new again," Seven commented dryly. Isis purred in agreement. Seven bent over and carefully placed the cat on the floor. "Unfortunately, we're not here for sight-seeing."

Party pooper, Roberta thought. Her annoyance turned to alarm, however, as she saw Seven casually remove his servo from the inside pocket of his jacket. The slim silver device looked deceptively harmless, but Roberta knew just what Seven's weapon was capable of. *Oh-oh,* she thought, experiencing a twinge of guilt. *Here we go again.*

"What's that?" McCoy asked, glancing at Seven. "Some sort of—" Before he could even finish his question, Seven pointed the tip of the servo at the doctor. There was a brief hum, then McCoy's entire body began to sag slowly toward the floor. A dreamy smile broke out on his face.

"Wait! What are you doing?" Chekov said, reaching for the weapon attached to his belt. Some sort of ray gun, Roberta guessed. Seven was too fast for him, though. The servo hummed again, and Chekov's arms dropped limply to his sides.

"That's all right," Seven said soothingly as he gently guided Chekov's drooping body onto the floor next to the slumping form of Dr. McCoy. He removed Chekov's weapon and handed it over to Roberta, who looked at it warily. The Russian crewman offered no resistance; the servo's tranquilizing beam, she knew, left its victims quite suggestible. "Pleasant dreams, gentlemen."

"Did you have to do that?" she asked. The two future-men had been very pleasant and hospitable; it seemed a shame to ambush them like that.

Isis mewed sarcastically, perhaps anticipating Seven's response. "We cannot afford to wait for the captain's cooperation," he announced. Stepping away from the fallen crewmen, he placed his ear against a sealed doorway built into the corridor wall. "Sounds empty," he said. "Excellent." Roberta scowled, unsure if he was talking to her or the cat. Sometimes it was hard to tell.

He adjusted the setting on his servo, then directed it at the closed door. Roberta heard something sizzle inside the door just before it slid open. Peering into the shadowy chamber beyond the door, she saw what looked like ordinary living quarters. Unoccupied, thankfully.

"Over here," Seven instructed. Placing his arms under Chekov's shoulders, he dragged the sleeping Russian into the empty room. "Help me with the other one."

Roberta stuck the stolen ray gun into her belt, then grabbed hold of McCoy and pulled him toward the now-open doorway. Adding insult to exertion, Isis paced along beside her, meowing emphatically. "I don't require any supervision, thank you very much," Roberta grunted, straining to get the doctor's body out of the corridor as quickly as possible. What if someone came along and caught them in the act? She could just imagine explaining *this* to Captain Kirk.

"I don't get it," she said as the doctor's heels disappeared into the chamber. "Why didn't we just wait until we got where we were going before you zapped them? Why pull this stunt in the hall?"

Straightening from a crouched position, Seven returned the servo to his pocket. "To be honest, I wasn't entirely sure how large a staff served the ship's medical facilities. I didn't want to have to deal with any possible nurses or interns." Isis padded across the floor and jumped back into Seven's arms. "An excellent question, though, Miss Lincoln. Your strategic instincts are improving."

Yeah, that's me, Roberta thought. *The Girl from U.N.C.L.E.* She cast a guilty look back at the snoozing crewmen, easing her conscience by remembering that the tranquilizer effect was quite harmless, not to mention distinctly pleasant. *Sleep tight, guys,* she thought. *Sorry we had to knock you out.*

At the doorway, Seven peeked cautiously around the edge of the door, then withdrew his head back into the chamber, looking around speculatively. "There must be a manual control," he murmured, either to himself or to Isis. "Ah, here it is." He slid the smooth metal door back into place.

Roberta quickly assessed their surroundings. The stateroom consisted of a bedroom, a work area, and a private bathroom with a weird-looking shower. *Pretty cozy,* she decided; frankly, it was bigger and cleaner than her apartment in the East Village. *And I bet they don't get cockroaches, too.* Was this strictly the VIP quarters, or did everyone aboard get one of these nifty little compartments? *If so,* she thought, *where do I sign up?*

Seven dropped Isis onto the bed, then removed his jacket. "I'm going to borrow the ensign's uniform," he said. He gestured towards what looked like some sort of futuristic closet. "See if you can find an appropriate disguise for yourself."

"What are the odds of that?" she asked out loud, turning her back while Seven changed. "Just how sexually integrated is the future anyway?"

"You may be surprised," Seven commented from somewhere behind her. "I estimate there must be over a hundred humanoid women serving aboard the *Enterprise.* It shouldn't be too hard to find a uniform for you. If not in this cabin, then perhaps one nearby."

"A couple hundred?" she blurted. This was one big ship. To her relief, though, Roberta discovered that the current occupant of the stateroom apparently wore dresses. Retrieving a bright red outfit like the ones she'd seen on some of the female space-travellers, she disappeared into the bathroom while Seven contemplated what looked like a small, portable television set. "Computer," he addressed the machine, "display interior schematics of U.S.S. *Enterprise,* highlighting the most efficient route from this location to main engineering."

"Working," the machine replied in a feminine voice that Roberta thought sounded rather warmer and more human than the Beta-5's artificial voice. Maybe because it was actually programmed by humans?

"That little thing is a computer?" she asked a few minutes later, emerging from the bathroom. The red uniform was snug in a few places, but it seemed to fit enough to pass casual inspection, or so she hoped. The boots squeezed her toes as she walked, making Roberta pine for her comfy sneakers. She sighed. Nobody said being a time-travelling secret agent was going to be easy.

Seven did not look up from the illuminated screen, which cast a bluish glow upon his face. Although Chekov's golden shirt and black trousers barely fit him, he looked very much at home in this era. "A computer terminal, to be precise," he explained, "but it's told me everything I need to know. The ship's engineering section is just a turbolift away."

Isis was curled atop Seven's neatly folded pile of twentieth century garments. "Let's go," he said, and the cat leaped from its newfound bed to rendezvous with Seven in front of the door. "Are you ready, Miss Lincoln?"

"I guess so," she replied. *Ready for what, exactly?* She often wished Seven wasn't so secretive by nature. "What should I do about the purse? It doesn't really match the uniform."

Seven squinted at the brightly colored Peter Max

Greg Cox

design on Roberta's handbag. "I see what you mean."
He scanned the compartment until his gaze landed
upon a black leather bag resting on a shelf above the
computer station. "What about that?" he suggested,
pointing at the bag.

She hurried over as fast as her ill-fitting boots
permitted and lifted the bag from its shelf. There was
a shoulder-length black strap attached to the bag and
a folded-over flap held closed by a snap. She unfas-
tened the flap and peeked inside, spotting a piece of
metal hardware about the size of a small record
player. "What's this?" she asked, lifting the device
from the bag. It was surprisingly lightweight.

"A tricorder," Seven declared. Observing the puzzled expression on her face, he added, "Don't worry
about it. I'll explain later. For now, just transfer the
multipurpose controller to the black bag."

Roberta nodded. She knew he meant the green cube
that had sunk to the bottom of her handbag; she
didn't think he'd want her to leave it behind. She dug
through the scattered contents of her bag, overturning
pieces of wadded-up kleenex, a spare set of keys, a
pack of spearmint gum, loose change and subway
tokens, tickets to an upcoming Bob Dylan concert,
nail clippers, and a paperback copy of *Stranger in a
Strange Land* before she finally located the polished
crystal cube. Pacing back and forth in front of the
sealed doorway, Isis hissed impatiently.

"I'm coming, I'm coming!" Roberta said, dropping
the cube into the tricorder bag, then slinging the bag
over her shoulder. "Keep your fur on, okay?"

Operating the manual controls, Seven slid the door
open. He stepped furtively into the hallway, then
beckoned for Roberta and Isis to join him. His servo
was tightly gripped in his other hand, she noted. Once
Roberta and the cat were in the corridor, Seven
carefully closed the door behind them, concealing the
dormant bodies of McCoy and Chekov from any stray

passersby. "This way," he said. Isis jumped into his arms.

They had almost reached the nearest elevator—*turbolift,* Roberta corrected herself—when a pair of crewmen, one tall, one short, came around a corner, walking directly toward them. Roberta gulped. Would their borrowed uniforms fool these two? It was hard to imagine that the *Enterprise* was so big that a couple of unfamiliar faces could go unnoticed, but maybe it was. *I should probably think in terms of the* Queen Mary, she thought, *and not an old-fashioned Saturn rocket.* Her heart pounding, she glanced over at Seven, but he kept his gaze fixed straight ahead of him. His face betrayed no sign of anxiety.

Chatting casually, the two men drew nearer to Seven and Roberta. They seemed to be paying no attention to either she or Seven, and, for a second, Roberta experienced a surge of relief. They were going to get away with it! Then the tall man halted in his path and stared at Seven. "Hey," he said, and Roberta felt her mouth go dry, "where'd you get that cat?"

Figures, Roberta thought. *I always knew that damn cat was going to get us in trouble someday.*

The man came closer, peering at the sleek black animal in Seven's arms. "I used to have a cat just like that, named Midnight, but I left her with my sister in the Andromeda system." He leaned his face in toward the cat's. "Hello, girl. Are you friendly?"

"That depends," Roberta said. *Just our luck. We have to run into a cat-lover.* The man reached out to pet Isis's head, but the cat backed away, nestling in against Seven's chest.

"Now, now, Isis," Seven chided her. "Be good." The cat snorted, then grudgingly allowed the man to stroke the top of her head. *Maybe we can still bluff our way through this,* Roberta thought.

The other man wandered over to join his buddy.

Roberta noted that the tall man had a yellow shirt, while the short man wore red; she wondered what the significance was. Some sort of military ranking, or simply a fashion statement? There was still too much she didn't know about this future society. She felt like she was flailing around in the dark. *Can't they tell,* she fretted, *that I don't belong here?*

"I've been tempted to get a new cat," Isis's admirer said, "but I heard that the captain isn't too keen on having pets aboard, especially after that tribble business."

Tribble? Roberta wondered. *What's a tribble?*

"Isis and I have been together a long time," Seven volunteered. "I can't imagine going anywhere without her. Isn't that right, girl?"

Tell me about it, Roberta thought ruefully. She wasn't sure how much longer she could fake all this friendly chitchat. Her smile was feeling more and more forced with each passing second. What did they do to spies in deep space, she wondered. Toss them out an airlock? "Say, shouldn't we be checking on that . . . tricorder?" she improvised.

"Tricorder?" the other crewman said. He glanced at the bag hanging from her shoulder. "Looks like you got one already."

"Er, it's not working right. We're taking it in for repairs," Roberta said, kicking herself mentally. Tricorders, tribbles . . . how was she supposed to keep up with all this kooky future jargon?

"Here, let me take a look at it," the short man offered, reaching for her bag. "I've got a knack with tricorders."

"He does," his friend confirmed, still stroking Isis's fur. "I once saw him recalibrate a medical tricorder to detect subspace vibrations—and in three minutes, no less."

"No!" Roberta said, holding on tightly to the strap of her bag and trying not to look too alarmed. "I mean, thanks a lot, but you really don't need to bother. It's not an emergency or anything." Out of the corner of her eyes, she saw an almost imperceptible scowl appear on Seven's face. They were rapidly losing control of the situation, and losing time as well. Was anyone expecting them in sickbay? How long could they remain at large before the captain realized they were up to something? Her free hand drifted toward the ray gun stuck in her belt. *Like I really know how to use it,* she scolded herself.

"It's no problem," the overly helpful crewman insisted. Maybe all these future people were just a little too friendly and hospitable, Roberta decided. Why couldn't they be more like New Yorkers? He reached again for the bag. "What sort of trouble is it giving you?"

"A bad case of tribbles?" she guessed. Both men looked surprised by her response. "Subspace vibrations?" she tried again.

. Seven sighed loudly. "Go ahead, Isis," he murmured. "Say hello to the nice man."

Without warning, the cat leaped from Seven's arms, hissing and striking out. "Hey!" the cat-lover cried out, staggering backwards as Isis sunk her extended claws into the man's golden shirt, hanging on to the man's chest with all four paws. The man tried to pull the enraged cat away from his body, but Isis snapped at his hands, drawing blood. *Now you're seeing that cat's real personality,* Roberta thought. *Nasty, isn't she?*

"Hey!" the other crewman shouted. He lunged for the cat, but Roberta tripped him by sticking out her leg. The man stumbled forward, almost losing his balance. The distraction gave Seven time to pluck his servo from inside his boot and zap the short man with a powerful dose of the tranquilizer beam. A beatific smile replaced the anger on the man's face as he slid peacefully onto the floor.

Seven instantly turned his attention to the remaining crewman, still grappling with Isis. So far, the cat had succeeded in leaving five bloody scratches down the man's cheek. "That's enough, Isis," Seven barked, and the cat sprung away from her opponent, landing on all fours several meters away. Seven pointed the servo at the other man and fired. Midnight's proud owner slumped to the floor beside his friend. "Hurry," Seven said to both Isis and Roberta. He rushed to the turbolift entrance and pressed the call-switch.

Roberta ran after him. "Shouldn't we dispose of the bodies?" *Listen to me,* she thought. *We sound like Bonnie and Clyde.*

"No time," Seven declared. The turbolift arrived almost immediately. The doors slid open with a hiss, and Roberta followed Seven inside. Isis was the last one in; the automatic doors almost closed on her coiled black tail. While Roberta looked unsuccessfully for a button to press, Seven grabbed onto a handhold position at waist-level. "Main engineering," he requested.

The turbolift started moving without even the tiniest bump. Compared to some of the creaky, bouncy, jerky elevators Roberta had ridden in Manhattan and elsewhere, the turbolift's progress felt almost motionless. Roberta couldn't tell if they were traveling horizontally, vertically, or both. "Pretty neat," she commented. Isis squawked back, perhaps irked by the close call with her tail.

They arrived seconds later, coming smoothly to a halt. "Here we are," Seven announced, turning to face Roberta. He retrieved Chekov's ray gun from her belt. "Create a distraction," he instructed.

Sure, she thought sarcastically. *No problem.* The doors slid apart and she stepped out into what she assumed was the ship's engineering section. Isis trotted between her legs.

Roberta's eyes widened in amazement. Engineering was more impressive than anything she had seen on the ship so far. It was at least two stories high and as large as an airplane hanger. Computer banks adorned with all sorts of flashing lights and monitors lined the walls, except at the far end of the chamber where a huge pane of tinted glass or plastic offered a breath-taking view of several huge turbinelike structures. Those *have* to be the ship's engines, she thought. She hadn't seen anything like them since she'd toured the gigantic hydroelectric generators at Grand Coulee Dam as a child.

A least a half-dozen men, most of them clad in red or brown jumpsuits, scurried back and forth, attending to the vast machines. They seemed too busy to notice her at first, then a stocky, dark-haired man wearing a red shirt and black trousers noticed her standing in front of the turbolift entrance. "Hello there, lassie," he called out with a thick Scottish brogue. "What can I do for you?"

A distraction, Roberta recalled. *What in the world—whatever world—did Seven have in mind? Surely he couldn't zap all these people before some-body sounded an alarm.* "Uh, hi," she said. "I was trying to find sickbay, but I think I got lost." At her feet, Isis added a chorus of meows. *That's right,* she thought, giving the cat a hostile glare, *upstage me, why don't you?*

"Looks to me like you need a vet more than a doctor," the Scottish man said. He walked toward her. "If you don't mind, lassie, I like to keep wee animals away from my engines." He gestured at the turbolift—just as Gary Seven stepped out from behind the curved walls of the turbolift. He seized Roberta by the waist and held Chekov's stolen ray gun to her temple.

"This phaser is set on kill," Seven said grimly. His tone was so icy that Roberta actually felt a bit nervous for a second. "Don't move a muscle, or I'll fire."

"You!" the engineer exclaimed. He obviously rec-ognized Seven from before, although Roberta didn't

41

remember him. "What the devil are you doing here?"

"Never mind that," Seven barked. "Where are the controls for the warp engines?"

"Just put the phaser down, mister," the engineer said. By now, the apparent hostage drama had attracted the attention of the entire engineering section. The other men stood by helplessly, a few of them producing phasers of their own and occasionally glancing at the man in the red shirt. Roberta couldn't be sure, but she got the impression that the Scottish guy was in charge.

"Please, sir," Roberta pleaded, playing along with the gag. *What do I call him? Officer? Lieutenant? Sergeant?* "Don't let him kill me. Ohmigod, I'm too young to die!"

"Don't overdo it, Miss Lincoln," Seven whispered in her ear. "Remember, you're a Starfleet officer."

Everyone's a critic, she thought, half-expecting Isis to put in her two cents worth, too.

"The warp controls," Seven repeated. He pressed the muzzle of the ray gun—scratch that, *phaser*—against her skull. Roberta hoped he knew what he was doing. "Now."

The head engineer hesitated, clearly unsure what to do. "Blast it," he muttered, "I should have recognized the bloody kitty." He stared at Roberta, perhaps trying to identify her place in the crew. *He's onto us,* she thought suddenly, convinced that the Scottish guy had seen through their ruse. Without removing his gaze from Seven and Roberta, the man addressed his staff. "Someone hail the captain," he ordered. "Let him know what's happening."

Bad idea, Roberta thought. Kirk would guess who the "hostage" was instantly.

Seven shook his head. "Don't try it." Roberta let out what she hoped was a heartrending moan.

The engineer still looked suspicious, but apparently he decided not to call Seven's bluff. "Over there," he said gruffly, indicating a bank of computer controls on the left. Keeping his hold on Roberta and his eyes on the engineering staff, Seven sidled over to the controls. Isis kept pace with him, eliciting a puzzled expression from the Scottish guy, who was obviously trying to figure out how the cat fit into all this craziness. *Join the club,* Roberta thought.

Isis sprang from the floor to land atop the control panel. She mewed happily, as if she'd just discovered the mother lode of catnip. "Yes, Isis," Seven said, scanning a row of sliding knobs. "A very basic system. It shouldn't be too hard to adapt at all." He withdrew his hand from Roberta's waist, although he kept the phaser aimed at her with his other hand. He adjusted one of the knobs, then glanced at a monitor positioned at eye level. Looking at the same monitor, Roberta was faintly distressed to see a thin black arrow moving into a bright red area of the display clearly labeled DANGER. "Good," Seven murmured. "All we need to do now is invert the matter/antimatter ratios, then factor in a negative compensation . . ." Isis squawked in response and slunk toward a large white lever with a highly visible warning label affixed to its handle.

"Wait! Stop that!" the Scottish engineer cried out, clearly horrified by what he could see of Seven's actions. Throwing caution to the wind, he snatched a phaser from the hand of one of his subordinates and fired at Seven without hesitation. A brilliant burst of energy struck Seven in the back, who stiffened suddenly, then collapsed against the console. Chekov's phaser dropped from his fingers, striking the floor with a harsh metallic clang. "Thank heaven," the engineer gasped, thinking the danger past. "Please step away from those controls, miss," he instructed Roberta.

Isis shoved her body against the white lever, pushing it all the way down.

A violent vibration shook the floor almost immediately, sending Roberta staggering away from the controls, nearly tumbling head over heels. Seven's unconscious body was thrown to the floor, while Isis's claws scratched futilely at the polished steel surface of the control panel as the cat tried to keep from sliding from its perch. A shrill siren started blaring as, all around the engineering sections, circuits began to pop and explode. Tottering uncertainly, Roberta happened to observe the head engineer's shocked expression. To her dismay, she saw that the man's face looked utterly white.

"God help us all, lads," he said softly.

Chapter Four

"WORMHOLE!" Sulu shouted as the bridge was suddenly buffeted by a series of floor-shaking jolts. Kirk grabbed his armrests with both hands to keep from being thrown from his chair. He glanced quickly at Spock and Uhura, desperate for information on the status of the ship; despite the turbulence, both officers had succeeded in staying seated at their respective posts. Spock was already studying his monitors with a look of intense concentration on his face. The warning siren went off, for the second time in as many hours, as the ship's computer automatically went to red alert.

"Ship's structural integrity intact," Spock reported. "Shields holding."

Yet another shock wave hit the *Enterprise,* rattling the ship and making the overhead lights flicker. Kirk felt the jarring impact all the way through to his bones. "On screen," he ordered, trying to keep the vibration out of his voice. He didn't quite succeed.

The main viewer lit up. Instead of the expected

starfield, it showed a swirling vortex of cosmic forces directly in front of them. Space-time itself was being warped by the wormhole, churned up into overlapping layers of dimensional reality that disappeared into the voracious black maw at the center of the wormhole like muddy, foam-flecked water disappearing down a drain. Kirk's eyes widened. He'd heard about wormholes before, read about them in his theoretical physics courses back at the Academy, but he'd never actually seen one before, nor been so dangerously close to its transdimensional boundaries.

"Fascinating," he heard Spock intone over the rumble of the shock waves. Kirk was impressed once again by the Vulcan's ability to remain dispassionate and analytical even during the midst of a catastrophe. *I can always count on Spock,* he thought.

"Change course," he ordered Sulu. "Keep us out of that thing."

"I'm trying," the helmsman replied, strain evident in his voice, "but it's not working. The gravitational pull is too strong. It's got us trapped."

"Full reverse," Kirk ordered, shouting to be heard over both the siren and the throbbing of ship's duranium framework. Going from full warp to reverse would be hard on the ship, but safer than getting sucked into the wormhole. *Scotty will never forgive me for this,* Kirk thought, *if we get out of this alive, that is.*

Sulu manipulated the helm controls, a line of sweat beading upon his brow. Their ride was getting bumpier by the second; it was like the *Enterprise* was being carried through white-water rapids straight towards the lip of a cascading waterfall. "No good, sir," Sulu said a few moments later. "We're still going in."

Damn, Kirk thought. *Where the devil did this thing come from? Why didn't our sensors detect the wormhole before we got too close?* "Spock?" he called out. "How did this happen?"

"According to my readings," Spock reported from

the science station, "this is not a natural phenomenon. The wormhole ahead was artificially generated."

"By whom?" Kirk demanded. Were they under attack by some strange new weapon?

"By ourselves, Captain," Spock said evenly. "The wormhole was created by an imbalance in our own warp engines."

What? Before Kirk could respond, the *Enterprise* was rocked by another jarring shock. On the main viewer, the wormhole appeared to be growing at a geometric rate; it was almost impossible to see the surrounding space. The lightless black tunnel filled the screen. *We're getting closer to the falls,* Kirk realized. There was no way to avoid the wormhole now. They'd have to ride it out. "Divert power to the deflector screens," he ordered. "Maximum strength!"

"Affirmative," Spock said. His voice sounded thin and very far away. As they approached the event horizon of the wormhole, distortion effects permeated the bridge, scrambling Kirk's senses. Everyone appeared to be moving in slow motion, their bodies stretched and twisted like figures in a funhouse mirror. To his right, Uhura opened her mouth but the words seemed to hang in the air, muffled and mangled beyond comprehension. The wormhole was warping time, light, and sound, even before they passed beyond the point of no return. Kirk saw Spock rise from his chair and step toward the auxiliary control station next to Sulu; the Vulcan's body seemed to expand, then broke apart into over a dozen separate images of Spock, stretching from the science console to the forward station in a continuous ribbon of Spocks, each one thinner than the finest sheet of paper. Were all these Spocks existing in the same moment, Kirk wondered, or was he seeing several consecutive moments at the same time?

On the main viewer, the wormhole appeared to pulsate, expanding and contracting like a dilating eye exposed to rapid changes of light. Sulu frantically worked the helm controls, sweat running down his face, his head and upper torso seeming to stretch light-years away from his hands, tapering away to a pinpoint beyond Kirk's ability to discern, but the wormhole only grew nearer. Kirk braced himself for the impact as the screen went totally black. *Here we go,* he thought as the *Enterprise* plunged into the abyss.

There was a blinding flash of light, strong enough to override the safeties on the viewer, and Kirk felt himself starting to black out. Tremendous g-forces pressed him into his chair, pulling his skin tightly over the bones of his face. Kirk forced his eyes open, just in time to see colors of unimaginable intensity burst upon the viewer in prismatic explosions of light. It looked nothing like ordinary space, like nothing he had ever seen. The ship started spinning, rotating around its axis faster and faster until his vision blurred. Nausea gripped him. He had to bite down on his lip to keep from vomiting. He tasted blood upon his tongue. For an instant, his skin felt like it was on fire, then he was so cold he trembled. *The deflectors,* he thought desperately. *Were the shields holding up?*

Then the light faded. All Kirk's blood seemed to rush to his head, and he had to close his eyes for an instant. When he opened them again, the vivid colors—and the brutal g-forces—were gone. He looked around the bridge. The distortion effects had vanished, too; everything looked back to normal. On the main viewer, Kirk was relieved to see ordinary space once more, the stars zipping past the prow of the *Enterprise* as they usually did.

But which stars? Kirk wondered suddenly. *Where are we now?*

He checked on his crew. Sulu's head rested against the helm controls. He appeared to have lost consciousness for a time, but was beginning to stir. He lifted his head and looked around. Elsewhere on the bridge, Kirk saw Uhura shake her head groggily and retrieve her earpiece from the floor. Only Spock seemed to have avoided passing out entirely. He was already back at his science station, observing the readouts on his monitors. They cast a faint blue glow upon his face.

"Captain," Sulu asked, looking a little dazed. "What happened?"

"We went over the falls in a barrel," Kirk declared, "but we seem to have reached the bottom intact." He turned toward his science officer. "Mr. Spock? Any conclusions?"

"A unique experience, Captain," the Vulcan commented. "I regret that the physiological effects impaired my ability to observe the phenomenon with complete accuracy. Still, a review of the sensor logs should prove most informative."

"First things first," Kirk reminded him. "Where in blazes are we?"

"I am attempting to determine that," Spock said, "by comparing our present readings against the star charts contained in the ship's memory banks." He worked with maximum efficiency; using one hand to access the ship's sensors and scanners while the other hand keyed instructions into the library computer control panel. Kirk heard the hum of information being transferred between the two systems. "We appear to be quite distant from our former location, possibly outside the Federation entirely."

How distant? Kirk worried. Although their trip through the wormhole had been brief in duration, they could have ended up anywhere in the universe. What if they were lost countless light-years beyond known space? He didn't like the idea of spending, say, seventy-five years or so trying to get home.

On the other hand, he thought, *that could be quite an adventure. . . .*

"Mister Sulu," he asked. "What is our present speed?"

The helmsman checked his controls. "Er, full reverse, sir."

Of course, Kirk thought. "Slow to impulse. Let's not go rushing around until we know just where we are."

"I believe I can provide that information now," Spock said. He rose from his station and addressed Kirk. *Here it comes,* the captain thought. Although Spock's voice offered only the most minute indications of his feelings at any given moment, something about his tone and bearing told Kirk that this was not going to be good news. *After three years in space,* Kirk thought, *I've gotten pretty good at reading that poker face of yours.*

"According to my calculations," Spock continued, "our present coordinates are located well within the boundaries of the Romulan Star Empire."

Kirk heard an involuntary gasp from Uhura. He didn't blame her. He was also shocked to discover that they were on the wrong side of the Neutral Zone, deep behind enemy lines—right where Seven wanted them. "That arrogant bastard," Kirk cursed, suddenly realizing who had to be responsible for the wormhole.

"Captain," Uhura announced, interrupting Kirk's bloody-minded musings. "It's Chief Engineer Scott again. He says there's been a disturbance in engineering. Something about an intruder."

"Why am I not surprised?" Kirk said, clenching his fist. *The Romulan Empire,* he thought, appalled. *Why couldn't Seven have sent us someplace safer, like maybe the heart of a nova!* "Lieutenant, contact Security. I want to see Gary Seven. Now."

There was an empty chair at the head of the conference table, but Kirk remained standing. He was too angry to sit down. "I should lock you up and throw away the key," Kirk barked at Seven, who stood at the opposite end of the table, flanked by two unsmiling security officers, "or, better yet, turn you over to the Romulans myself. What were you thinking, tossing my ship into an wormhole?"

"For that matter," Scotty said, sitting at the table, "I still want to know *how* he did it?"

Seven, still clad in a blue Starfleet uniform, did not look contrite. His pen-shaped weapon rested on the tabletop in front of Kirk and out of Seven's reach. "I apologize, Captain, but I had no alternative. As I explained earlier, my mission is extremely urgent."

"*Your* mission," Kirk said. "*Your* priorities. I'm getting pretty tired of hearing about *your* secret agenda. You've used trickery and violence to put my ship in a very hazardous situation. It will be a miracle if we make it back across the Neutral Zone without being detected by the Romulans. For a so-called peacemaker, you don't seem to mind bringing both the Federation and the Romulan Empire to the brink of war."

Déjà vu, he thought. It had been less than a year since he had been in Romulan territory on an unusually dangerous assignment. Even though he had succeeded at his mission of espionage, it had been a damn close thing. *I never expected to be back here again so soon.*

"You overestimate your importance, Captain," Seven replied, "in the overall scheme of things." He ignored the two guards looming over him. "Peace is a delicate thing. Sometimes it requires risk to preserve it."

A third security officer stood watch over Roberta, who looked very uncomfortable, under the circumstances. Seven's black cat rubbed against the young woman's legs until she finally bent over and picked the cat up. "Okay, okay," Roberta muttered. "This better?"

The cat watched the proceedings with wide yellow eyes.

Kirk glanced around the table. McCoy, Chekov, and Scotty had all testified as to Seven's activities.

McCoy rubbed his eyes, still looking a bit groggy, despite a stimulant administered by Nurse Chapel. Chekov, wearing a fresh uniform to replace the one stolen by Seven, glowered at the unflappable time traveler. Kirk guessed that the ensign was probably furious at letting Seven ambush him so easily. Scotty looked angry as well, and anxious to get back to his engines and inspect them for whatever damage the trip through the wormhole may have caused.

Yawning loudly, McCoy picked up Seven's silver device from the table and inspected it. "I don't know what he's got in this thing, but it sure packs a punch."

"I assure you, Doctor," Seven commented, "that the tranquilizer beam has no negative side effects." He turned his attention back to Kirk. "Captain, you must believe me. My mission is too important to let your anger over this incident distract you from the larger picture. The future is too important."

"I don't have time to debate philosophy with you," Kirk told Seven. "I have a ship in jeopardy and a mission of my own to complete." He had left Spock in charge of the bridge, but he didn't want to stay away too long. The Romulans could discover the *Enterprise* at any minute. "Mr. Chekov," he said, giving the ensign an opportunity to regain some lost face, "see to it that Mr. Seven is confined to the brig for the time being." He shot a glance at the sleek black animal nestled in Roberta's arms; Scotty had sworn that, back in the Engineering, the pet had actually followed Seven's commands. "Without his cat," Kirk added.

"Captain." Seven started to step forward, but was restrained by the guards. "Since we are here already, we ought to proceed to the coordinates I can provide. If I induced the wormhole correctly, and I believe I did, it should not be too far away. I respect your feelings on the matter, but you should not allow this opportunity to go to waste."

Kirk ignored Seven. He had made his decision, and his first priority was to get the *Enterprise* back to

Federation space as quickly as possible. Seven had proven himself untrustworthy; Kirk wasn't inclined to listen to the man's self-serving warnings anymore. "Gentlemen," he said, heading for the exit, "I will be on the bridge."

"Captain Kirk, wait!" Roberta said. "What about me?"

Good question, Kirk thought, pausing to contemplate the young woman in the red yeoman's uniform. She had kicked her boots off for some reason, and was now barefoot. To tell the truth, he wasn't quite clear on her exact relationship to Seven. When he'd first met them both, either several months ago or three hundred years ago, depending on how you counted it, she and Seven had seemed like fairly recent acquaintances; indeed, she had appeared almost as suspicious of Seven as he had been. Yet, according to Spock's historical research, conducted shortly after Kirk's first encounter with both Seven and Roberta, the pair had later enjoyed a long association, although how far that association may have developed at the time Seven brought her forward into the future was not clear. One thing seemed certain, though; unlike Seven, she had not been raised by manipulative aliens from an unknown planet. She was a native-born Earthwoman, circa the late 1960s.

"Honest, Captain," she insisted, "I had no idea what he was planning. I was as surprised as anyone." She gave a nervous sideways glance at the massive security guard standing beside her. "I don't even know what a wormhole is, aside from something you find in bad apples."

She sounds convincing, Kirk thought. Then again, as McCoy never failed to remind him, he had a definite weakness for a pretty face. "The question is, Miss Lincoln, would you have stopped Seven if you'd known what he was up to?"

She looked guiltily at Seven, who stared calmly at a sloping blue wall, seemingly unconcerned by the question. "Well," she hedged, "he—Mr. Seven, that is—goes a bit far sometimes, but he usually knows what he's doing. Most of the time. I think."

A triangular computer node rested in the center of the conference table. A yellow light flashed on all three sides of the node, attracting Kirk's attention. "What is it?" he asked.

Spock's voice emerged from the lighted terminal. "Captain, forgive the interruption, but our long-range scanners have detected several Romulan ships in this vicinity, although they do not yet appear to have detected us."

Damn, Kirk thought. "Thank you, Mr. Spock. I will be with you shortly." He looked back at Roberta. *I don't have time for this.* "Confine Miss Lincoln to her quarters. I'll deal with her later."

"Yes, sir," the security guard said. He took Roberta firmly by the arm. At first, she looked relieved to have gotten off so lightly, then she recalled the cat in her arms.

"Oh, no," she gasped. "Wait, Captain, please. You can't lock me up with . . . her." She glared balefully at the animal, who looked back at her with an equally disdainful expression. "It would be cruel and unusual punishment."

"You don't like the cat?" Kirk asked, amused despite the ongoing emergency.

"We don't get along," Roberta explained. She lowered the cat onto the table. "Please, I'd much rather have solitary confinement."

The cat stared at Kirk with unblinking yellow eyes. It kind of made his flesh crawl, especially when he remembered how a similar black tabby, albeit several times larger, had nearly had him for lunch on Pyriss VII. *That,* he thought, as a certain shape-changing alien witch came to mind, *was enough to turn me off cats permanently.*

Especially black ones.

"Fine," Kirk informed Roberta. "You don't have to

keep the cat." He nodded at the security officers, who escorted both her and Seven out of the conference room, leaving the feline in question resting atop the table.

"Well, I'm not going to take her," he declared to all concerned. He looked at McCoy and Scotty. The engineer shook his head. Kirk wasn't surprised; the only pets Scotty approved of came with circuit boards and blueprints. "Bones?" he asked.

"Me?" McCoy asked, looking askance at the feline in dispute. Then a crafty smile appeared on his face. "Sure," he said. "I'll take her." He lifted the cat from the table and draped it over his shoulder. "I know just what to do with it: put it in Spock's room."

"Bones . . ." Kirk started.

"Hey, he said he liked it last time," the doctor said. "I remember. For a Vulcan, he was practically cooing at it."

Kirk eyed the cat skeptically. The last thing he needed was a stray animal getting into trouble. "I have a better idea," he declared. "You have cages in sickbay, Doctor, for handling biological specimens. Lock her up."

"Sickbay?" Realizing his joke had backfired on him, McCoy looked appalled. "Wait a second, Jim. I'm a doctor, not a vet!"

But Kirk was already out the door. He had more important things to worry about than a cat.

Spock rose from the captain's chair the minute the turbolift doors hissed often. "Situation, Mr. Spock?" Kirk requested as he strode onto the bridge.

"We have identified the nearby vessels," Spock stated, returning to the science station, "as a Romulan battle cruiser, of Klingon design, accompanied by two warbirds. There appear to be no other spacecraft in the vicinity, although I must remind the captain of the Romulans' cloaking capabilities."

"I'm hardly likely to forget them," Kirk said. He

paced in front of his chair, too full of adrenaline to sit down. "Although I'm not sure why they'd want to fly cloaked within their own borders."

"That would seem to be a logical assumption," Spock agreed. "Barring any internal conflicts, of course."

Spock had a point there, Kirk thought. It was possible that the Romulan government used cloaked ships to police their own people. He wished he had more information to work with; unfortunately, what he didn't know about the internal workings of the Romulan Star Empire would fill several supercomputers. Hell, up until a few years ago, the Federation hadn't even known that the Romulans were an offshoot of the Vulcans. Since then, Federation intelligence had learned precious little else, even if he and Spock had managed to abscond with some cloaking technology a while back. "Any sign that they've recognized us?"

Spock shook his head. "Not yet. Lieutenant Uhura is monitoring their communications. So far they have raised no alarm at our presence."

"Keep your ears open, Lieutenant," Kirk said, glancing at Uhura before returning his attention to Spock. "It may be that the sheer unlikeliness of our circumstances may be working in our favor. The Romulans have no reason to suspect that any Federation vessel could get this far beyond their borders without being detected. Security is probably tighter closer to the Neutral Zone than here at—" Kirk paused and looked at Sulu. "Do we know exactly where we are at the moment?"

"Yes, sir," Sulu said crisply. "At maximum warp, we are approximately twelve hours away from the Romulan side of the Neutral Zone."

"Twelve hours, seventeen minutes," Spock added, "to be precise."

"How far are we from the Romulan homeworlds?" Kirk asked.

"Two full sectors," Sulu reported, much to the captain's relief. The last thing he wanted to do was present a possible threat to either Romulus or Remus. That would be equivalent to thrusting a sharp stick into a nest of hornets.

"Mr. Sulu," he said, "set a course for the Neutral Zone. Let's get back to the Federation as quickly and as quietly as possible." *Easier said than done,* he thought. As he'd already acknowledged, Romulan security would invariably grow tighter the nearer they got to the border. Sooner or later, an armed confrontation with one or more Romulan starships was inevitable.

"Maximum warp?" Sulu asked, adjusting his helm controls.

"No," Kirk said, finally taking his seat in the captain's chair and considering the matter carefully. "That might attract the attention of our friends out there. We don't want to look too guilty or suspicious." He quickly weighed speed versus stealth and arrived at what he thought was a reasonable compromise. "Warp factor six, Mr. Sulu."

"Aye, aye, Captain," the helmsman answered, but Kirk barely heard him. He had too many other concerns on his mind. Twelve-plus hours, and then some, was a long time to elude detection. The *Enterprise,* he knew, was living on borrowed time. *What will I do when they catch us?* he brooded. *Shoot our way out? Activate the self-destruct system?* One way or another, there was no way he could let the Romulans get their hands on a *Constitution*-class starship.

He didn't even want to think about the disaster unfolding on Duwamish right now. Unfortunately, the endangered colonists were on their own; it would be a small miracle if the *Enterprise* made it back to the Federation intact, let alone arrived at Duwamish in time to rescue the colonists. *Damn you, Gary Seven,* Kirk thought. *How dare you play games with people's lives?* He wondered if he had misjudged the man entirely the first time they met; after all, Kirk reminded himself, Seven had been willing to detonate nuclear satellites in Earth's upper atmosphere just to further his own political agenda. Was Seven merely a well-intentioned meddler—or a dangerous fanatic?

"Mr. Spock," Kirk said, "you conducted some historical research regarding Gary Seven after our first encounter with him. Perhaps you can refresh my memory on the subject while we're waiting for the Romulans to wake up." He spoke with a casual flippancy he hardly felt, the better to keep up morale on the bridge. It was part of a captain's job to rally the spirits of his crew. Why should Chekov or Uhura have to share his anxiety?

"In fact, Captain," Spock replied, "I began preparing a report shortly after our visitors's arrival."

Kirk's smile was quite genuine; Spock was nothing if not reliable. "Give me the highlights."

Spock inspected a computer printout affixed to a magnetic clipboard. "As you may recall, Mr. Seven claims to have been raised by unknown aliens who abducted his ancestors six thousand years ago for the purpose of training human operatives who could then intervene during crucial points in Earth's history. He also implied that these same aliens have sponsored similar operations throughout the galaxy, although there is insufficient evidence to either confirm or refute this assertion."

A scary idea, Kirk thought. Whoever these anonymous aliens were, their activities seemed far removed from the spirit and wisdom of the Prime Directive. Painful experience, including mankind's disastrous first contact with the Klingons, had taught Starfleet how dangerous it could be to interfere in the natural development of an alien culture. Who were Seven's enigmatic masters to think that they could disregard such risks? *Granted,* Kirk admitted privately, *I've been known to push the limits of the Prime Directive a time or two, but I never set out to do it on purpose.*

"Following our initial encounter with Mr. Seven in the late 1960's," Spock continued, "historical evidence indicates that Gary Seven, accompanied by Miss Roberta Lincoln, continued their work for many more years. Much of this information, however, is speculative, and possibly apocryphal, due to the covert nature of their activities and Mr. Seven's demonstrated talent for working behind the scenes of history. Indeed, many of the instances I have uncovered may have not yet happened to the individuals who beamed onto the bridge not long ago. Nevertheless, Mr. Seven and Miss Lincoln have been linked to a number of significant incidents, including the averted assassination of Chairman Mao Tse-tung at the Great Wall of China, the apprehension of the so-called Watergate burglars in the District of Columbia, a well-publicized near-disaster at the Three Mile Island nuclear facility, the defeat of the so-called 'cybernauts' in conjunction with a pair of British intelligence operatives, the successful elimination of a top-secret conspiracy to clone world leaders, the publication of a best-selling treatise on global cooperation, the destruction of fourteen deadly biological weapons, including one spaceborn virus, the birth of a future Nobel prize-winning diplomat, three successful motion pictures of socially transforming value, the crash of the Skylab orbital facility (and subsequent lack of terrestrial casualties), the 'accidental discovery' of an AIDS vaccine, the creation of the first true artificial intelligence . . ."

"I get the drift of it," Kirk said, a bit impatiently. "It sounds like Seven may have known what he was doing in the late twentieth century, but what's he up to now, in our time and on my ship? Even he admits that humanity is not rushing to blow itself to bits anymore."

"Judging from our present location," Spock said, "it may be that Mr. Seven's current mission has little to do with *human* history at all."

Was that it? Kirk wondered. *Did Seven deem twenty-third century Romulan civilization in need of his services?* But, if that was the case, why hadn't his superiors trained a Romulan operative to work within their society? Wasn't that how it was supposed to work? There was too much he didn't know about Seven's shadowy organization.

"What about the young woman?" Kirk asked. "Where does she fit in?"

"That is not entirely clear," Spock told him. "Her background prior to meeting Mr. Seven is well-documented, though. She was born and raised in the United States of America, and is indeed what she appears to be: a typical human female of the late twentieth century."

"Not too typical, I suspect," Kirk said, remembering how close Roberta had come to accidentally killing him with Seven's own weapon back in 1968. For someone raised centuries before the dawn of warp travel, she had adjusted to Vulcan time travelers and talking computers with remarkable speed.

"That may be so," Spock conceded. "Historical records confirm her presence on or near the sites of Seven's few verifiable exploits, although her precise role in these events remains open to dispute." Spock raised an eyebrow as he scanned the data produced by the ship's computer. "Odd. Some records suggest that Seven had another female associate, although the evidence recording this second woman is ambiguous and frequently contradictory."

"I'm not interested in his personal life," Kirk said, frustration tingeing his voice. "I want to know what Seven is not telling us, and I want to know how much Miss Lincoln knows about his plans." He rested his chin upon the knuckles of his clasped hands, considering his options. "Spock," he said finally, "I know it's a lot to ask, but . . . a mind meld?"

Spock's expression did not change, but Kirk thought he saw a flicker of something in the Vulcan's eyes. Regret, perhaps, or reluctance. "As you know, Captain, a Vulcan mind meld is a very personal thing. I would be . . . uneasy . . . about resorting to such methods in this instance, especially without the consent of either Mr. Seven or Miss Lincoln."

"I know that, Spock," Kirk said. He felt guilty about pressing his friend on such a touchy subject, but he couldn't help thinking that the safety of everyone aboard the *Enterprise* might depend on the secrets locked in Gary Seven's skull. "But you've used your telepathic abilities in emergency situations before, like that time on Eminiar VII. This may be one of those instances where we don't have any choice, not if we want to survive this mess."

Spock's face remained as fixed as granite. "Your point is well-taken, Captain," he stated flatly. "If, in your judgment, a mind meld is necessary to preserve the ship, that is your decision as captain."

I don't want to order you to do it, Kirk thought. He knew what it cost Spock to perform a mind meld. He had personally witnessed the enormous physical and emotional toll the Vulcan endured whenever he lowered the boundaries between his mind and another's, seen the anguish that contorted Spock's face and soul when he melded with the Horta on Janus VI. A mind meld could be an extraordinarily intimate and traumatic experience, especially for someone like Spock, who had spent his entire life carefully concealing his emotions from the world. How could he command his friend to undergo such an ordeal simply because of some vague suspicions regarding Seven?

Besides, Seven was safely stowed away in the brig.

"Well, we probably haven't reached that point just yet," Kirk reassured Spock, looking in vain for any trace of relief on the Vulcan's features. "I'm merely reviewing our options, just in case."

"As is only proper," Spock said with a nod. Kirk felt like he'd been let off the hook, and was grateful that he apparently hadn't imposed too much on his friendship with Spock. *Good thing McCoy's back in sickbay,* he thought. He could just imagine the good doctor's views on Vulcan mind melds as a means of interrogation.

Kirk's shoulders sagged. Suddenly, all the fatigue and tension of the last few hours caught up with him. *Over twelve hours to safety,* he thought. It was tempting to close his eyes for a few minutes, very tempting, but how could he relax while the *Enterprise* was still in Romulan territory? He considered paging a yeoman to fetch a cup of hot coffee. He generally frowned on food or drinks being consumed on the bridge, but right now he was inclined to make an exception. He reached for the call-button on his portside armrest.

"Captain!" Uhura called out. "I'm detecting priority transmissions between the Romulan ships. They've gone to battle alert!"

"Confirmed, Captain," Chekov reported. "All three vessels have changed course—and are heading toward us."

Kirk sat up straight in his chair. "This is it," he said. "They're on to us. Raise deflector shields . . . now!"

Chapter Five

ROBERTA WAS IMPRESSED by the size of the guest quarters on the *Enterprise*. The roomy suite was definitely larger than her own pad back in Manhattan. That apartment was probably long gone in this era, she realized, wondering briefly if there even was a New York City in the twenty-third century. *Maybe the whole town's been made into an historical exhibit by now, or maybe a theme park.*

It was encouraging to see firsthand that there was a future, though, considering all the turmoil and unrest back home, including the ever-present threat of thermonuclear annihilation. She had seen movies like "Fail-Safe" and "Dr. Strangelove" and even "Planet of the Apes," all of which seemed to accept as given that humanity would inevitably destroy itself in a full-scale nuclear war. Yet here was Captain Kirk and his crew, confidently exploring the universe generations after all the wars and unrest of her own time. Seven had told her several times that the two of them (and, okay, Isis, too) were working to bring about a better future. Was this strange new world what he had always had in mind?

Granted, she thought as she explored her surroundings, discovering her own clothes folded neatly on the bed, the future seemed to have its problems, too. She had no idea who the Romulans were, but from all Captain Kirk's talk about borders and Neutral Zones, she gathered they weren't exactly Earth's best friends. Kirk talked about Romulans the same way Americans of her time talked about the Russians or the Red Chinese. *The more things change,* she thought, *et cetera, et cetera.*

She remembered the face of the agent who had appeared on the viewscreen back on the Beta-5. He'd looked like he'd been in a fight or something. Had the Romulans, whomever they were, caused his injuries? She wished she'd had more of a chance to quiz Gary Seven before they'd zoomed off to the future. How come the guy on the screen had looked like Mr. Spock? As nearly as she could figure out, the same people who had attacked Agent 146 were planning to do the same thing to Mr. Spock, but not for another twenty years or so. She was kind of surprised Seven hadn't warned Mr. Spock when he had the chance, but she guessed that would've been tampering with history or something. *So how come history always has to revolve around assassinations and things like that?* It really was just like the bad, old days back home.

But at least mankind was still around to deal with the same old stuff. That was something.

Upon inspection, the suite appeared largely identical to the single-occupant stateroom she had scoped out while "borrowing" her Starfleet uniform, complete with the same funky-looking shower. She felt slightly guilty for securing such comfy accommodations while Gary Seven languished in the brig. She guessed that Seven's cell was nowhere near as hospitable. *I suppose it's up to me to get him out of jail,* she thought, *but how?*

A computer terminal resembling the one she saw in the conference room rested in one corner of the stateroom, positioned atop a triangular tabletop that fit neatly in the juncture between two walls. Roberta pulled up a hard plastic chair and inspected the terminal. She would have been impressed by how small and compact the device was, compared to the bulky computers of her own era, if Seven hadn't taught her to use even smaller devices. She patted her purse automatically, confirming that the crystalline cube was still safely stored inside. The young Russian crewman, Chekov, had searched her bag for weapons, but hadn't paid much attention to the cube. *Probably thought it was just a shiny twentieth century knick-knack,* Roberta guessed. *A paperweight from a more primitive era.*

She quickly ran her hands over the cool metal exterior of the terminal, seeking unsuccessfully for an on/off switch. Having no luck in that endeavor, she leaned back in the chair and crossed her arms thoughtfully. The Beta-5 back home responded to voice commands, she recalled. Maybe the computers on the *Enterprise* had caught up with Seven's weird alien science?

"Er, hello," she addressed the terminal. "Anybody there?"

The terminal beeped in response.

The Romulan warships were already within visual range. Kirk stared at the main viewer, gazing intently at the image of the Romulan battle cruiser, flanked by the two smaller birds-of-prey. The cruiser resembled the one he and Spock had boarded last year; green in color, its bulbous command center was linked with its rear warp nacelles by a slender, elongated neck. Kirk knew the cruiser was roughly the same size as the *Enterprise,* while the warbirds, each painted to resemble a feathered raptor, were only half as large as either the battle cruiser or the *Enterprise*. Kirk reminded himself not to underestimate the two smaller ships. Another warbird had come dangerously close to destroying the *Enterprise* during his first encounter with the Romulans.

"Phaser banks powered," Chekov reported. "Photon torpedoes loaded and ready to go."

"Deflectors at maximum strength," Spock added.

"Thank you, gentlemen," Kirk said grimly, prepared to go down fighting if it came to that. Red alert lights flashed all around the bridge, just as they did throughout the entire ship, he knew. His crew were at their posts. They were as ready as they'd ever be. Kirk just wished the odds weren't so much against them. *Three against one,* he thought, *and on their home-ground to boot.* He carefully excised any trace of apprehension from his voice as he spoke, "Lieutenant Uhura, hail the commander of the battle cruiser." Maybe it was still possible to talk his way out of this mess, although he wasn't very hopeful about it.

"Yes, sir," Uhura said crisply, her dark eyes fixed on her console as she deftly manipulated the external communications controls. "Transmitting on all known Romulan frequencies . . . Captain, I have a response."

"Put it on the screen," he instructed, glad that the Romulans hadn't chosen to shoot first and ask questions later.

The image of the three oncoming warships was replaced by the head and shoulders of a Romulan officer. Kirk was struck by how much the man resembled Spock, albeit a few years older; he had the same arched eyebrows, dark hair, and pointed ears, although the lines of his face were etched deeper, making the Romulan's stern scowl look even more severe. Kirk found it impossible to estimate the officer's age, especially given the sizable disparity between the human and Romulan lifespans; the man on the screen could have been anywhere from fifty to a hundred years old. A heavy red sash was draped over the man's right shoulder. It seemed to be made from the same thick, quilted fabric as his gray military uniform.

"I am Commander Motak of the Imperial battle cruiser *Gladiator*. You have been identified as the U.S.S. *Enterprise*, in direct violation of the Treaty of Algeron. You are hereby ordered to surrender immediately and turn your ship over to my command."

Just once, Kirk thought, *I'd like to run into a Romulan ship when I wasn't in violation of some treaty. It made it hard to take the moral high ground—and refute the smug self-righteousness of the enemy commander.* He knew he couldn't surrender, though, regardless of the circumstances. The Federation would never see the *Enterprise* again, and Romulan Intelligence would receive a bounty of military secrets from the captured ship.

"This is Captain James T. Kirk," he said, "in command of the *Enterprise*. I apologize for our unexpected arrival within your borders, but I can assure you it was an accident, entirely beyond our control. We had an unfortunate encounter with a wormhole that knocked us badly off course." He chose not to mention Gary Seven's involvement in the creation of that wormhole; that would just complicate matters.

"Ah, Captain Kirk." A very unVulcanlike smirk appeared on Motak's face. "I was hoping you were still in command of this ship. As you may or may not be aware, there is an outstanding warrant for your arrest on charges of espionage and crimes against the Empire. The Praetor himself has offered a sizable reward for your capture. I look forward to collecting it."

Easier said than done, Kirk thought. "It's gratifying to know that I'm so popular these days, but I don't intend to do anything except return to Federation territory as quickly as possible. You're welcome to escort us to the Neutral Zone if that will make you feel more comfortable."

"Your very presence here constitutes an illegal incursion into our space," Motak declared harshly. "You will surrender, or you will be destroyed."

"I told you, we're here by accident," Kirk protested. "We have no military objectives." He glimpsed a portion of the Romulan cruiser's bridge behind Motak. Romulan soldiers wearing golden helmets manned their posts, ready to fire upon the *Enterprise*.

"Captain," Chekov interrupted, keeping his voice low. "The other ships are spreading out around us. They have us blocked in three directions."

Let me guess, Kirk thought. *All three ships are positioned between us and the Neutral Zone.* Keeping his hands well below the usual boundaries of the viewer, he silently pointed to the lower righthand corner of the screen. Chekov responded to his signal by projecting a tactical display onto that corner of the screen while the remainder of the viewer continued to be dominated by Motak's grim visage. Sure enough, Kirk noted, the warbirds had positioned themselves above and below the *Enterprise,* leaving the battle cruiser directly in their path. The only available escape route led even deeper into Romulan territory, not exactly a direction he was eager to explore. He could feel the pincers closing in. "There's no need to fight a battle over this," he insisted, consciously averting his eyes from the tactical display so as not to alert Motak. "We just want to return home without starting a war."

"What you intend, and why you are here, no longer matters," Motak replied, his smirk giving way to a look of cool Romulan determination. "The fact remains that you are here. You have no choice except to surrender. Let me demonstrate that I am quite serious." He nodded to an offscreen subordinate and

Kirk felt a chill run down his spine. He sensed the time for talking was running out.

"Captain!" Chekov called out, confirming Kirk's fears. "The cruiser is firing its disruptors!"

"Hello? Computer?" Roberta repeated, encouraged by the way the screen on terminal had lit up, until an abrupt shock rocked the entire room, sending her tumbling out of her chair onto the floor. It felt like an earthquake, although she didn't think you could have earthquakes in outer space.

Good heavens, she thought, glancing up at the lighted computer terminal. *Did I do that?*

"Deflectors down to seventy-three percent," Spock announced calmly. Kirk held on tightly to the armrests on his chair, anticipating another jolt. On the screen in front of him, Motak's head and shoulders had been replaced by a view of the attacking battle cruiser. A flash of violet energy at the prow of the ship alerted Kirk to another attack. Strategic options raced through his brain, none of them very appealing.

Worst-case scenario: the combined efforts of the trio of Romulan warships reduce the *Enterprise* to spacedust. Casualties: one hundred percent.

Best-case scenario: beating the odds, he destroys all three Romulan vessels, almost certainly sparking an interstellar war. Casualty: peace throughout the galaxy.

Another disruptor blast shook the bridge. Bright blue sparks flew from a control panel near Uhura, who jumped away from her seat to avoid the energy discharge. "Are you all right, Lieutenant?" Kirk asked.

"I'm fine, Captain," she replied, eyeing the console carefully as she rerouted the communications systems through the auxiliary circuits. She listened intently to her earpiece. "Commander Motak is calling again for our surrender."

"I guess he's not joking," Kirk said.

"In my experience," Spock commented, "Romulans are not known for their humor."

Violet energy burst once more from the battle cruiser.

In the brig, confined behind an invisible wall of repulsive energy, Gary Seven felt the third blast knock the ship about and wondered when he should make his move. His brow furrowed in thought, he remained seated on the simple bench provided by his cell.

Obviously, the *Enterprise* had encountered hostilities, just as Captain Kirk had feared—and Seven had anticipated. He wasted no thoughts on guilt or self-recrimination; he had done what he had to do, and he was confident in Kirk's ability to defend the *Enterprise* for as long as was necessary to reach their ultimate destination. So far the mission was going exactly as planned. The only question was whether they would arrive in time to rescue Agent 146. Time travel, alas, was not an exact science, even for his superiors. Seven regretted momentarily that Isis had not been confined with him; he would have appreciated her advice.

Isis did not like being caged. The rectangular carrier was designed for transporting biological specimens, not pets or honored guests, and was far from luxurious. She paced around and around in the cage, although there was only barely enough room to do so, nor could she even extend her tail fully. And as for her other form . . . well, that was just impossible under the circumstances. The floor of the cage was layered with some sort of absorbent synthetic pad that smelled vaguely medicinal. Her ears bumped into the hard metal lid of the cage every time she tried to raise her head. It was cramped for a cat, let alone anything else.

The cage was frustratingly effective as well. The

metal lattice that surrounded her on all four sides was tight enough that she could not stick more than a single claw out through the bars, and the metal had already proven resistant to both her jaws and her claws. The lid itself was held down by some sort of magnetic locking mechanism that was both out of reach and difficult to outwit. These humans, alas, were much more clever than the ones she usually encountered.

Resigned, for the moment, to her captivity, Isis settled down on the spongy floor of the cage to inspect the world outside her prison. The carrier had been placed on a shelf overlooking the sickbay. Empty beds, equipped with elaborate displays of monitors, lined the wall opposite her perch. There were at least three such beds in view, separated from each other by one or two cat-lengths, but very little activity to watch. The cross-sounding human who had brought her here after they'd taken Seven and the other one away had left the premises almost as soon as he had locked Isis into the carrier. The only human left was a blonde-haired female who seemed to work here. At the moment, she appeared to be checking the inventory of a built-in cabinet at the far end of the room. Isis meowed experimentally, and the female turned around to look at the cage.

Intrigued, Isis made another sound and the human female came closer. Hmmm, this had possibilities. Isis wondered if, perhaps, this particular human might be a cat-lover, and if, just maybe, she could be persuaded to undo the lock and let Isis free.

Stranger things had happened. . . .

How many Romulan vessels was Kirk engaged with, Gary Seven wondered. Not for the first time, he wished that he could have beamed directly from his own base in 1969 to Supervisor 146's base in the Romulan Empire, instead of depending on the *Enterprise* for transportation, but that would not have been wise, not while hostile forces apparently held dominion over the transporter controls at the receiving end of his trip. Under the circumstances, the last thing he wanted to do was beam directly into a trap, or, worse yet, be scattered to atoms due to interference from this base.

Now, when the guards posted to the brig were distracted by the larger battle beyond these walls, would be an excellent opportunity to escape the brig, but, Seven decided, it was doubtful that he could elude capture until the *Enterprise* reached the proper coordinates. Better to wait for an occasion when he can put his freedom to better use. Besides, the last thing he wanted to do was distract Captain Kirk at such a perilous juncture.

He waited patiently in his cell while yet another jolt buffeted the ship, shaking the guards outside off their feet.

"Shields down to sixty-two percent," Spock reported. Wisps of smoke from one or two small fires irritated Kirk's nostrils and added a slight haze to the atmosphere upon the bridge. Automatic flame suppression systems snuffed out the flames before they could consume too much oxygen, but Kirk knew that the burning circuitry were merely minor symptoms of the wholesale battering the *Enterprise* was receiving. The ship couldn't take many more blasts. He could just imagine what Scotty had to be going through down in engineering, trying to keep the warp engines on-line despite the damage done by the Romulan disruptor beams.

"Captain?" Chekov asked anxiously. "Shall I return fire?"

Kirk hesitated for only a heartbeat. What he was about to say went against his instincts and disposition, but, as Spock would surely say, it was the only logical alternative.

"Hold your fire," he instructed Chekov. The *Enterprise* was precious, but it wasn't worth starting a war for. "Mr. Sulu, full retreat. Head away from all three ships as fast as we can go."

"Yes, sir," Sulu said, responding immediately. Kirk felt a slight tug of centrifugal force as the *Enterprise* spun around on its axis, then leaped forward at warp speed, pushing the limits of its inertial dampers. On the main viewer, the attacking battle cruiser was replaced by an open starfield.

Here we go, Kirk thought. *Zooming off into the unknown.* He hated to turn and run like this, but it was the only way to avoid a fight with the Romulans without risking his ship and crew. He couldn't help wondering if this was all part of Gary Seven's unknown mission. He felt like a sheep being herded toward the slaughter. "Rear view on screen," he commanded, restoring the battle cruiser to the main viewer. *Gladiator* fell behind them, still in pursuit but shrinking as the *Enterprise* gained a lead on the other ship. But where were the warbirds? "Position of the other ships?" he demanded.

"They are pursuing us at impulse speed," Chekov stated, "but the big cruiser is still hot on our tail."

So far, so good, Kirk thought. At least they were leaving the smaller ships behind, but how long would it be before Motak called in reinforcements—or set up a blockade in front of them? For all they knew, they could be heading straight toward a Romulan armada. As fast as the *Enterprise* flew, they couldn't outrace a subspace message sent ahead of them by Motak. Or could they?

"Lieutenant," Kirk called to Uhura. The communications specialist had returned to her chair after bringing the short circuits at her console under control. "Is there any way we can block transmissions from *Gladiator?*"

Uhura gave him a skeptical expression. "I can try to set up a countermodulation on their known frequencies, Captain, but it's going to be difficult to get a proper fix on the Romulan ship when we're both travelling at warp speed, plus I'm down to the backup communications array anyway." She shook her head. "I can't guarantee anything."

"Understood," Kirk said. "Do what you can, Lieutenant." At best, he knew, Uhura could only buy them time. Ultimately, they had to get out of the Romulan Empire—or else find a safe place to hide until the Romulans stopped looking for them. What they could really use right now, Kirk realized, was another convenient wormhole.

"Chekov," he asked urgently, rising from his chair, "is the cruiser gaining on us?"

"No, sir," the young ensign reported. "We are maintaining a steady lead, although they remain in pursuit."

Good enough for now, Kirk thought. "Mr. Spock, you have the bridge." He stepped into a waiting turbolift. "I'm going to have another talk with Mr. Seven."

Chapter Six

"I'M SORRY, CAPTAIN, but we cannot return to the
Federation yet. I still have to complete my mission."

The entrance to the detention cell appeared open.
Only a string of bright white lights ran along both
sides of the empty doorway. In fact, a powerful force
field confined Seven to the spartan, simply furnished
cell, which contained only a simple bench and a pair
of double bunks built into the wall. Kirk stood so
close to the force field that he could feel the repulsive
energy of the field tingling his skin. Seven faced him
on the opposite side of the invisible wall, looking Kirk
in the eye. They were only centimeters apart, but
more than an energy field divided them.

"Maybe you didn't notice," Kirk snarled, "but this
ship is already under attack by the Romulans. Perhaps you thought you could slip in undetected, take
care of your assignment, then sneak out again without
the Romulans knowing, but that is no longer an
option. There's a Romulan battle cruiser out there
that would like nothing better than to blow us all

apart, and the longer we remain behind enemy lines, the more dangerous our situation becomes. Pretty soon we're going to be surrounded by the entire Romulan fleet. If you know a way to return us to the Federation, you better show it to me now."

Seven shook his head. "I regret that my actions have placed you and your crew in jeopardy, but my mission takes priority."

"Your mission, whatever it is, has obviously failed," Kirk said. Two security officers stood at attention at the entrance to the brig, each with a type-2 phaser pistol hanging on their belts. Seven was the only prisoner they were guarding right now. The other cells were empty. "Or are you determined to get me, my crew, and Miss Lincoln killed?"

"My mission has not failed, Captain," Seven replied. "It has barely begun." Seven walked away from Kirk and sat down on his bench. "Believe me, the effects of my failure would be catastrophic to the time line itself."

"So you keep saying," Kirk said, slightly unnerved by Seven's eerie certainty. Even Spock seemed more human than Seven at times, more subject to doubt and human frailty. Could it be, Kirk permitted himself to wonder, that Seven actually knew what he was talking about? Kirk knew from personal experience just how fragile the time line could be. He had once sacrificed the life of a woman he loved to preserve the proper course of history; how different from that was Seven's apparent willingness to sacrifice the *Enterprise?* It was a disturbing comparison, one that only grew more so the more he turned it over and over in his mind. Seven's unrelenting secretiveness tested Kirk's patience to its utmost. *Then again,* he thought, *how much did I explain to Edith?* The only difference seemed to be that Kirk had come from the future in that instance, whereas Gary Seven had come from the past, but in a universe subject to the mind-twisting paradoxes of time travel, how much of a difference did that make?

Kirk forcibly expelled such doubts from his mind. He couldn't afford to let himself get caught up in all sorts of speculative abstractions. He had to focus on his primary responsibility: the safety of his ship and his crew.

Obviously, Seven wasn't about to listen to reason, so Kirk switched tactics. "Listen to me, Seven," he snarled, letting all his pent-up frustration and rage out into the open. "You have effectively taken my ship hostage, and I am not above using deadly force to get my people safely home. Either you reverse your wormhole stunt and take us back to the Federation, or I will personally have you beamed into space." He smacked his hand against the force field, letting the crackle of discharged energy punctuate his threat. "Do you understand me, Mr. Seven?"

Seven blinked, caught off guard momentarily by the sizzling flash of the force field. Kirk felt encouraged by Seven's surprise, but his hopes were dashed by the prisoner's next words. "I understand you, Captain," Seven replied, swiftly regaining his customary composure, "but I do not believe you. You are not a barbarian, Captain. You are not even a relatively undeveloped human of the twentieth century. I cannot accept that a Starfleet officer of this era would carry out a threat of that nature, especially against someone such as myself, who has previously demonstrated his good intentions where the future is concerned."

"Maybe you don't know me as well as you think," Kirk insisted, but with less vehemence. *Damnit, he's called my bluff.* He remembered Spock's long list of Seven's accomplishments in the twentieth century. *How harshly can I really treat him? Earth may not have survived without him.*

"I've dealt with cold-blooded killers before," Seven

said. "Assassins. Executioners. You're not one of them."

And thank God for that, Kirk thought. Even if it meant that there were limits to his powers of coercion, limits that Seven seemed all too aware of. *Too bad this wasn't a first-contact scenario. It's always easier to bluff an alien than a member of your own species.*

And if Seven refused to clean up his own mess, then Kirk would have to do it for him. "All right," he said to Seven. "I don't have time to argue with you anymore. If you change your mind about helping us, tell one of the guards. In the meantime, I'm going to do my best to keep all of us out of a Romulan prison camp."

"Good luck, Captain," Seven replied. "I mean that."

I'll bet you do, Kirk thought, turning his back on the prisoner. He was only a few steps away from the exit when a whistle from the ship's intercom attracted his attention. He approached a speaker mounted in the adjacent wall and pressed the activation button. "Kirk here. What is it?"

Spock's voice emerged from the speaker. "I apologize for disturbing you, Captain, but our long-range sensors have detected a highly unusual phenomenon. You might want to return to the bridge."

On his bench, Seven looked up at Kirk the moment Spock mentioned locating something odd. He seemed particularly interested in Spock's discovery, his entire body seemingly going on alert. Noting Seven's reaction, Kirk wondered if they were getting closer to the temporal threat Seven kept talking about. "What about the Romulans?" he asked Spock.

"Gladiator remains in pursuit at warp factor 5.88. I estimate that we are about twenty-five-point-six minutes ahead of her at present."

"Any sign of more Romulan ships?" Kirk asked.

"Negative," Spock replied. "The sector we are now

crossing appears uninhabited. Indeed, on first inspection, it appears quite desolate and unremarkable."

"Aside from your intriguing phenomenon, that is," Kirk said, relieved to hear that the *Enterprise* continued to evade her pursuers, at least so far. He had no idea what kind of oddity Spock had discovered, but he knew his first officer would not have mentioned it unless he thought it was important. "I'll be right with you," he said. "Captain out."

He walked once more toward the exit, then turned around in the doorway to look back at Gary Seven in his cell. "I don't suppose you have anything you'd like to add to Spock's report?" Seven stayed as silent as the Sphinx. "I didn't think so," Kirk said.

Kirk was surprised to find both Scotty and McCoy standing by Spock's science center on the bridge. Scotty's presence was particularly unexpected. Kirk would have guessed that the engineer would have been hard at work undoing whatever damage was done by *Gladiator's* disruptors. Usually, wild horses couldn't drag Scotty away from his beloved engines, especially when there were repairs to be made.

"I suggested that Mr. Scott join us," Spock explained as he turned over the captain's chair to Kirk. "I have reason to believe that the phenomenon I mentioned may be technological in origin, so Mr. Scott may be able to provide some insights into this enigma." Spock's gaze shifted toward the two other men. "Dr. McCoy invited himself," he added dryly.

"I figured Chapel could hold down the fort in sickbay," McCoy said, "while I found out what sort of fix we were in this time. We came through that last fracas without any serious casualties, but I'm not sure how much longer our luck can hold out."

Kirk was relieved to hear that his crew was still intact, but eager to find out whatever Spock had discovered. "What sort of enigma?" Kirk asked his first officer, glancing at the main viewer. The screen revealed nothing exceptional, only a routine—if unfamiliar—starfield. Romulan space looked no different from any other void explored by the *Enterprise*. *Makes you realize,* he thought, *just how artificial all our borders and claims to territory really are.*

Spock returned to his science station. "I was scanning for wormholes, in hopes of reversing the circumstances that brought us to this region, when I noted some puzzling gravitational readings in this sector. The discrepancies were quite subtle; if I had not been specifically searching for gravimetric distortions, I doubt if I would have detected them."

Spock pressed an illuminated yellow button on his science console and the starscape on the main viewer was replaced by a two-dimensional diagram of a solar system. Colored spheres indicated suns, moons, and planets, while elliptical lines charted their respective orbits. Kirk peered at the diagram, trying and failing to uncover its significance. He didn't recognize this particular solar system, but there didn't appear to be anything remarkable about it.

"This system," Spock stated, "lies directly before us, approximately thirty-three-point-five-six minutes away at our current speed. Direct observation indicates the presence of a single class-L sun surrounded by six planets, none of them habitable by life as we know it. Precise gravitational readings, however, suggest the existence of a seventh planet, undetectable by most conventional scanning techniques."

Scotty's eyes widened in disbelief. "Mr. Spock, you cannot be saying what I think you're saying."

"Indeed I am, Mr. Scott," Spock replied. "The only logical conclusion is that an entire planet has been concealed by means of a cloaking device of almost unimaginable power."

"Good Lord!" McCoy exclaimed.

Scotty shook his head vehemently. "It's impossible to hide a planet!"

A sudden memory flashed through Kirk's mind.

"You said the same thing," he reminded Scotty, "when our friend, Mr. Seven, claimed to be able to do just that." According to Seven, Kirk recalled, his alien sponsors had used their unearthly technology to elude discovery even in Kirk's own time. *Could it be,* he wondered, *that Seven's superiors' home base resided in the middle of the Romulan Empire?* That seemed unlikely, but he couldn't dismiss the possibility. Then again, it was the Romulans who had originally developed the cloaking technology now used by both them and the Klingons. Maybe this was some sort of top secret Romulan project?

"That thought had occurred to me as well," Spock commented, referring to Kirk's memories of their first encounter with Seven. "It is perhaps significant that the planet's presumed location is exactly where one would expect to find a class-M planet in a solar system of this nature."

"I find that *very* significant, Mr. Spock." Kirk stared at the diagram on the screen; an empty circle now indicated the probable location of the seventh planet, according to Spock's calculations. Kirk didn't even want to think about how much power would be required to cloak a whole planet, but he couldn't help wondering what sort of secret the Romulans—or Seven's people—could have gone to so much effort to hide. If the Romulans were responsible for the cloaked planet, it was possible that whatever they were concealing might constitute a serious threat to the safety of the Federation. *Since we're stuck here anyway,* he thought, *it might not be a bad idea to check this out.*

He brooded for only a minute before making his decision. "Mr. Sulu," he instructed the helmsman, "set a course for this mystery planet. Mr. Spock can give you the coordinates."

"What?" McCoy blurted. He hurried across the bridge from the science station to Kirk's side. "Jim, you can't be serious!"

"What's the matter, Bones?" Kirk asked, although he was none too surprised by the doctor's reaction. "Aren't you at all curious about what's lurking behind that cloaking field?"

"Curiosity killed the cat," McCoy drawled, "and I'm not just talking about that fuzzy feline Seven brought aboard. Don't you think we've got enough problems without sticking our noses in where we're obviously not wanted?"

"That's exactly why I want to investigate," Kirk said, a determined expression on his face. "We didn't ask to be here, but now that we are I'm not about to turn my back on what might be some new Romulan super-weapon."

"You don't know that for sure," McCoy objected.

"No I don't," Kirk said. "I don't even know if it's the Romulans or Gary Seven who are responsible for this enigma, as Spock calls it. But someone's obviously gone to a whole lot of trouble to keep us from finding out, and that's what worries me."

"And what about those poor settlers on Duwamish?" McCoy's concern was written all over his face. "Never mind the danger to the crew; we're needed desperately on Duwamish. Those people are in trouble now. We don't have time to mess about with sneaky Romulan mysteries."

Kirk winced inwardly. He had not forgotten about the imperiled men and women he had been sent to protect.

Spock came to his rescue. "Regrettably, Doctor, time for us has already run out. Even at maximum warp, the Duwamish system is now many days away. We could not hope to arrive in time to make a significant difference. Logically, our needs and priorities have changed." Spock pressed a button and the diagram on the main viewer was replaced by a deceptively empty-looking starscape.

"Logic!" McCoy's face looked as though he had just

bitten into an unusually sour lemon. "How can you talk about logic when we're looking at a catastrophe?"

"Extreme circumstances are often when clear thinking is most required," Spock responded.

Kirk decided to interrupt the familiar argument between Spock and McCoy. "Starfleet has other ships," he announced. "They may not be as near to Duwamish as we once were, but they'll have to do what they can. Spock is right; thanks to our friend Mr. Seven, we've lost our chance to be the first on the scene." Kirk peered at the image on the screen; he could see the system's sun shining in the distance, but none of its planets were visible yet. He stared into the approaching darkness as if he could penetrate its mysteries by sheer will alone. Somewhere ahead, he knew, was that invisible seventh planet, and who knows what else. *This is the right thing to do,* he thought. *So why do I feel like I'm playing into Seven's hand?*

Chapter Seven

I THINK I'm starting to get the hang of this, Roberta thought. She perched on the edge of the plastic chair, munching on a slice of pizza while she experimented with the computer. At first, the so-called "food synthesizer" had professed its ignorance of even the simplest varieties of pizza, but, after a bit of trial and error, she had not only managed to reprogram the synthesizer to produce passable slices of pizza, but she had also succeeded in teaching it to provide a wide assortment of toppings. *Yum,* she thought, biting into the sweet and crispy result of her labors. *You just can't get a decent pineapple pizza east of the Mississippi—except on starships, I guess.*

The floor was littered with earlier, failed attempts at pizza, some of them topped with alien substances that Roberta couldn't even begin to identify, especially that wiggly orange stuff that appeared to be, well, alive. Interplanetary brotherhood was all very well and good, but Roberta wasn't sure she wanted to meet any being that considered that orange goo a condiment. Extending a bare foot warily, she shoved the writhing slice further away from her. "I'll make you a deal," she said to the pizza. "I won't eat you if you won't eat me."

The slice, thankfully, left her toes alone.

Enough fooling around, she thought. *Time to get down to business.* The green cube rested atop the triangular computer terminal, flashing periodically. Establishing a link between the cube and the computer had been easier than she expected, at least once the ship stopped shaking; she wondered just how similar the *Enterprise*'s computer was to Seven's good old Beta-5.

Despite her initial fears, she was now convinced that the tremendous jolts that had rocked the *Enterprise* had not been caused by her first experiments with the computer. The ship must have run into some sort of turbulence, she guessed, remembering that one time she'd had to fly a 747 through a thunderstorm after accidentally knocking out both pilots with a tranquilizer beam. Boy, had that been a bumpy flight! *If I can survive that trip, I can survive this one,* she thought, although she couldn't help wondering exactly what sort of rough weather you could run into in space?

"Computer," she said, focussing on the tiny viewscreen, "identify location of the jail . . . I mean, brig."

"The brig is located on Deck Seven," the terminal answered. Yes, Roberta decided upon hearing it again, the voice of the *Enterprise*'s computer was definitely warmer and less snooty than the Beta-5's.

"Deck Seven, right," Roberta muttered. Like she knew where that was. She took another tack. "Show me what it looks like."

The terminal emitted a stern beep. "Access to security monitors is limited to command personnel."

"Darn," Roberta said. It made sense, though.

Captain Kirk wouldn't want to give any old visitor the run of the ship. Hopefully, though, she had resources nobody had counted on.

She gave the blinking green cube a friendly tap. "Okay, buddy, it's your turn. Override the ship's computer."

The flashing emerald light within the cube turned into a continuous green glow as the cube went to work. Roberta held her breath while a furious humming emerged from the interior of the three-sided terminal. "Unauthorized interface," the computer announced, its voice sounding almost alarmed. "Unauthorized interface, unauthor—interface, un—interface, interface, interfacing . . ."

The lighted viewscreen went blank for a moment, then came on again. Roberta gasped as she saw what appeared to be a row of doorless cells, observed from the vantage point of what she guessed was an overhead camera. A string of white lights outlined the entrances to each cell, all of which appeared to be unoccupied except for one in the middle, which held the unmistakable figure of Gary Seven, still clad in his stolen gold and black uniform. Seated on a simple, utilitarian bench, he glanced up at the ceiling outside his cell. Roberta had the eerie feeling that he was looking directly at her.

"Security protocols overridden," the terminal announced, its previous voice replaced by the cold, imperious tones of the Beta-5.

"Groovy," Roberta said, staring into the cryptic depths of Seven's icy blue eyes. She swallowed one last gulp of pizza, then absentmindedly wiped her greasy fingers on her skirt while she tried to figure out what to do next. She licked her lips; the tangy pizza had left her feeling thirsty. "Get me a Fresca," she said, "with ice."

"Please supply the chemical components of this foodstuff," the computer replied.

* * *

"Almost there," Sulu declared a bit hesitantly. He peered through a binocular viewing mechanism attached to the helm console by a telescoping metal arm. "I think."

Kirk shared the helmsman's uncertainty. According to Spock's calculations, they should be within sight of the seventh planet, yet the screen before him displayed nothing but empty space. "Mr. Spock?" he inquired, rapping his fingers impatiently upon the armrest of his chair.

"The planet should be dangerously close by," the Vulcan confirmed. "I recommend slowing to impulse speed."

"Do it," Kirk ordered Sulu. He squinted at the main viewer as the distant stars appeared to slow to a stop. "I don't see anything ahead, Spock."

Spock approached Kirk's chair. "According to most conventional scanning techniques, there is nothing there. Nevertheless, slight aberrations in the orbits of the other planets in this system imply the presence of a celestial body at these coordinates."

"That's incredible," Kirk murmured, genuinely amazed by the concept. Cloaked ships were one thing, but an entire planet? "How far out do you think the cloaking field extends?"

"Beyond the outer atmosphere of the planet at the very least," Spock surmised. "Otherwise we would be able to see a thin, gaseous shell around the location of the planet."

"I still cannot believe it," Scotty said, scratching his head. The engineer had remained on the bridge, manning an auxiliary station behind Kirk's left shoulder. "The energy demands alone are inconceivable. Where do you find that kind of power?"

"I don't think I want to know," McCoy said, holding on tightly to the handrail surrounding the command module. "The sooner we get out of here, the better."

"All in good time, Doctor," Kirk said. He leaned

forward in his chair. "Mr. Sulu, take us closer . . . carefully."

"Aye, sir," Sulu said with a nod. He kept his gaze glued to the screen in front of him, as did everyone else on the bridge. *You could hear a pin drop,* Kirk thought. He hoped that the invisible planet didn't have any equally invisible moons that Spock had somehow overlooked, or they could be in for an extremely unpleasant collision.

"I don't suppose," he said, turning his head towards Lieutenant Uhura, "that anybody on this hypothetical planet is trying to get in touch with us yet?"

"Negative, sir," Uhura reported. "No hails at all."

Figures, Kirk thought. He wondered if the inhabitants of the planet, assuming any existed, had detected the *Enterprise's* approach. *We'll find out soon enough,* he decided. He wasn't expecting a friendly reception, not this deep into Romulan space. "Go to yellow alert," he announced.

Before anyone could respond to his order, though, Chekov called out to him. "Captain! The Romulan vessel is closing on us!"

Damn, Kirk thought, not too surprised. Commander Motak was not going to give up until the *Enterprise* was captured or destroyed; it was just how Kirk would have dealt with a Romulan warship in Federation territory. "How much time do we have?"

Chekov wiped a trickle of sweat away from his eyes. "*Gladiator* will be within firing range in less than ten minutes."

Kirk quickly weighed his alternatives. He might be able to outrace *Gladiator* again, but only by leaving the mystery planet behind and heading even deeper into the heart of the Romulan Empire. *Forget it,* he thought. *We've come this far, we're not going to leave until I get some answers.*

A provocative question sprung to mind: *Did Motak know about the cloaked planet?* If this was a Romulan military experiment, then *Gladiator's* commander was probably aware of its existence and location, but if Gary Seven or his mysterious associates were responsible for cloaking the world, as Seven had claimed they could . . .

"Mr. Sulu," he ordered. "Take us into that cloaking field, into the planet's atmosphere if necessary." If there was even a chance that Motak did not know about the cloaking field, then Kirk had to risk it.

"But, Captain," Sulu said, looking away from his personal viewing unit, "I'm not even sure where the planet is."

"Best guess, Mr. Sulu," Kirk told him, wishing he could offer the helmsman better prospects. He had never crashed the *Enterprise* into a planet before, Kirk realized, but maybe there was a first time for everything.

"Eight minutes, Captain," Chekov shouted.

"Mr. Sulu," Spock said calmly, scanning the readouts on his sensor control panel, "I have estimated the mass and diameter of the planet in question, based on the precise gravimetric distortions observed. I am feeding that data into your navigational sensors."

"Acknowledged," Sulu replied, glancing down at his control panel. Kirk saw the helmsman expel a sigh of relief.

"Just how reliable are these estimates of yours, Spock?" Kirk asked, anxious to know the worst.

"Approximately sixty-eight-point-four percent," the Vulcan stated. "The key variable is the planet's density. If the planet's core is less massive than is customary for a Class-M planet, then its diameter may be larger than estimated."

And we end up like a fly on a windshield, Kirk thought, keeping the grisly image to himself.

"Six minutes," Chekov called out.

"Good Lord," McCoy whispered. "We're being chased into a brick wall. Made of invisible bricks, no less!"

"Take a sedative, Doctor," Kirk suggested. He felt

his heart pounding in his chest, but he kept a confident expression locked firmly on his face. It took plenty of self-restraint to keep from springing from his seat and taking the helm controls himself, even though he knew Hikaru Sulu was fully up to the challenge, if anyone was. "Mr. Sulu?"

"Coming closer," Sulu reported, intent on his task. Even at mere impulse speed, the margin between safety and disaster might be a matter of seconds.

"Five minutes," Chekov counted down.

Kirk nodded at the nervous young ensign. The big question now was whether Kirk would destroy the *Enterprise*, by ramming it into an invisible planet, before Commander Motak got a chance. *Look out below*, he thought.

For one endless moment, the viewer displayed nothing but the diamond-speckled blackness of interplanetary space. Then, as if the *Enterprise* was passing through a gauzy curtain, the view on the screen shimmered briefly before giving way to an entirely different scene. Kirk suddenly glimpsed vaporous white mists, billowing clouds, turquoise seas, and huge continental land masses, all rushing towards them at frightening speed. "Pull out!" Kirk barked.

A collision seemed inevitable, but Sulu was already way ahead of his captain. The view on the screen tilted vertiginously and Kirk felt inertia yank him into his seat as the *Enterprise* leveled off its flight path above the planet's surface. A wave of nausea gripped Kirk, and he had to clench his teeth together to keep from vomiting. Caught off guard by the ship's abrupt change in course, McCoy gasped and staggered back and forth a few steps before grabbing onto the security of the handrail once more. "Fascinating," Kirk heard Spock observe.

Kirk's stomach settled back into place as their flight stabilized. "Everyone in one piece?" he asked. A chorus of affirmative responses came from all around the bridge. Kirk nodded and took a deep breath before speaking again. "Excellent work, Mr. Sulu, and you, too, Mr. Spock."

"I'll send you the bill for my shattered nerves in the morning," McCoy groused, his dour features more than a little green. "Next time you want a ride like that, I recommend you check out the Coney Island Historical Amusement Center instead."

"Why, Bones," Kirk joked, "I didn't know you liked roller coasters."

"I don't," the doctor declared, but Kirk was no longer listening. He turned toward Chekov. The young Russian still sat at his post about a meter to the right of Sulu. Like the rest of the personnel on the bridge, he looked shaken but steady.

"What about our pursuer?" Kirk demanded. This was the moment of truth: Would Motak realize where the *Enterprise* had gone? Kirk held his breath.

"*Gladiator* has slowed to impulse and is now scanning the vicinity. They do not appear to be following us." Chekov grinned wolfishly at the captain. "I think we've lost them, sir."

"Good," Kirk said, breathing a sigh of relief. He had gambled and won. If nothing else, this ploy would buy them some much-needed time. He wondered what Motak thought when the *Enterprise* suddenly disappeared from his sensors. Was there any chance that the Romulan commander would figure out where they were hiding? Even at impulse speed, a starship could cover a lot of distance in five minutes. Kirk didn't want to stick around long enough to find out.

"Captain," Uhura spoke up. "Commander Motak is hailing you on all channels."

"Let's hear what he has to say," Kirk instructed, "but don't respond unless I say so. Audio only."

Uhura flicked a switch and Motak's voice rang out from the bridge's loudspeakers: "Captain Kirk, the Treaty of Algeron specifically forbids the use of cloaking technology on Federation starships. Despite your earlier protestations of innocence, you are now in flagrant violation of the Treaty on several counts. I demand that you turn yourself and your ship over to my authority immediately."

"In a pig's eye," McCoy muttered.

Uhura cut off the transmission. "That's all there is, Captain, although the Commander's message is being repeated at regular intervals." She removed her earpiece and put it down on the communications console. "Do you wish to reply?" she asked, although she clearly guessed what his answer would be.

"Not just yet, Lieutenant," Kirk said. The last thing he wanted to do was let Motak get a fix on his position. He felt encouraged, though, by the Romulan Commander's mistaken assumption that the *Enterprise* itself possessed some manner of cloak; better that he should hunt for a cloaked ship, which could be anywhere, than guess at the existence of the cloaked planet.

Satisfied that Motak had been thwarted for the time being, Kirk turned his attention to the newly revealed planet. He contemplated the image on the screen. So near to the planet's surface, he could see only part of one hemisphere; it was strange to see the thinning blue atmosphere hanging over the planet instead of the open space he was accustomed to viewing. A heavy layer of clouds, dark with moisture, partially obscured the topographical features below. Rivers, lakes, and oceans of clear blue water divided large stretches of lush green landscapes. "One Class-M planet," Kirk said, exchanging a glance with Spock, "just as predicted."

The more he thought about it, the more intriguing he found it that Motak was apparently unaware of the cloaked planet's presence. Whatever was hidden here had been kept secret even from the commander of a Romulan battle cruiser. Now, more than ever, Kirk wanted to know what was up on the planet below— and just how much Gary Seven knew about it.

"Scan the planet for any signs of recent habitation

or unusual activity," he ordered. He peered again at the sunlit sky in front of them, then addressed Sulu. "How close to the planet are we, anyway?"

"Close enough," Sulu informed him. "We're cruising approximately twelve thousand meters above the planet's surface."

Kirk whistled appreciatively. He'd never been this close to a planet in anything larger than a shuttle. "How stable is our orbit?"

Sulu shrugged. "We can maintain this orbit indefinitely, as long as our power doesn't run out."

"I hope we're not going to be around here *that* long," Kirk said. *Just long enough to find out what's hiding down there, and why it was important enough to hide a whole world, and for Gary Seven to hijack my ship and throw it halfway across the known universe.* Deep down inside, he knew that this impossible, invisible planet had something to do with Seven's mysterious mission.

I don't know what the connection is, he thought, *but I'll bet I won't like it when I find out.*

Chapter Eight

ROBERTA GOT UP off the floor and righted her chair, which had tipped over backwards during the *Enterprise*'s last abrupt change in course. The back of her head still stung where it had smacked against the floor. She winced and felt beneath her hair, searching for a bump. *Just who is flying this spaceship anyway?* she thought irritably. *Isis?*

She pulled the chair back into place before the computer terminal and plopped down in front of the screen, only to discover that the screen had gone black and that her green cube had also tumbled to the floor. She had to get down on her hands and knees and crawl under the desk to retrieve it. *The glamorous life of a time-travelling secret agent,* she thought. *I bet Mrs. Peel never has to go poking around under the furniture.*

Inspecting the cube, she was relieved to see that the fall had left it completely unscratched. *I shouldn't be too surprised,* she thought. *After all, Seven's office back in New York had been blown up twice and* attacked by killer robots once, and the cube had come through intact each time. One of these days she'd have to ask Seven what exactly it was made off.

"Restore image of brig," she said, placing the cube back atop the computer terminal. The green cube flickered momentarily and Roberta found herself peeking at the row of detention cells once more.

Like the cube, Gary Seven appeared none the worse for wear. He stood patiently in front of the illuminated entrance to his cell. The doorway appeared open, which made Roberta wonder why Seven couldn't just walk out of the cell. Were twenty-third century jails based on the honor system or what? For the brig of a starship, security seemed to be pretty lax.

As if in answer to her questions, Seven stepped closer to the doorway and held out his hand. To her surprise, Roberta saw coruscating flashes of white energy appear where Seven's hand intersected the plane of the doorway. "Oh, my goodness!" she whispered, realizing she had severely underestimated the ship's resources. Apparently, there was something holding Seven in his cell after all.

Grimacing, Seven attempted to push his hand through the invisible barrier. Judging from his clenched teeth and contorted expression, Roberta guessed this was far from easy. For a few tense moments, the tips of his fingers extended beyond the rectangular doorway and she actually thought he was going to break free from his cell; then, with a blinding surge of energy, Seven was thrown backwards, slamming into the rear wall. Looking slightly dazed, he slumped down onto his bench, cradling the hand that had initiated the jolt. Roberta suspected that he had just received a nasty shock.

This was not good. She knew she had to do something to help. "Computer, can you turn off that force field thingie?"

"Affirmative," the cube replied. As she watched, a guard came into view on the screen. He was a beefy, blond man wearing a red shirt and black trousers, and he eyed Seven suspiciously through the invisible barrier; Roberta guessed that Seven's escape attempt had not gone unnoticed. She was still seeing spots before her eyes from the incandescent flash that had repelled Seven.

She waited until the guard had turned his back on Seven. "Now," she breathed. "Turn it off now."

"Please specify which detention cell," the cube prompted her.

Which one? Roberta had no idea how the cells were numbered, and she didn't have time to figure it out. Captain Kirk was bound to figure out what she was up to eventually. "All of them," she said. "Hurry." She held her breath, waiting anxiously to see if her plan would work.

Instantly, the lights outlining the entrance to each cell blinked off. Breathing a sigh of relief, Roberta hoped the guard wouldn't notice.

No such luck. The guard pivoted around quickly, his eyes widening at the sight of the unlighted doorways. He reached for the futuristic-looking weapon on his hip. *What was it called again?* she wondered. *A laser? No, not quite, a . . . phaser! That was it.*

Seven's reflexes were even faster than the guard's. He sprang through the now-open entrance and delivered a blow to the guard's wrist with the edge of his hand. The gun spun through the air, hitting the floor a couple yards away, then skidding to a stop inside one of the empty detention cells. Roberta watched it land, wishing she were there to grab it. It was maddening to watch the conflict unfold on her little computer screen and not be able to take part.

The guard shoved Seven away and backed towards the wall opposite the cells. His fist slammed a button next to a circular metal grille mounted in the wall. *The intercom,* Roberta guessed immediately. He was going to raise an alarm.

"Computer," she blurted, "kill the intercom in the brig."

"The internal communications system is not a living organism." The green cube flickered again. "Please clarify meaning of 'kill.'"

"Jam it, stop it, shut it down!" Roberta stared at the guard on the screen, watched him open his mouth to call for reinforcements. Seven charged at the guard again, but he clearly wasn't going to be able to shut the guard up in time. Roberta chewed her lip and crossed her fingers.

"Affirmative," the cube reported. On the screen, the guard shot the intercom a confused look. He pressed the speaker button repeatedly, getting no response.

"Yes!" Roberta exulted as Seven barreled into the unlucky guard, knocking the breath out of him. The two men grappled next to the malfunctioning intercom, pitting Starfleet muscle against Seven's specialized training, until Seven managed to seize his opponent by one arm and flip him onto the floor. Unfortunately, the guard landed right outside the nearest detention cell, only inches away from where his flung ray gun had come to rest. "Uh-oh," Roberta muttered. She saw the danger immediately, but had Seven managed to keep track of the weapon as well?

The guard scrambled on all fours into the cell and reached for the gun. His fingers wrapped around the weapon's grip and he spun around swiftly, sat up, and fired. A beam of brilliant red energy shot toward Seven, who *ducked* out of the way at the last second.

Roberta's jaw dropped. She knew that Seven kept himself in peak physical condition for a human being, but she'd never realized he could dodge a laser beam. *I want to see that in slow motion,* she thought, wondering how she could get the screen to show her an instant replay.

The guard looked even more surprised. He gulped

and fired again, but Seven dived beneath the beam. His hand reached out and struck a lighted panel next to the cell entrance. *Wait a minute,* Roberta thought. *What's he doing now?*

Without warning, the lights came on again around all the doorways into the cells. This was bad news for the unfortunate guard, who still had part of one leg in the entrance when the invisible barrier returned. Glowing white sparks erupted all around his limb, which was forcibly squeezed back into the cell with the rest of him while he howled at the sudden shock. He grabbed onto his injured leg and glared at Gary Seven through the invisible prison bars.

Alerted by the sounds of the struggle, a second security officer ran into the brig, laser gun in hand. But Seven was waiting for him just inside the door. With practiced efficiency, Seven disarmed the man and blasted him with his own weapon. The burst of crimson energy dropped the second guard to the ground. Roberta winced in sympathy; she wasn't sure exactly what those glowing rays did, but their effect looked a lot less humane than the tranquilizer beam Seven was accustomed to using.

Seven stepped away from the detention cell and inspected his borrowed Starfleet uniform for rips or tears. Apparently, he judged it in satisfactory shape, since he straightened his gold shirt, tucked the pur- loined ray gun in his belt, and headed for the exit to the brig. Before he disappeared from Roberta's sight, however, he paused and looked up directly at the overhead camera lens. Once again, she had the dis- tinct impression that her cryptic employer was mak- ing eye contact with her, an impression confirmed when he winked at her once, then stepped out into the corridor beyond the brig.

Roberta sagged back into her chair, feeling as if she'd just been through a fight herself—which, in a weird sort of way, she had. *Okay,* she thought, *now what?* Seven was on the loose again, but what was Captain Kirk going to do when he found out? Or had he caught on already? Roberta decided she needed to check on the opposition.

"Computer, show me the bridge."

"Confirmed, Captain," Uhura reported. "There is definitely an installation near the planet's equator."

"What kind of installation?" Kirk asked. So far, this installation Uhura had detected was the only sign of habitation on the cloaked world below them. He looked over Uhura's shoulder, anxious to get down to the planet and find out what was going on, preferably before that Romulan battle cruiser figured out where the *Enterprise* had disappeared to.

"It's hard to tell, sir," Uhura said. She adjusted the knobs on the emissions blanking control, filtering out the atmospheric background noise. "I'm picking up some transmissions, but they're in some sort of Romulan code."

Kirk peered at the readouts on the external communications panel, even though he knew Uhura could read them better than he could. "Are you sure they're Romulan?" Motak's apparent ignorance concerning the cloaked planet had half-convinced Kirk that Seven's people, not the Romulans, were responsible for hiding the world. *So why would they be using a Romulan code, unless this project is so top secret that not even a Romulan starship commander knows about it?*

"I think so, sir," she said. "I studied Romulan cryptography at the Academy, and these transmissions fit those algorithms. They're specially designed to baffle the universal translator, not to mention the rest of us."

"I see," Kirk said, stepping away from the communications console. As he recalled, Starfleet Intelligence had never succeeded in cracking Romulan codes, not even during Earth's first hardfought war with the Empire in the twenty-second century. "Do what you can to decipher them, Lieutenant."

What were the Romulans up to, not to mention Gary Seven and his organization? *Looks like there's only one way to get to the bottom of this.* He marched toward the turbolift doors, his mind made up. "In the meantime, I'm leading a landing party to check things out for myself. Mr. Spock, I'm leaving you in command. Sulu, Chekov, you're with me."

"Captain," Spock said, rising from his science station. "Now is not a logical time to embark on a potentially hazardous mission. Are you sure that is wise?"

"Maybe not wise," Kirk replied, "but necessary." Spock was right; this was not a decision to make lightly. He couldn't help thinking, though, that vital matters were at stake. Why else would Seven be here, in this day and age? The last time their paths had crossed, back in the twentieth century, Seven had been instrumental in preventing a nuclear war. Did the present now face a similar threat? The terrible tragedy of an old-fashioned global conflict paled against the possibility of an all-out war between the Romulans and the Federation, especially if the Empire had pushed their cloaking technology to a whole new level. This was about more than just the *Enterprise* and its crew now. The entire galaxy might be in danger.

He still had a responsibility to his crew, however. "One thing more," he instructed Spock, "if anything happens to me, if you don't hear from me for over an hour, I want you to take the *Enterprise* and get back to the Federation as quickly as possible."

"Jim!" McCoy protested. "That's suicide! You have no idea what's waiting for you down there."

Kirk ignored the doctor's objections. "I repeat: You are not to mount any sort of rescue mission on my behalf. Your first and only priority is to get this ship and its crew safely home. Understood?"

"Understood, Captain," Spock answered. If the possibility of abandoning his friend light-years behind enemy lines disturbed him, he did not show it. Kirk wasn't sure if he should be reassured or offended.

Not wanting to beam down into the middle of a potential firing squad, Kirk had Scotty transport the landing party to a site roughly half a kilometer from the perimeter of the presumed Romulan installation.

This region of the mystery planet resembled other tropical jungles that Kirk had visited. A dense canopy of leaves, vines, and branches blotted out the sky while moist ferns and bracken covered the ground between abundant tree trunks wrapped in layers of moss. Thank goodness, he thought, for the safety scanners built into the transporter equipment; otherwise, they could have been easily beamed inside one of the gigantic towers of timber all around them.

A light rain was falling, the tiny droplets streaming down his face, but the air remained warm and humid. Kirk wore only his usual shipboard uniform, but he felt decidedly overdressed. He assumed Chekov and Sulu felt the heat as well. Deep, bassy croaking came from the surrounding jungle brush; frogs, Kirk guessed, or something similar. Probably harmless, but he kept one hand on his phaser just in case.

He stepped forward experimentally, gauging the planet's gravity. It was a little heavier than he was used to, more like the gravity on Vulcan, but not excessively so. *I wouldn't want to run a marathon here,* he decided, *but this should be fine for a little covert reconnaissance.* He sniffed the air: plenty of oxygen, along with the ripe, pungent smell of rotting underbrush. A real equatorial rain forest, all right. He wondered what the Romulans thought of the climate.

If they were as similar to Vulcans as they looked, they probably liked the gravity and the heat, although this jungle was considerably damper than most sites on Vulcan.

He glanced at his companions. Both Sulu and Chekov appeared to have acclimated themselves to this new environment. He saw Sulu, the amateur botanist, bend over to inspect the toadstools growing near the base of a looming tree trunk about twelve centimeters in diameter. "Grocery shopping, Mr. Sulu?" Kirk asked.

"Just collecting samples," Sulu said. He rose, placing one of the toadstools in a pocket of his trousers. "There are some interesting specimens here. Too bad there's not time for a complete botanical survey."

Unless Spock has to leave us behind, Kirk thought. Then Sulu might end up with more than enough time to catalog the planet's proliferating flora, assuming they didn't land in a Romulan prison camp, or worse. His gaze travelled up the length of one moss-covered tree until he stared into the complex tapestry of vines and branches overhead. The leafy cover and light precipitation made it hard to judge the time of day, but, from the failing light, he guessed that night was approaching. *Just as well,* he thought. Spying was easier accomplished under the cover of darkness than in broad daylight. "Mr. Chekov, do you have the proper coordinates?"

A tricorder hung on a strap over the young Russian's shoulder. Chekov unslung the instrument and unsnapped the protective head cover. Wiping his rain-dampened bangs away from his eyes, he examined the illuminated video display next to the sensor controls. "Yes, Captain," he said, pointing into the underbrush behind Kirk. "According to this, the Romulan base is that way."

"Very good," Kirk said, contemplating a vigorous hike through the jungle. With luck, the thick foliage would conceal their approach from whomever might be guarding the installation. "Mr. Chekov, you lead the way. Sulu, you keep an eye out behind us for snakes, sabre-toothed tigers, or Romulan storm troopers." Kirk grinned. "That should just about cover everything."

"*Almost* everything, Captain," an unexpected voice added. Kirk drew his phaser and twisted his body toward the source of the voice: a dimly glimpsed figure stepping out from behind the bole of an enormous tree. The shade concealed the figure's features, but Kirk recognized the voice instantly. *Damn,* he thought. Things had just gotten a lot more complicated.

"Mind if I join you?" asked Gary Seven.

Chapter Nine

Kɪʀᴋ's ᴄᴏᴍᴍᴜɴɪᴄᴀᴛᴏʀ beeped before he could reply. Keeping both eyes and his phaser on the visitor from the twentieth century, he lifted the device to his face with his free hand and snapped it open. "Kirk here. What is it?"

Spock's voice emerged from the communicator. "You should be aware, Captain, that Mr. Seven has somehow escaped from the brig. Two security officers were immobilized, but neither has been seriously injured. A ship-wide search is now in progress, but—"

"Don't bother," Kirk interrupted. Raindrops ran down his hair, dripping onto the back of his neck. "I know just where Mr. Seven is at the moment. About seven meters in front of me, in fact."

"Indeed." Kirk couldn't see Spock, but he could imagine the Vulcan raising an eyebrow as he spoke.

"I suggest you inspect the transporter rooms," Kirk suggested. "You may find one or two more 'immobilized' personnel." Seven shrugged, looking none too apologetic. "Then I want you to beam Mr. Seven right back to the brig."

That got a reaction from Seven. "I can't let you do that, Captain. Not yet." He drew a thin silver instrument from his pocket. Kirk's eyes widened.

"Don't move!" he ordered. Chekov and Sulu followed his lead, aiming their own phasers at Seven. "Drop it," he told Seven.

"Captain Kirk," Seven began. He didn't point his weapon at Kirk, but he didn't let go of it either. "You don't understand. . . ."

"Drop it," Kirk repeated. Seven had jeopardized his crew for the last time. "I don't care how good you are. You can't knock out all three of us, before one of us stuns you with a phaser. You're outnumbered."

Seven paused, as if mentally evaluating his chances. Kirk found himself grateful that at least Roberta Lincoln was apparently not within the vicinity. "Perhaps you're right," Seven said finally. The silver device slipped from his fingers, splashing gently into a rain-filled puddle at Seven's feet.

"I thought we took that thing away from you," Kirk commented, lowering his phaser. Sulu and Chekov kept Seven under guard while Kirk retrieved the weapon from the puddle. It was just as lightweight as it looked, even more so than a standard issue phaser. *Starfleet science would probably love to get a look at this gadget,* he thought.

"Servo has a homing device," Seven explained. "It was easy enough to lock onto it with your transporter and beam it back to me at the same time that I transported down to this planet."

"A simple, one-step process, right?" Kirk asked, impressed despite himself. He doubted that even Scotty could manage to transport two objects simultaneously with that much precision.

"Something like that," Seven said. "Captain, I gave you my tool as a gesture of good faith. I would much rather work with you than against you. Now that we're this close to my goal, we can't afford to keep getting in each other's way."

So Seven's mission does *involve this cloaked planet,* Kirk thought. He didn't feel surprised, just manipulated. "Sorry, Mr. Seven. Your intentions may be sincere, but your methods seem to involve assaulting my crew whenever it strikes you as convenient to do so. I can't afford to trust you, and you don't deserve it."

"But this isn't about me," Seven said. "It's about the future." He approached Kirk, his boots sinking into the muddy earth between them. Chekov rushed, phaser raised, in front of Seven and forced him to back up a few steps.

The rain was coming down even harder now, reminding Kirk of the flood victims back on Duwamish. Seven had endangered them as well. Kirk slipped the servo into his pocket, then brought his communicator up to his lips. "Spock? Are you still there?"

"Yes, Captain." Static distorted Spock's voice. Kirk wondered if the turbulent weather was interfering with the transmission, or if something more ominous was responsible for the static, maybe some kind of jamming technology? "Is the situation under control?"

"For now," Kirk said, "but I'll feel better when Mr. Seven is back in the brig. Beam him up."

"You're making a mistake, Captain." Seven glared at the phaser in Chekov's hand. "Trust me, you have more to lose than almost anyone else."

Kirk felt a chill run down his spine that had nothing to do with the weather. *What did Seven mean, I have the most to lose?* He watched as the familiar sparkle of the transporter effect enveloped Seven. His angular frame began to dissolve into a column of golden sparks.

Then something went wrong. Without warning, the process reversed itself. The smell of ozone permeated the air and the usual hum of the transporter turned into a harsh, screeching noise, like the sound of a phaser on overload. Raw energy and information was forcibly crammed back into tight, restrictive patterns, abruptly displacing a man-sized volume of wind and rain. Kirk felt a splash of moisture against his face as the disrupted transporter beam stirred up the already stormy atmosphere of the jungle. Golden sparkles dimmed abruptly, their radiance snuffed out, and, blinking the rain from his eyes, Kirk saw the outline of a humanoid body thrashing wildly amidst a disintegrating column of energy, a scream of agony blending with the grating screech of the distortion. Through a haze of chaotic particles and mist, he thought he discerned a pair of dark eyes, alive with shock and anguish. *Dear God,* Kirk thought, *can he feel what's happening to him?* The once-shimmering, now shadowy beam of light collapsed into a writhing, radiant figure composed of billions of agitated electrons rushing together, reintegrating into solid matter, into a being called Gary Seven, who let out a cry of pain before falling forward into the mud.

Sulu ran over to the prone figure, lifting Seven's face from the mucky water before he could suffocate. A sticky layer of mud adhered to Seven's features, partially masking his expression. A thin, brown slurry streamed from his lips and nostrils. Sulu rolled the man over onto his back and placed his ear against Seven's chest. The enigmatic time traveller appeared to be breathing, but it was difficult to tell through the rain. Did he need a doctor? Did they dare risk beaming McCoy down after watching Seven implode like that? "Spock, what happened?" Kirk shouted into the communicator. "Spock! Spock?"

There was no answer. The transmission had been cut off. But was his communicator malfunctioning, Kirk wondered, or had something happened to the *Enterprise?* He had to know the answer. "Chekov, try to contact the ship! Can you get through?"

The young ensign spoke into his communicator,

then shook his head. *"Nyet,* Captain," he called out. Tossing the worthless communicator aside, he consulted his tricorder. "Captain, I don't believe it." He swung the tricorder in a full circle around him, his gaze glued to the readout on the instrument's display screen. "It's a force field, many kilometers across, all around us, cutting us off from the ship. I don't know where it came from. It wasn't there a minute ago, I'm sure of it."

"Understood," Kirk answered. He understood all too well.

They were trapped on the planet—with no way out.

Roberta watched the monitor in her room with growing dismay. On the screen, the woman in the red uniform, whose name she had learned was Uhura, tried relentlessly to get hold of the landing party, but without any success. Mr. Spock and Dr. McCoy looked on grimly while they spoke of a "force field" that apparently had them stumped. She didn't need to be on the bridge physically to sense the tense mood that had come over the scene.

Great, she thought bitterly, *just great.* Now that the crew of the *Enterprise* had lost contact with both Gary Seven and Captain Kirk, how was she supposed to keep track of what was going on? Granted, Mr. Spock had been prevented from beaming Seven back onto the *Enterprise,* but that was hardly reassuring. All she knew was that Seven was stuck on the planet below— assuming that he had even survived that botched transporter job. Judging from the tense conversations she had overheard via the computer, not even Mr. Spock or Scotty the engineering guy were quite sure if Seven was still alive and well on the planet. *I have to do something,* she thought, *but what?*

She contemplated the illuminated green cube sitting atop the computer station. So far the device had acted as an all-purpose skeleton key to most of the

Enterprise's computerized systems. How far was she willing to push it?

"Computer," she said. "Show me Supervisor 194. Code name: Gary Seven."

The cube blinked furiously for less than ten seconds before responding. "Subject is not within range of ship's scanners."

She scowled and tried again. "How about Captain Kirk, then?"

"Subject is not within range of ship's scanners."

"Great," she muttered sarcastically. It made sense, though; the cube was limited to whatever resources were available to the *Enterprise*. If Mr. Spock and the others couldn't locate the landing party, then neither could she. The cube could only override whatever technology already existed aboard the ship; it wasn't Aladdin's lamp.

Leaning back against her chair, she pushed away from the computer station and looked over at the closed door to her temporary quarters. She was starting to feel a little stir-crazy. There was only so much she could do cooped up in this comfy little interstellar hotel room. Perhaps it was time to stage another breakout. She studied the green cube from a few feet away. Maybe it was no crystal ball, but it might work as a get-out-of-jail-free card.

But what could she do once she was loose? Where should she go? The planet itself was one possibility. She could probably figure out the *Enterprise's* transporter system if she had to; how different could it be from the one she and Gary Seven used all the time? Granted, there was still that force field to deal with, but surely it couldn't be covering the whole world? With a little bit of luck and a lot of hiking, she might be able to hunt down Seven on Planet Romulan or whatever it was called. She refused to accept that he had been permanently disintegrated by the interrupted transporter beam, not after all they had both survived back on Earth.

Yeah, she thought, *that's a plan. Maybe I can even hook up with Isis before I vacate the ship. Or not.* After all, *someone* had to stay behind to keep an eye on the ship, and she nominated the cat.

She hurried to retrieve her old sneakers from the bedroom, then dropped back into the chair to pull them on. She was just lacing up the last shoe when she heard an angry voice come from the computer screen. Something about the tone of the speaker's voice caught her attention, and she stared at the screen, which continued to look in on the ship's bridge. Doctor McCoy seemed to be having some sort of confrontation with Mr. Spock, and he didn't look happy.

"You can't be serious, Spock!" he objected strenuously. "We have to organize a rescue party, not plan our escape! What about Jim and the others?"

The alien first officer appeared unmoved by the doctor's outburst. "We are making every effort to reestablish contact with the captain, despite the ongoing problem of the force field. However, if we do not succeed in reaching him within the agreed-upon time period, I will have no choice but to set course for the Federation, just as Captain Kirk instructed."

"Leaving him behind, you mean," McCoy snapped, "along with Chekov and Sulu and Seven! You cold-blooded, procedure-spouting machine, these are human lives we're talking about!"

Roberta jumped to her feet, newly energized by what she had just heard. *This changes everything,* she thought. If the *Enterprise* took off for Earth, as Mr. Pointy-Ears clearly intended, Seven would be marooned on an alien planet so far from Earth that not even NASA could bring him home. *Forget it,* she resolved. That wasn't happening as long as she had something to say about it.

She snatched her control cube off the top of the computer, relieved that she didn't have to detach any wires or cables connecting the cube to the computer station. *Let's hear it for trouble-free technology,* she thought. Now that she had established a link between the cube and the ship's computerized brain, proximity shouldn't matter. In theory, that is.

No time like the present to check it out, she thought, approaching the closed door confining her to the guest quarters. She rapped gently on the metal door, but nothing happened; the door remained shut. "Computer," she instructed, "open door."

The cube blinked once, the green light reflecting off the polished steel surface of the door. "Doorway to Suite 14-J ordered shut under security protocols gamma-xy-5," it announced.

Roberta rolled her eyes. She could have predicted that. "Override security protocols."

"Working," the cube reported. Moments later, the door slid open, revealing the corridor beyond. *So much for house arrest,* she thought. *These future people shouldn't depend so much on their computers.*

Then she noticed the guard posted outside her door. *Oh,* she thought, *I should have known it wouldn't be that easy.*

The guard was an athletic-looking Asian man wearing a red shirt, black trousers, and a surprised expression on his face. He obviously hadn't expected her to find a way out, although Roberta was relieved to note that he didn't immediately reach for his gun. "Excuse me," he said. "I'm afraid I have to ask you to step back into your room. Captain's orders."

Talk fast, Roberta thought. "But my food processing whatchamacallit isn't working." She pointed back at the open doorway. "Maybe you can take a look at it?"

The guard shook his head. "I can't leave my post," he explained. He crossed his arms over his chest. "If you want, I can call for a technician."

"But I'm starving to death," Roberta lied, conveniently forgetting her groundbreaking experiments in pizza processing. "I haven't eaten since 1969!"

"Well . . ." he said hesitantly, thinking it over. He gave her a quick once-over and relaxed his posture somewhat. *That's right,* she thought, *I'm just a poor, primitive waif from the twentieth century. No threat to anyone, let alone a highly trained starship trooper.* He uncrossed his arms and stepped toward the door. "Maybe you're just overlooking something obvious."

Like a transparent escape attempt, maybe? She moved to one side to let the guard enter her quarters, then waited until he was all the way inside. "Hey, what kind of trouble were you having?" he asked. "There's food all over the floor in here."

You won't be hungry then, she thought, and darted into the hall, blurting instructions to the cube even as she ran. "Seal Suite 14-J immediately! Security Protocol, er, lincoln-roberta." The cube flashed rapidly, its flickering green radiance escaping through the cracks between her fingers.

"Stop!" the guard shouted, rushing after her. "Wait!" He grabbed for his phaser, but the steel door came whooshing shut, trapping him half in and half out of the doorway, like a New York commuter stuck between closed subway doors. "Come back! Captain's orders!"

He'll get free in a minute, Roberta knew, *but that may be enough. All I need to do now is find one of those turbolift thingies and take an express trip straight to the bridge, just in time to keep Mr. Spock from stranding Gary Seven on the wrong side of the universe.*

You know, maybe the twenty-third century wasn't so complicated after all. . . .

"C'mon, kitty, what do you want?"

Nurse Christine Chapel offered the caged animal another piece of nutrient bar. They didn't actually have much in the way of pet food in sickbay, but the all-purpose emergency ration couldn't do the cat any harm. Unfortunately, the animal wasn't showing any interest in the snack, although she clearly wanted something.

Just like Zoe, she thought, her old cat back in her Academy days. Zoe was more tortoise-shell-colored than midnight black, but she could be just as finicky. And opinionated.

The cat emitted a singularly plaintive yowl and tried to stick its paws through the steel grating between it and Nurse Chapel. Golden eyes stared longingly into the nurse's.

"I know, I know," Chapel said, "you want out of that cage. But Doctor McCoy said that the captain wanted you locked up." She didn't know the full story behind the animal; the doctor hadn't even mentioned the cat's name, just muttered under his breath, then stormed off to the bridge, saying something about "keeping an eye on that green-blooded robot." Chapel winced slightly at the thought. She didn't exactly share McCoy's acerbic opinion of the ship's first officer.

The pads of the cat's front feet protruded through the metal lattice hemming it in. The caged feline made a sound that sounded heartbreakingly like a whimper. Chapel glanced at the magnetic lock on the lid of the carrier. All she needed to do was key in the right three-character combination, which McCoy had programmed to be simply C-A-T. She looked again at the unhappy animal. She always was a sucker for a sob story. "Well, maybe it wouldn't do any harm. Just for a few minutes . . ."

She reached for the lid and typed in the first two characters. Inside the cage, the cat watched her with eerie concentration. Then Chapel noticed the yellow alert lights flashing above her head, just as they had been flashing since the captain beamed down to the planet. *Maybe this isn't such a great idea,* she thought. They were in enemy territory, after all. What if the Romulans caught up with them again? Casualties might come flooding into the sickbay, and there would be this cat getting in the way, contaminating the sterilization fields . . .

"Sorry, kitty." She reset the lock and stepped back from the cage. "I'm afraid you're going to have to stay where you are until things are a little less crazy."

To her surprise, the cat hissed angrily and turned its back on her.

Their communicators wouldn't work, but nothing was stopping the rain from pouring down. *A force field,* Kirk thought, *located somewhere in the stratosphere. That makes sense.* The field must have gone up just in time to block the transporter beam from the *Enterprise,* forcing Seven's molecules to reintegrate violently. It had been a close thing; another second, plus or minus, and Seven would have been safely aboard ship, or else too far gone to solidify again. Seven had nearly become background radiation, permanently.

Kirk felt a pang of relief. *Nobody deserves that,* he thought, *not even Gary Seven.* Grudgingly, he recalled Spock's list of Seven's various accomplishments in the twentieth century, then watched as Sulu helped the stricken man assume a sitting position next to the puddle of mud. Apparently, he was still alive after all. Muck trickled from Seven's mouth as he coughed violently, shaking his entire body.

Okay, he amended privately, *especially not Seven.*

But who was responsible for the force field? Kirk's mind raced through the possibilities. Not Seven, surely; Seven didn't want to be transported back to the *Enterprise,* but Kirk couldn't imagine that Seven would subject himself to such an ordeal, risking his very corporeal existence, just to avoid a detention cell. Hell, he had *seen* the shocked look in Seven's eyes when the beam jerked him back to the surface. The man had been just as caught off guard as the rest of them.

It had to be the Romulans, then. Not Commander Motak of *Gladiator,* but whoever was in charge of this top secret installation on this supposedly nonexistent planet. *Cloaks* and *shields,* Kirk thought. *Someone really doesn't want to be found.*

And if the shield just went up, that could only mean two things. Either they had detected the *Enterprise* in orbit around the planet, or they had noted the arrival of the landing party. *One way or another, they know we're here,* Kirk thought. For all he knew, they could be closing in on him and the others at this very moment—and/or attacking the *Enterprise.* He didn't like either notion.

"Mr. Sulu," Kirk called to the helmsman. To his surprise, Sulu was already helping Gary Seven onto his feet; Kirk couldn't believe the man was still conscious after what he'd been through. "Can he be moved?"

"I think so, Captain," Seven answered for himself. His voice sounded a bit shaky, but determined. He used his sleeve to wipe some of the mud away from his mouth and eyes. "We have to try."

Kirk nodded. "Let's get going. Sulu, you help Mr. Seven. Chekov, watch out for ambushes, but keep us heading toward that installation." *If nothing else,* he thought, *we have to shut down that force field before Spock can beam us back.*

Part of him hoped, however, that Spock would follow his orders to the letter and flee with the *Enterprise* within an hour, if not earlier. The sudden appearance of the force field clearly indicated the presence of hostile forces responding to their arrival; the smart thing for Spock to do would be to get the ship out of here—and out of Romulan territory—as quickly as possible. Surely, Spock wouldn't risk the *Enterprise* just to wait for Kirk and the others—or would he? Despite his professed devotion to logic, Spock could be remarkably unpredictable at times, not to mention stubbornly loyal to his friends. Just look at all he had risked for the sake of poor Chris Pike. *Don't do it, Spock,* Kirk thought, wishing that the Vulcan's telepathy was strong enough to hear him even from so far away, *don't wait for me.* With any luck at all, the ship was already en route to the Neutral Zone. *Good luck,* he thought, imagining all the obstacles between the ship and the Federation and recalling the friends he might never see again: Spock, Scotty, McCoy, Uhura . . . if any crew could give the Romulans the slip all the way back to the Federation, then they were the crew who would do it. *Godspeed,* he thought.

Then he was running after Chekov through the rain and the mud and the dark. The underbrush was not too thick to traverse; the leafy canopy overhead kept sunlight away from the jungle floor, cutting down on ground-level biomass. Still, stringy vines and exposed roots tugged on his legs as he jogged behind Chekov, while thorny brambles snagged onto his trousers. His boots splashed through puddles, sometime ankle-deep in thick, clingy ooze. The extra gravity only made the trek harder. The available light grew even fainter as the rain became a downpour. Soon he could barely see Chekov in front of him. The young ensign was only a vague, gray silhouette, dimly glimpsed through the pouring sheets of rain and ever-darkening shadows. Kirk glanced back over his shoulder, worried about leaving Sulu and Seven behind. He saw them trailing behind him. Seven still had one arm draped over Sulu's shoulders and was limping slightly. Kirk was amazed the man could move at all, after the ordeal he'd been through.

"Keep your eyes on each other," he ordered Chekov and Sulu, raising his voice to be heard over the deluge. "We don't want to lose anyone."

Muffled acknowledgments came from the two crewmen. Maybe even from Seven, too; the voices were difficult to make out. The only good thing about the foul weather, he thought, was that it would help conceal them from any Romulan search parties. He tried to listen for any sounds of pursuit, but heard only the rain cascading in his ears. His uniform, soaked through, stuck to his skin as he ran, weighing him down even more. He wiped trickles of cold rain water from his eyes and kicked his way through the clotted jungle growth.

A roar cut through the night, followed by a cry of alarm. Kirk spun around just in time to see a dark shape drop from the trees onto Sulu and Seven. He got a quick impression of four outstretched legs, green-and-black striped fur, and a glimpse of something that looked like ivory, before he yanked his phaser off his belt, disregarding the sticky brambles that hindered his arm as he did so.

The beast had knocked both men to the ground and now had one of them pinned beneath its heavy paws. Kirk couldn't tell if the creature's prey was Seven or Sulu; all he could see was a confusion of flailing human limbs and emerald fur. Worried about hitting the downed man by mistake, he fired a warning shot just above the creature's head. The incandescent beam burned through the air between Kirk and the beast, momentarily dispelling the shadows so that Kirk got a brief glimpse of enraged green eyes, a maw full of gleaming white fangs, and a glistening ivory horn in the center of the creature's forehead.

The beam got the creature's attention all right, distracting it from its fallen prey. With a fierce growl, the predator sprang off the other man and charged toward Kirk, who aimed his phaser at the attacking beast. Before he could fire, though, something sprayed from the tip of the creature's single long horn. Half liquid, half gaseous, the foreign substance stung like acid. The spray burned Kirk's hand where it touched his exposed flesh; caught by surprise by the sudden pain, he let go of his phaser, which went flying into the underbrush. Fumes stung his eyes and throat. Tears streamed down his face, mingling with pelting raindrops, as he coughed the noxious vapors away from his lungs.

A heavy weight slammed into him with the force of a meteor. Kirk landed on his back in the mud with the full mass of the creature on top of him. Ignoring the pain from the creature's venomous spray, he grabbed onto the animal's throat, digging his fingers into the thick, corded muscles beneath the creature's matted coat. The pungent odor of the creature's fur filled his nose and mouth. Sharp talons sank into Kirk's chest as he fought to keep a set of snapping jaws away from his neck. The beast's jagged fangs were only centimeters away from his jugular, and getting closer.

"Captain!" Kirk heard Chekov splashing through the rain-drenched jungle. The alien predator raised its head long enough to release another dose of its venom at the Russian. Chekov cried out in pain and Kirk saw the flash of a phaser beam, wildly off target, zip by overhead, missing the creature entirely.

The ensign had distracted the beast for an instant, though. Kirk took advantage of the animal's inattention by rolling over onto his side and tossing the creature's massive body into the surrounding foliage. The beast's claws left bloody streaks down the front of Kirk's shirt as he leaped away from the animal and scrambled to his feet.

The predator regained its bearings just as swiftly. Landing on its feet, it turned around and confronted Kirk once more. Its jaws opened wide to roar its challenge; Kirk found himself looking straight down the creature's gullet, past forbidding rows of pointed teeth. He could smell the animal's breath, as hot and fetid as the swamp that sheltered it. The creature's ferocious roar filled his ears.

"J'sshwato ormeur! Ki agbo Seven!" a voice called out. Kirk glanced away from the beast long enough to see Gary Seven rising from the mud where he had fallen. His voice, though tremulous at first, gained

strength as he called out to the animal. He staggered through the muck until he was only centimeters away from the creature, who turned its head to watch him quizzically. *"Kiy sora sta-riis-nokta!"*

Kirk expected the monster to tear Seven apart. Instead it lowered its head and padded over to Seven's side, suddenly looking no more ferocious than a kitten. Seven stroked the creature's fur-covered skull and the animal closed its eyes. Kirk wasn't sure, but he thought he heard . . . *purring?*

"Lower your weapons, gentlemen," Seven said to the Starfleet officers. "Osiris poses no threat to us."

Kirk approached Seven and the animal warily. Now that he had a moment to catch his breath and take a better look at the creature, Kirk could see that Seven's friend was quite definitely feline in nature, despite the ivory horn that sprung from its forehead like a mugato's. A thin trickle of venom leaked from the tip of the horn. The green and black stripes upon the animal's pelt, well-suited to camouflage in this verdant rain forest, resembled a Terran tiger's markings, just as the quivering whiskers beneath the creature's muzzle bore further evidence to its similarity to terrestrial felines. Kirk stared into the big cat's emerald eyes, looking for some sense of its intelligence. Was this beast Seven called Osiris actually sentient, he pondered, or was that merely animal cunning peering back at him? Kirk remembered the sleek black cat that accompanied Seven everywhere and wondered, for the first time, whether Isis might be more than a mere pet. He wished there was some way he could warn Spock to keep a closer eye on the cat.

Osiris emitted a throaty squawk. "He apologizes for the misunderstanding," Seven translated, "but Osiris is suspicious of strangers, especially these days. Thankfully, no one was seriously harmed."

"More or less," Kirk said. His eyes and throat still burned from the cat's toxic spray, but the symptoms seemed to be fading away. He inspected his right hand. The skin was red and irritated, as from a sunburn or minor allergic reaction, but otherwise undamaged. Osiris's venom was intended to stun its prey, he deduced, not finish them off. He stretched out his hand, letting the cool rain soothe the reddened skin. "Chekov," he called out, remembering that the young ensign had been sprayed as well, "are you all right?"

"I think so, Captain," Chekov answered, coughing mildly and rubbing the tears from his eyes. "It stings some, but that's all."

"How about you, Sulu?" Kirk asked. He watched the helmsman slowly lift himself from the soggy ground. A thick layer of mud coated the front of Sulu's uniform, which looked torn and shredded around his shoulders. Kirk looked for bite or claw marks, and was relieved not to spot any.

"I'm fine, sir," Sulu reported. "I just had the wind knocked out of me."

"Your men got off easy," Seven commented to Kirk. "Osiris can be quite lethal, under the proper circumstances."

"Such as?" Kirk prompted. His mind raced ahead furiously, as he dug through the underbrush, searching for his phaser. Seven's familiarity with this animal, so reminiscent of Isis the cat, only confirmed Kirk's suspicions that Seven and his mysterious alien supervisors were intimately connected to this entire cloaked planet. But where did the Romulans fit in? Kirk still couldn't figure it out. "Exactly what sort of circumstances are we dealing with here? And why would Osiris be, as you said, unusually jumpy these days? What's going on?"

Seven sighed wearily. A growl rumbled in the big cat's throat. "I know, I know," he murmured to Osiris. "I suppose there isn't any choice." He fixed his gray eyes on Kirk and took another deep breath before speaking again. "Now that we've come this far, you need to know something of the facts."

Finally, Kirk thought. He retrieved his phaser from beneath a leafy fern. It was a bit muddy, but looked still in working order.

"It all started," Seven began, "back in 1969. . . ."

Chapter Ten

"DAMNIT, SPOCK, you can't just abandon Jim!"

Dr. McCoy's face reddened as he spoke; Spock found it singularly unflattering, even for a human. He was quite accustomed to the doctor's volatile nature, however. At times he even found it amusing, on an intellectual level. This was not one of those times.

"The captain's orders were quite clear," he observed. He kept his gaze fixed on the viewscreen, where the unnamed planet slowly rotated before his eyes. It looked deceptively innocuous and ordinary. "Should anything happen to him, I was to use my best efforts to return the *Enterprise* to Federation space." It was not by his choice that Spock now occupied the captain's chair on the bridge. Indeed, he would have preferred otherwise, but with the captain missing there was no other alternative. His duty was clear.

I am sorry, Jim, Spock thought, permitting himself a rare moment of regret. *You will be missed.* He was aware of a greater sorrow, caged behind the wall of his intellect, yet he was cautious not to let it demand too much expression, lest it break free and overpower his logic just when his duty most required a clear and unencumbered mind.

"Lieutenant Rodriguez," he said, addressing the crewman who had taken Sulu's place at the helm, "prepare to depart orbit."

"But we lost contact with Jim and the others only an hour ago!" McCoy said, his tone growing even more vehement. He grabbed the armrest of the captain's chair and spun Spock around to face him. "You have to give him a chance to turn things around. God knows Jim's gotten out of stickier situations than this."

There was some validity to the doctor's argument, Spock conceded. In the past, Captain Kirk had demonstrated a consistent ability to extricate himself from seemingly hopeless circumstances. Indeed, Spock could immediately recall numerous instances where the captain had defied odds that Spock had calculated at ninety percent or higher, including his triumphant encounters with the Gorn, the Horta, and the so-called Squire of Gothos. The odds were against him doing so again, but the captain had always managed to defy the odds before. To believe otherwise, in the face of the documented evidence of past events, would be illogical.

"Lieutenant Uhura," he asked, "have you been able to reestablish contact with the landing party?"

"I'm trying," she insisted, making minute adjustments to her instrumentation even as she spoke, "but I can't get past the force field, no matter what frequency I use."

"Acknowledged," Spock said. "Continue your efforts for as long as we remain within communications range of the planet." He intended to give the captain every chance to contact the ship in the time remaining, but he could not delay their departure indefinitely. By his own estimation, it was extremely unlikely that the captain would be able to elude capture by those responsible for the sudden appearance of the force field, although the involvement of Mr. Seven, an unknown factor of a distinctly unpredictable nature, made it impossible to calculate the odds precisely.

The Romulans, on the other hand, were quite predictable. They would show the captain no mercy if they apprehended him. On some level, Spock privately admitted to himself, he always found it . . . unsettling . . . to deal with Romulans, more so than during comparable interactions with such adversaries as the Klingons or the Tholians. In many ways they were more similar to him than any human, yet their aggressive militarism and negative emotions made them each a living repudiation of the Vulcan ideals to which Spock had devoted his life. *If even the Romulans, who are genetically indistinguishable from Vulcans, cannot live according to the teachings of Surak, what hope does a half-breed such as myself have to attain a state of perfect logic?* The Romulans were a mirror that offered him only the most disturbing reflections.

Nor had his last encounter with the Romulans left his mind untroubled; although his duty to Starfleet had been clear, he regretted the deception he had been forced to practice upon the Romulan commander, whose trust he had both won and betrayed. It had felt much like deceiving another Vulcan. The incident, although undeniably necessary, still plagued his conscience.

I must be careful, he thought, *not to let such concerns cloud my reasoning in this instance.* "Mr. Rodriguez, plot an evasive course that will put as much distance as possible between *Gladiator* and ourselves."

"Aye, sir," Rodriguez answered. The crewman was new to bridge duty and looked verifiably nervous. Next to him, on the other side of the astrogator, Ensign Sheryl Gates filled in for Chekov at the navigation console. She, too, looked concerned and anxious. Spock found such naked emotional distress unseemly and vaguely embarrassing; he wondered if humans realized how obvious their emotions were, or if they even worried about that.

Dr. McCoy, certainly, was not one to hide his feelings. "Spock," he whispered hoarsely, "Jim will find a way to get back to us. You know he will."

"I wish I could share your certainty, Doctor, but that would not be logical." It would be unwise to make such a decision without considering all available data, but no new information appeared to be forthcoming. "Lieutenant Uhura?"

She shook her head. "Still nothing, sir."

"Acknowledged," Spock said. His mind weighed the probabilities concerning the captain's possible survival, trying to establish logical criteria by which he could judge how long a delay might be *too* long. It was difficult, he admitted, to balance the equations; Captain Kirk's resourcefulness—what he called his "luck"—was a variable that was difficult to quantify. The safety of the entire crew outweighed that of any single individual, but what about when that individual was Jim? He turned his head away from McCoy and contemplated the screen ahead of him. "Is our course plotted, Mr. Rodriguez?"

"Yes, sir." The crewman looked back over his shoulder at Spock. "Shall I engage the engines?"

Spock hesitated. *I cannot decide Jim's fate with so many variables undetermined. More data is required, but where can it be found? What would Jim himself do under these circumstances?* He doubted that the captain, whose actions were often more admirable than logical, would ever leave any member of his crew behind, least of all Spock.

The captain's orders were clear, but Spock had disobeyed orders before, had once even risked a court-martial and the death penalty for the sake of another captain. Logic and loyalty, he had learned, sometimes took precedence above the chain of command, but what was he to do when logic and loyalty pointed him in opposite directions?

"Captain?" Rodriguez asked again, reminding Spock that more than Kirk's life was at stake here. The lives of everyone aboard the *Enterprise* depended on Spock's decision. There seemed only one logical decision he could make, no matter how hard he searched for a plausible alternative. Deep within his soul, he felt a terrible sorrow struggling to break free.

"The captain must be abandoned," he announced, his voice holding only the icy coolness of his irrefutable logic. "Set course for the Neutral—"

"Whoa there!" a female voice called out. "Wait just one minute." Spock turned around to see Roberta Lincoln emerge from the turbolift at the back of the bridge. She hurried toward him, clutching a translucent crystal cube in one hand. The cube, Spock observed, emitted a faint green glow.

"Nobody's going anywhere just yet!" she declared.

"A base of operations?" Kirk said.

Seven nodded. "For the entire Romulan Star Empire and beyond. My Romulan counterpart initiates all his activities from here."

They crouched behind a sprawl of bushes, peeking through the branches at a building that occupied the center of a circular clearing about a kilometer in diameter. The structure was not much to look at: a squat, rectangular bunker seemingly constructed from large blocks of some granitelike material. Kirk had never visited Romulus, nor did he know of any human who ever had, but the look of the building reminded him of the massive stone buildings he had seen in covertly obtained spy photos of the Romulan capital. A mural worked its way around the two walls Kirk could see from his vantage point. Painted, two-dimensional cats of many sizes and colors stalked across the mural. *What is it with these people and cats?* Kirk thought, although the mural added credence to Seven's claim that his own organization had built this installation.

Green-tinted searchlights, inactive now, were mounted on each corner of the building's roof. Additional lamps, sitting atop elevated posts, were situated at regular intervals around the clearing. Obviously, there was no point in waiting for the sun to go down; the bunker and the surrounding area would be thoroughly illuminated at night.

Romulan soldiers, armed with disruptor rifles, patrolled the perimeter of the bunker. Their golden helmets were streaked by raindrops, but the guards appeared oblivious to the weather. Their thick, padded uniforms seemed ill-suited to the tropical climate until Kirk remembered that Romulans, if they were as much like Vulcans as they looked, probably preferred hot environments. *Besides,* he thought, *those uniforms probably keep out all the rain.* He ducked lower behind the bushes as a guard marched past them, about four or five meters from their hiding place. So far, Kirk had counted at least four guards.

"As I recall," Kirk whispered to Seven after the guard had passed, "all you needed was an apartment in New York City. Why cloak this entire planet?"

"The Romulan Empire is essentially a police state," Seven explained, "and one equipped with far more advanced surveillance techniques than I ever had to worry about. There's no way Agent 146 could conceal this base in the midst of a Romulan population center."

That had the ring of truth to it, Kirk thought. Certainly modern-day Romulans were harder to spy on than ancient humans; Starfleet Intelligence would attest to that. "But I thought your people were leaving us alone in this century?"

"The internal affairs of the Federation no longer

concern us," Seven clarified, "but the Romulan Empire will remain a threat to galactic peace for at least a generation beyond your own time."

There's discouraging news, Kirk thought. He would have liked to have seen peace in his lifetime, as unlikely as it seemed where the Romulans or the Klingons were concerned. "Even still, a whole planet?"

"There were other considerations," Seven admitted. "We hoped to preserve this world's natural treasures, its abundant forests and wildlife, for future generations. The Romulans of this time would not hesitate to despoil this planet to further their military agendas."

"I didn't realize your people went in for that sort of environmental campaign," Kirk said, glancing at the green-striped tiger lurking beside them in the underbrush. He noticed that both Sulu and Chekov were keeping a safe distance from Osiris, a reasonable enough strategy given the big cat's formidable-looking fangs and claws.

Seven gave Kirk a wry smile. "There are other ways of protecting the future besides sabotaging nuclear satellites." His smile vanished as he contemplated the guards stationed around the bunker. "In any event, it appears that even the cloaking field was not sufficient to hide this base from the Romulans forever. 146 must have made a crucial mistake, alerting the Romulans to his activities. Captain, we cannot allow the Romulan Empire to retain control of the technology employed in this complex. That would . . . severely alter . . . the balance of power throughout this quadrant."

Is that all? Kirk thought. He suspected that, as usual, Seven wasn't telling him the whole truth. He was tempted to ask Seven exactly what technology he had in mind, but he doubted that Seven would give him a straight answer anyway, so all he could do was speculate—and worry. What could the Romulans do with Seven's super-advanced equipment? Remembering Seven's ship-shaking, galaxy-hopping transporter beams, Kirk could all too easily imagine worse-case scenarios that ended with the total conquest of the Federation. "All right then," he asked, "what are our options?"

"Most of the complex is located underground," Seven said. "The nerve center is located on the lowest level, about four stories beneath the surface. If we can get there, I can activate the self-destruct system. After it detonates, there won't be any equipment left for the Romulans to analyze."

"What about the force field controls?" Kirk asked. As long as the field was in place, there was no way Spock could beam them back to the *Enterprise,* assuming the *Enterprise* was even in transporter range. In the best of all possible worlds, the ship was halfway through the Neutral Zone by now. *Maybe we can hijack a Romulan vessel to escape in,* Kirk thought, *or use one of Seven's super-transporter beams to get home.* There had to be some way to come out ahead in the end; he didn't believe in no-win scenarios.

"I should be able to disable the force field as well," Seven answered, then turned his head to address Kirk face to face. "Captain, I want to make my intentions perfectly clear. Destroying this complex is my primary responsibility. If I can ensure a safe escape for all of us, I will be happy to do so, but not if it means endangering my mission. If I have to destroy us along with the complex, then I am willing to make that sacrifice."

Kirk shook his head. "You're not in charge of this mission, Seven. If it comes to that, I'll make the decision, not you." He wasn't afraid to die. He'd accepted that possibility the instant he'd decided to beam down to an uncharted planet behind enemy lines, but he'd be damned if he'd let Seven turn this into some sort of kamikaze run without his permission. *I'm going to beat the odds and get us all back to safety, whether Seven likes it or not.* He owed that much to Chekov and Sulu at least; he owed them a captain who refused to give up.

Still, he prayed that his earlier decision had not doomed his two crewmen. *If I'd known I would have Seven and Osiris on my side down here,* he thought, *maybe I wouldn't have brought along Sulu and Chekov for backup.*

But it was too late for second thoughts now.

"I assure you, Captain," Seven declared, "I don't have a death wish, but there might not be any other choice."

I wonder if that's why he left Roberta and the cat behind? Kirk thought. *Was this what he was planning all along?* "We'll blow up that bridge when we come to it," Kirk said, preferring to focus on the task at hand. "So how do we get past the guards?"

Seven patted the green cat's massive skull. "I think Osiris has some ideas concerning that."

"Mr. Spock," Lt. Uhura stated dryly, with more than a trace of humor in her voice, "Ensign Cho reports that Miss Lincoln has escaped from her quarters."

"That fact is self-evident, Lieutenant." Spock rose from the captain's chair to face the young human who had just dashed out of a turbolift. She was panting slightly, as though she had just sprinted a short distance. "Miss Lincoln, I must ask you to leave the bridge."

"No way, Mister Martian." Hopping down into the command module, she walked around him and quite confidently planted herself in the seat Spock had just vacated. She leaned against the padded black vinyl back of the chair, holding the glowing crystal cube in the palm of her hand. Spock noted that she had exchanged her Starfleet-issue boots for a pair of antique tennis shoes. "Like I said, no one is going anywhere until I hear from Mr. Seven." She glared at

Lt. Rodriguez at the helm controls. "And that means you, buster!"

Had he been human, Spock would have been surprised by her audaciousness. As it was, he was slightly taken aback by her unexpected behavior. Dr. McCoy, standing on the other side of the captain's chair, looked positively dumbfounded—and maybe a bit amused.

"Mr. Spock?" Rodriguez asked, glancing from Roberta to Spock and back again.

"Remain at your post, Lieutenant. You will have your orders shortly." Spock approached Roberta. Although he would never admit it, he experienced what a human might term a distinct sense of relief. Roberta's intervention had provided a temporary reprieve from his dilemma concerning the captain's fate. Indeed, it occurred to him, the young woman might possess information regarding Seven's mission that would help Spock evaluate their situation. He recalled the captain's suggestion of a mind meld. . . .

Before he could address her, however, Roberta raised the cube in her hand until it was level with her face. "Computer," she said decisively. "Maintain orbit."

The cube blinked in response. "Warp engines at ready. Cancel previous command?"

"If that's what it takes," Roberta answered. "Do it."

"Commander Spock," Rodriguez called out. He stared with alarm at the systems status board at his station. "I've lost control of the helm. The warp engines are powering down!"

"Wow," Roberta breathed. "I wasn't sure that was going to work." A grin broke out on her face. "Cool."

Spock gave the cube a closer inspection. Searching his memory, he recalled seeing the same object, or its exact duplicate, in Gary Seven's offices in twentieth century Manhattan. At that time it had seemed of little significance, but obviously that judgment had been mistaken. The voice emerging from the cube he identified as identical to that of the highly advanced computer Seven had employed to take control of an orbital nuclear weapons platform. *Fascinating,* he thought, despite their dire circumstances. Either the cube provided a remote link to Seven's central computer, he theorized, functioning across the gulf of time, or else it served as a piece of advanced cybernetic hardware in its own right. Either way, the cube was apparently capable of overriding the command functions of the *Enterprise*'s own computer systems.

This constitutes a serious threat to the security of the ship, he concluded. *The prospect of placing the* Enterprise *under the command of a primitive human from three centuries ago, especially under the present hazardous circumstances, is not one that should be encouraged.*

"Miss Lincoln," he said sternly. "You have no authority to command this vessel. Please return control of the computer systems to the ship's personnel."

Roberta's face betrayed a twinge of guilt, but she didn't budge from the captain's chair. "Listen, Dr. Spock—"

"Mr. Spock," he corrected.

"Sorry. *Mr.* Spock, I mean." She leaned forward earnestly. "I've been playing J. Edgar Hoover for the last hour or so, listening in on you from my quarters back in the guest wing. I know what you're planning to do, namely head back home and leave Mr. Seven and Captain Kirk and the rest of your buddies stranded on that planet down there. I can't let you do that, not until I hear from Seven and find out what he wants me to do next."

Regrettably, Spock thought, a nerve pinch was not an option. He could not risk immobilizing Roberta while she remained in control of the ship. Even if he took the cube from her, he doubted if the device would respond to his own verbal instructions. *A mind meld,* he thought, *may well be the only way to resolve this conflict.*

Years of training, however, had taught him that a mind meld, especially with a nonVulcan, was something to be undertaken only in the most dire of circumstances. Reason and discourse must always be the first resort.

"I am no more eager to leave my fellow officers behind than you are to abandon Mr. Seven, but the facts remain. A force barrier has cut off all communications with the landing party, including Gary Seven. It is very possible that there will be no further instructions for you from Mr. Seven." Spock saw Roberta flinch at the thought. "But while we delay, the *Enterprise* and everyone aboard remains in extreme danger. The longer we wait, the more we risk detection by either hostile warships or by the unknown parties responsible for the force field." Did Roberta understand what a force field was, he wondered. Clearly, she was more technologically adept than she had first appeared.

"Miss Lincoln, you must let us take whatever actions are necessary to preserve the ship. Any other course would be unwise in the extreme."

Roberta's face betrayed her distress. "Look, you don't need to lay a guilt trip on me. I know I'm putting you folks in hot water, but there isn't anything else I can do." She looked at Spock beseechingly. He saw both anguish and intelligence in her eyes. "I don't pretend that I know exactly what's going on here. Jeez, I'm just a hippie chick from the Village who'd never even heard of a Romulan before today. But I do know that Mr. Seven wouldn't have come all this way unless his mission was massively important to the history of the world, maybe even to the whole freakin' universe, and he's counting on me to cover his back and bail him out if he gets in too deep."

"Miss Lincoln, self-deprecating remarks aside, you

and I both know that you are far more than merely a 'hippy chick.' Nevertheless, there may be nothing you can do in this instance." He felt, curiously, as though he was arguing with himself. Could his own doubts so closely resemble this eccentric young human's? *Fascinating*, he thought.

"Yeah," Roberta answered, "but I don't know that for sure. Besides, I've seen Seven get out of tighter fixes than this. There was this one time, when he had to slip over the Berlin Wall and back without using his transporter, that I thought I was never going to see him again. But you know what? He came back."

"Listen to that, Spock," McCoy spoke up. "Sound like anyone we know?"

It occurred to Spock that, like himself, the doctor undoubtedly had mixed feelings about Roberta's activities. If nothing else, she had succeeded in postponing the *Enterprise*'s departure, just as McCoy had hoped. "Miraculous escapes, by their very definition," he observed, "cannot be anticipated or relied upon."

"Yeah, but there was this other time, while we were teamed up with this wise guy reporter from Chicago, when Seven actually sneaked in and out of the Pentagon with the top secret plans for a new type of robot soldier. The Quasar Tapes, or something like that. Maybe that's not quite the same thing as some weirdo planet light-years from who-knows-where, but if Seven can pull that one off, maybe he could do the same here. I mean, it's not like your own force fields did such a great job of locking him up."

"She's got you there, Spock," McCoy chortled, clearly enjoying himself far more than Spock judged appropriate.

"Your remarks are not entirely helpful, Doctor," Spock stated, "nor are they convincing." He attempted once more to persuade Roberta. "Your confidence in Mr. Seven's abilities is commendable, but it is not sufficient reason to justify retaining control of this ship. You are not a Starfleet captain. You are a stranger to this era and this sector of space. Logic dictates that you return command of the ship to those more qualified to perform that task."

Roberta turned the cube over and over in her hands. "Logic never was my strong point, I guess, and I've been accused of having a problem with authority figures." She gave Spock a defiant look, and leaned back into the captain's chair.

"In my day, we call this a sit-in."

Chapter Eleven

NOCTURNAL BIRDS trilled in the treetops overhead. Now that the cooling rain had faded to a gentle drizzle, Kirk grew ever more aware of the sweltering heat of the jungle. Even though the sun had almost set, leaving the tropical forest at the end of twilight, the air felt as hot as a Miami afternoon. *No doubt the Romulans love this heat,* he guessed, scowling, unhappy at having to grant his foes yet another advantage in this situation.

They were circling the clearing, keeping safely behind the green curtain of the jungle brush. Branches flicked against Kirk's face and stringy vines tugged on his legs as he worked his way through the dense foliage. Osiris led the way, gliding effortlessly between the trees and bushes. Gary Seven followed behind the big cat, only a few paces ahead of Kirk, while Chekov and Sulu kept up the rear. "So far, so good," Seven whispered to Kirk. "Now might be a good time to return my servo to me."

Kirk shook his head. "You're here as a guide and

observer, not a combatant. I'm in command of this mission, and I'm not satisfied that you wouldn't turn your weapon on me and my crew if it suited your purposes." *Seven could not be trusted with his handy little sleep-inducer,* he thought. *Just ask Chekov and McCoy.*

Seven apparently knew better than to argue the point. With a resigned expression on his face, he silently followed Osiris until the cat came to a halt several meters later. Kirk glanced around; he had to admit that this swatch of jungle seemed indistinguishable from any other. For all he could tell, Osiris could have led them in a complete circle.

A throaty rumble came from the cat. Seven nodded and turned toward Kirk. "Osiris says this is as close as we can get to the entrance without being detected."

Kirk furtively crept to the edge of the underbrush and peered through the branches. He received a head-on view of one face of the bunker, and glimpsed a darkened indentation that could have been a doorway. Two Romulan guards stood at either side of the entrance, their disruptor rifles at the ready. Kirk grimly contemplated the guards, and the expanse of open clearing between him and the entrance. Nothing but a wide carpet of grass, no more than a few centimeters high, stretched in front of him. There was no way to approach the bunker without being spotted by the Romulans.

"We need a distraction," Kirk concluded. "Sulu, Chekov, I want you to circle back and attack the bunker from over there." He pointed to a location many meters away. "Do whatever's necessary to attract the guards, then let them chase you into the jungle. Keep them busy for as long as you can, but don't let them capture you. Understood?"

"Yes, Captain. Are you sure you will be all right on your own?" Chekov asked, giving Seven and Osiris a suspicious look. He clearly didn't like the idea of leaving Kirk alone with such uncertain allies. *I don't blame him,* Kirk thought. *Frankly, I'd rather have Spock at my side.*

"Your concern is noted," he said, "but I can take care of myself." He checked to make sure he still had his communicator. "Maintain communications silence until I contact you. With any luck, I'll be in touch after I've completed our mission."

Sulu nodded. "You can count on us, sir." He looked at Chekov and cocked his head in the direction Kirk had indicated. "Let's go."

Keeping their heads down, the two men scurried away into the surrounding jungle. Within seconds Kirk had lost sight of them. *Good luck,* he thought. As always, he regretted putting any of his crew into the line of danger, but, he considered, in the long run, getting chased through the jungle was probably safer than infiltrating the bunker itself. He and Seven faced the hardest part: getting into the Romulan-controlled base and destroying it without getting themselves killed or captured in the process. *Not exactly the* Kobayashi Maru, Kirk thought, *but no piece of cake.*

Seven stroked Osiris's head as he watched Chekov and Sulu disappear. "Now what?" he asked Kirk.

"Now we wait," Kirk responded.

He called himself Septos, but his colleagues knew him as Supervisor 146. While he resembled a Vulcan or a Romulan in appearance, he subscribed to neither the teachings of Surak nor to the warrior ethic of the Empire. His true loyalty was to the alien aegis who had trained and sponsored his family for countless generations, indeed since before the early Romulans broke away from their Vulcan roots. Throughout his career, he had always taken his duties very seriously—which made his ultimate failure all the more painful.

The fierce glare of a harsh white light added to his torment. He tried to close both his inner and outer eyelids against the illumination, block out what was happening to him, but a sharp slap against his face brought him back to the cruel reality of his captivity. Staring past the blinding glare, he could barely glimpse the outline of his assailant, but he knew all too well who she was: Commander Dellas of the Tal Shiar, the dreaded Romulan secret police.

"No, no, my friend," Dellas said. She was an imposing Romulan woman, a mere sixty years old, with short black hair cut well above the points of her ears. A thin white scar ran across her brow, intersecting both of her angular eyebrows. "You cannot escape my questions that easily. I demand your full attention." She raised her hand, prepared to strike him again. A faint olive bruise marked his cheek where she had slapped him.

Septos knew his tormentor well, having frequently perused her file in better days. The youngest daughter of a disgraced proconsul, she alone had survived the purge that had erased the rest of her family from existence. Raised from childhood in the harsh environment of a government detention camp on Barbaros IV, she had impressed her captors with her cunning and ruthlessness, rising swiftly from exile to centurion to commander of her own elite task force, charged with investigating any and all threats to the internal security of the Empire. It was said, in some circles, that even the Praetor feared her zeal and ambition.

"That's better," she said, meeting Septos's gaze. The small chamber with its bare, water-stained gray walls had once served as his private meditation room; Dellas had converted it to an interrogation cell. Septos sat on a hard metal stool with one of Dellas's men standing behind him, holding his shoulders down while Dellas paced back and forth in front of him. An older Romulan, paunchy and balding, stood to one side, using a tricorder to record the interrogation. This, Septos had learned, was Vithrok, Dellas's chief scientific advisor. Unlike most Romulan males,

Vithrok affected a beard, perhaps to compensate for his thinning hair. He wore a white lab coat over his military uniform, and looked mild enough, yet, in his own way, the scientist was quite as dangerous as his cold-blooded superior; it was he who had already deciphered too many of Septos's technological secrets.

So far he had not gathered any new information this session, a testament to Septos's continued resistance. Photon torches had been set up in a triangle around the prisoner. Their glare hurt his eyes and seared his skin. *You would think I would be used to it by now,* Septos thought. This was not the first time Dellas had subjected him to such an inquisition. He feared it would not be the last.

Stubble dotted his jawline. His eyes were bloodshot and streaked with green. A swollen lip concealed the gaps where several teeth had gone missing. *I must endure for as long as I can,* he thought. *I must survive to summon assistance, alert the others to what has befallen here.* The sheer enormity of the catastrophe nearly overwhelmed him. How could he have let the Tal Shiar come into possession of this base? How could he have been so careless?

It was Dellas who had discovered him. She must have been observing him for months before making her move. He had just returned from what had seemed like a routine assignment, helping key Romulan dissidents defect to Vulcan, when Dellas surprised him in his own headquarters. Her troops had seized him and taken control of the compound before he even had a chance to react. Only Osiris had managed to escape into the jungle, although Septos knew that there was little the cat could do without access to the equipment within the base. It was up to him to turn the tables on the Romulans somehow, if only long enough to sound an alert. *If only I'm not too late,* he thought. *They've already learned so much!*

"Your mental discipline is admirable," Dellas commented. A thick ebony cloak, indicating her rank in the Romulan intelligence service, was draped over the right shoulder of her uniform. "So far you have resisted many of our most dependable drugs. You have even defied a Klingon mind-sifter set at force three, which, you may be interested to know, is the highest level that does not yet inflict permanent brain damage on its subjects. But your suffering is pointless. You know I will learn everything I want, eventually. Even without your cooperation, my scientists have already mastered much of your technology, including your very impressive transporter device." Septos heard malevolent triumph in her voice. "I have plans for your time-travel equipment. Quite ambitious plans, although I suspect you would find them more than a little horrifying."

Time travel! Septos struggled not to let his shock show on his face. It was even worse than he thought. He tried to imagine all the damage a person like Dellas could do to history as he knew it, and was frightened by all the possibilities that came to mind. *I need to slow her down if I can, stall her for as long as I'm able.*

"What do you need from me then?" he asked hoarsely. His throat was parched and dry. His rumpled garments, the tan robes of an ordinary Romulan merchant, reeked of old sweat and spilled blood. His bare feet scraped the cold tile floor. It was hard to even string the words together. He had not slept in days.

Dellas shrugged. Septos glimpsed the emblem of the Tal Shiar on her collar; some said that it was Dellas who had actually founded that infamous organization, although Septos had been unable to confirm that rumor. "Maybe nothing. Maybe everything. Information is the life's blood of the Tal Shiar, and I want every scrap of data that may be hiding in that traitor's skull of yours." She laughed coldly. "One of the great advantages of time travel is that I can depart on my mission whenever I choose and still arrive at the ideal moment. That being the case, I prefer to know every variable, every possible snag, before I take action, including the names and locations of all your confederates and superiors." All humor disappeared from her voice as she leaned toward Septos until her face was only a few centimeters away from his. Her dark brown eyes held no trace of mercy. "Tell me now. Who do you work for? Who sent you here? Tell me!"

Septos met Dellas's stare and kept his jaws tightly shut. Bad enough that he had, through carelessness, betrayed himself. Nothing would force him to expose the others. He tried to stand up, but strong, unforgiving hands pressed him back down onto the stool. *I won't talk,* he vowed. *I will die first.*

Dellas did not take his silence well. "Don't be an idiot," she snapped. "Give in while there's still something left of you worth preserving." She grabbed hold of the duranium rod supporting one of the photon torches and tipped it toward Septos's face. The heat from the lamp felt dangerously close to his flesh. Vithrok winced and looked away; clearly, he did not share his commander's enthusiasm for threats and intimidation.

"There is no one else!" Septos protested. "I work alone!"

A cruel smile lifted the corners of her mouth. "You're a better martyr than a liar, Citizen Septos. In my experience, espionage is a social disease; no one ever contracts it alone."

"I'm not a spy," Septos insisted for the hundredth time. The heat from the torch was scorching. His face felt like it was sizzling. "I consider myself an anonymous philanthropist, nothing more. There is no one else."

"Perhaps he is telling the truth?" Vithrok suggested. He nervously stroked his whiskers.

"Silence," Dellas commanded. "This is my field of expertise, not yours." She returned her attention to her prisoner, glaring accusingly at Septos. "You are an enemy of the Empire and a liar." Dellas stepped away from her captive, returning the lamp to its original position. "I dislike mind-sifters. They're crude, brutal things. Typically Klingon. At their highest settings, they tend to destroy as much of a brain as they expose. I've seen them reduce a brilliant scholar or poet to a babbling imbecile." She paused to let her words sink in. "Nonetheless, I am not above using them when other forms of persuasion fail to bring me the information I desire. You should keep that in mind. My patience is not unlimited."

Septos permitted himself a bitter chuckle. His flesh and bones still ached from Dellas's previous displays of "patience." *How much more can I endure?* he wondered, close to despair. Although he didn't want to admit it, the thought of facing the mind-sifter again terrified him. It had taken all his training and mental discipline to resist the machine's intrusions before, and his strength had only diminished since then. Unable to lie to himself, he knew just how close he was to total collapse. He could only pray that Dellas did not realize this as well.

"Let's try this one more time," she began, sounding slightly bored but willing to stick with her task even if it took her all day. "Where did you get this technology?"

Vithrok averted his eyes once more.

Sulu caught the first guard by surprise. Bounding out of the jungle into the clearing, he fired his phaser at one of the Romulan soldiers guarding the entrance to the bunker. Crouching down amidst the underbrush several meters away, Kirk saw the incandescent red beam stun the guard, dropping him to the grass before the shocked eyes of his fellow guard. The other

Romulan raised his disruptor rifle, eager to return fire, but had to duck for cover when Chekov emerged from behind a tree and added his phaser fire to Sulu's. In the light of the energy beams, their Starfleet uniforms were clearly visible. The guard darted into the shadowy alcove that held the entrance to the bunker, then leaned out of the indentation just enough to unleash a volley of disruptor beams.

That's no good, Kirk thought. He needed to get that guard *away* from the doorway, not hiding behind it. Plus, where were the other two guards? He was sure he had counted four soldiers earlier. He raised a hand to signal Seven and Osiris, who were hiding further back in the greenery, to wait a little longer. *Come on,* he silently urged Chekov and Sulu. *Lure them out into the open.*

Certainly they were making enough noise to rouse the entire Romulan Star Empire. Besides the hiss of their phaser beams, Sulu let out a series of bloodcurdling whoops worthy of any ancient samurai, while Chekov yelled obscenities and invective in his native Russian. At least Kirk assumed they were insults; he couldn't make out a word of it himself. *I just hope the Romulans have got their universal translators working. It would be a shame if they missed the full effect.*

Their strenuous efforts produced the desired effect. Two more Romulan guards came running around the corner of the bunker, nearly trampling over their fallen comrade. They fired their disruptors as they ran, forcing the two men from the *Enterprise* to retreat behind the bole of an enormous tree whose mossy trunk stretched toward the cloudy night sky. The wooden giant was wide enough to conceal both humans as they took turns firing from either side of the tree. Kirk knew their phasers were set on stun. He doubted if the Romulans were returning the favor.

Now that they had the Federation officers outnumbered, the third guard crept out of the shelter of the entrance to join the other two soldiers as they rushed toward Chekov and Sulu, disruptors blazing. "Yes!" Kirk whispered to himself. He beckoned Seven and Osiris closer. "Get ready," he warned them. Osiris growled in anticipation.

Chekov scored a lucky shot, dropping another Romulan onto the floor of the clearing. The other two kept on coming, though. Chips of wood and bark flew where their beams struck the mighty tree. Sulu and Chekov fired back wildly, too busy dodging the disruptor blasts to bother aiming their phasers. Kirk knew they would have to retreat soon. The Romulans were getting too close.

"Paashol v'chorte," Chekov hollered in Russian, getting one last dig in before abandoning his position and heading deeper into the brush, Sulu right behind him. The Romulans got the message all right, shouting angrily as they took off in pursuit of the two humans, crashing through the matted twigs and vines like rhinos on a rampage. Kirk waited until they were entirely out of view, then counted to five, just in case one of them turned back.

Nobody did.

"Now!" he barked, jumping to his feet and racing out into the clearing. Seven and Osiris leaped forward as well, the big cat's powerful legs propelling him above and ahead of Kirk. As they approached the entrance to the bunker, Osiris veered toward the prone body of the stunned Romulan guard, still splayed out amidst the grass. Ivory fangs flashed before Kirk's eyes.

"Not now," Seven called out to his feline ally. "Maybe later."

Despite Seven's admonition, Osiris couldn't resist taking a single swat at the fallen guard with one of his massive paws before rejoining Kirk and Seven in front of the bunker. On closer inspection, Kirk observed that the humanoid-sized recess he had spotted before formed a narrow arch in front of a gleaming metal door. He rapped his knuckles experimentally on the door; it felt like solid duranium. There was no way his phaser could disintegrate the barrier before the guards returned. He glanced at Seven. "Your move."

Seven nodded. His hand resting atop Osiris's furry skull, he addressed the door. "This is Supervisor 194. Emergency access code delta-sine-delta."

With a hiss of released air, the steel door slid upwards, revealing a well-lit vestibule beyond. *Open sesame,* Kirk thought, impressed by the ease with which Seven had eliminated the obstacle. "Maybe you belong on this mission after all, Mr. Seven," he said as he entered the bunker with his phaser drawn.

The entrance chamber was large enough to hold all three of them, with marble tiled floors and stone walls that sloped upward at an angle. A decorative sculpture composed of parallel silver rods hung on one wall. A porcelain vase holding a few withered pink blooms sat atop a marble column. *Looks hospitable enough,* Kirk thought; clearly it hadn't been designed by the Romulan military. Dried flower petals littered the floor around the vase. Kirk guessed that no one had watered or replaced the flowers since the soldiers captured the base.

Seven tapped a control panel on the wall nearby the open entrance and the metal door slid back down into place, sealing them in. Kirk looked around quickly. He didn't see any more guards, but he knew they couldn't expect their intrusion to go undetected for long.

The vestibule opened onto three corridors, to the right, to the left, and directly ahead. "Which way?" Kirk asked.

Osiris answered by taking off down the left-hand corridor, his ivory horn pointing the way. "After you," Seven said, gesturing toward the hall the emerald cat had chosen.

Kirk shook his head. "You first." He trusted Seven to a degree, but why take unnecessary chances? He'd rather have Seven in front of him, where he could keep an eye on the unpredictable time traveller. Osiris disappeared around a corner, his tail trailing behind. "Better hurry. Our guide is getting ahead of us."

Seven conceded to Kirk's directive, pursuing Osiris down the empty hall. Glancing over his shoulder to make sure they hadn't been spotted yet, Kirk rushed after them. Despite the obvious danger and urgency of his mission, he couldn't help feeling a trace of amusement at the sheer unlikeliness of his situation: *How in blazes did I end up chasing a lime-colored pussycat through an alien outpost on the wrong side of the Neutral Zone?*

He could just imagine what McCoy would say.

"How many agents do you have in the Empire?" Dellas demanded. "What are their names?"

Septos tried to swallow, but his mouth was too dry. He stared at the floor, seeing dried streaks of his own blood upon the tiles. "No one," he whispered. "I told you before."

This was not entirely true. Over the years, he had inevitably established contacts throughout all levels of Romulan society, from the imperial senate to household servants and disaffected students. Aside from Osiris, though, few had ever suspected the full scope of his operations, nor guessed at the supremely advanced nature of his sponsors.

Until Dellas.

She frowned in frustration. "I grow tired of your lies. Perhaps your remaining secrets are not worth my efforts at gentle persuasion." She grabbed his hair and yanked his head back, forcing him to look up at her. "This is your last chance. Cooperate and you will be rewarded with your own disgraceful existence. Defy me and I will make you wish you had never heard of the Tal Shiar."

His heart sank. There was no question of his response. He was prepared to die to protect the aegis and its agents, but he dreaded leaving Dellas in control of this base. The more time she wasted interrogating him, the less opportunity she had to turn his technology against the safety of the galaxy. If she had truly exhausted her patience with him, what new horrors might she turn to? He had not forgotten her vague but chilling reference to plans involving time travel.

"I don't know," he stalled. "I can't think. Maybe if I had some water? Or a chance to sleep . . . ?" He coughed pathetically, spitting up globules of emerald blood. "Please, I need to rest."

Dellas did not appear sympathetic to his pleas. Could she see through his desperate attempt to buy more time? The Romulan commander stared at him silently, her eyes narrowing in suspicion as she tapped the toe of her boot impatiently against the hard stone floor. Finally, after a seemingly endless interval, she turned to the aging scientist at her side, recording the session on his tricorder. "Very well, Vithrok. Prepare the mind-sifter."

"No!" Septos cried out as loudly as his ravaged body allowed. He did not need to feign his alarm. "You cannot. I need only a little time to think."

"Your time is up, Citizen Septos," Dellas stated coldly. "I warned you and, unlike yourself, I mean what I say." She turned her back on him and took the tricorder from Vithrok, casually perusing its display. "Make sure any new data is triply encrypted," she instructed him. As befitted a high-ranking member of the secret police, the commander was paranoid about secrecy; even the lone guard wore ear plugs beneath his helmet to keep him from hearing any details of the interrogation.

Vithrok removed the mind-sifter from a pocket of his lab coat. Although of Klingon design, the device did not look intimidating, consisting of a collapsible metal ring affixed to a folded leather hood. The ring, Septos knew from painful experience, fitted over the dome of the subject's skull while the hood provided a degree of sensory deprivation that heightened the effects of the mind-sifter, which operated by passing modulated baryon waves through the cerebral cortex of its victims. The waves interacted with the brain's electrical impulses to produce interference patterns that could be recorded and translated into a crude approximation of the subject's personal synaptic pathways. The technology was not unlike that employed by the mnemonic teaching machines of the ancient Eymorgs of Sigma Draconis VI, but infinitely less subtle. When the device was set at its highest levels, the baryon waves provoked synaptic overloads that could lead to seizures, brain damage, and even death. Septos had already experienced the headaches and nausea, the blackouts and memory loss, caused by the mind-sifter at its lowest settings; he dreaded what was yet to come.

Delicate silver circuitry glittered around the metal ring. Miniature display lights flickered to life as Vithrok powered up the device, adjusting the energy levels by tapping gently on a touch-sensitive pad along the edge of the ring. If not for the ominous dark-brown hood hanging down from the metal band, the electronic interrogation device might have easily been mistaken for a decorative tiara or crown. "We'll start at Force Four," he suggested.

"No," Dellas instructed. She regarded Septos coldly. "Force Six."

Six! Septos lurched forward, reaching out to stop Vithrok from placing the ring upon his head, but the Romulan soldier standing guard behind him shoved him roughly back onto the stool, then smacked Septos against the head with the back of his hand, stunning the already battered and despairing prisoner. His chin sagged upon his chest. His arms drooped loosely toward the floor. The hood descended over his head, casting him into darkness as the metal ring was put in place above his ears, tightening automatically around his skull. The inside of the hood smelled like fear. His fear.

Forgive me, Osiris, my friend, he thought. *I did my best, but I have run out of strategies. All is lost.*

"*Jolan true,*" he whispered, invoking the traditional Romulan farewell. "*Jolan true.*"

Then, without warning, the communicator on Dellas's belt emitted a loud buzz. Septos heard her snatch up the device and hold it to her lips. "Dellas here. What is it?"

Septos leaned forward, straining his ears to listen to the voice coming from the communicator: "Commander, the installation has been attacked by Starfleet personnel."

Starfleet! Hope surged within Septos. He had no idea what Starfleet officers were doing here, but it could not be good news for Dellas and her forces. What was going on? Had Osiris somehow managed to alert the Federation to Dellas's no doubt catastrophic plans? Septos summoned up his last reserves of energy and concentration. *If nothing else, Starfleet's unexpected arrival may be the distraction I need.*

Disturbingly, Dellas sounded neither surprised nor alarmed by the news she had just received. "I see," she said, sharing a knowing look with Vithrok. "From the *Enterprise,* no doubt. I've been expecting something like this ever since we identified the ship on our sensors."

The Enterprise, Septos thought. That was James T. Kirk's ship, he knew, but what was it doing on this side of the Neutral Zone again? He didn't understand. If only he could see what was happening . . . !

"But the force field?" Vithrok said.

Dellas's voice betrayed no anxiety. "Clearly it was not sufficient to curb the infamous Captain Kirk." She spoke again into her communicator. "What is the status of the attack?"

"The perimeter guards repelled the initial assault,"

the voice reported. "They are now in pursuit of the humans."

"Acknowledged," Dellas said, handing the tricorder back to Vithrok. "Meet me at the entrance to Level One. I will be there at once." She snapped the communicator shut and headed toward the exit. Then her footsteps paused long enough for her to look back at her prisoner. *"Jolan true,* citizen. It seems you will have the time you requested. I suggest you do not waste it."

I don't intend to, he thought, being careful not to let his defiance show in his posture. Vithrok deftly rolled up the sides of the hood until Septos could see again, but he kept his gaze fixed hopelessly upon the floor even as the Romulan scientist lifted the mind-sifter off his head. Vithrok spoke not a word to Septos, nor did he look him in the face; no doubt, Septos guessed, the commander's scientific advisor preferred to think of their prisoner as merely another test animal. Septos waited until Vithrok hurried off to catch up with Dellas, taking the mind-sifter with him and leaving Septos alone with just the single guard. His mind worked furiously, trying to figure out how to best take advantage of this opportunity.

The first thing to do was immobilize the guard. Ordinarily, this would not be a problem; his ancestors had been bred for centuries to provide him with a Romulan body with the maximum possible genetic potential, potential he had been trained from childhood to realize. But weeks of captivity and physical abuse had sapped much of his strength. Even with his advanced fighting techniques, he was by no means certain that he was in shape to overcome a determined Romulan soldier. Stealth and surprise were what was needed here. . . .

A low moan escaped his lips, followed by a series of horrible, hacking coughs that shook his entire body. Suddenly he let out a ghastly cry of pain and toppled forward off the stool, crashing onto the floor with much noise and impact. He felt a sharp pain where his brow connected with the unforgiving stone floor. His body lay crumpled upon the tiles, twitching spasmodically and bleeding profusely from a gash in his forehead.

"Get up," the guard commanded. Reaching beneath his helmet, he popped the plugs from his ears and shoved them into a pocket in his uniform. His accent betrayed his origins in the outer colonies. "Get up, you traitor!"

Aside from the twitching of his limbs, Septos did not move from where he had collapsed, his head turned sideways on the floor. Greenish saliva bubbled at the corner of his mouth. His eyes rolled upward until only the bloodshot whites could be seen. His fingers and toes jerked repeatedly, scraping against the marble tiles, as though he was being subjected to a sequence of electrical shocks. A puddle of blood formed around his head, streaming from the wound on his brow.

"You! Can you hear me?" the guarded demanded, sounding more uncertain now. "What's the matter with you?"

The twitching subsided, leaving the unresponsive body limp and motionless. No sound escaped Septos's lips, only a thin trail of chartreuse drool that slid onto the floor, merging with the darker green blood from his head wound. It was impossible to tell if he was alive or dead.

Swearing under his breath, the guard shoved the stool out of the way and stepped closer to the figure on the floor. He nudged Septos with the toe of his boot, then kicked him cruelly in the ribs. The body remained inert. The guard drew his disruptor pistol from his belt and knelt cautiously next to the body. He shook the body by the shoulder, causing Septos's head to wag back and forth. Empty white eyes stared lifelessly across the floor.

The pool of blood spread beneath the guard's knee,

soaking the bottom half of one leg of his trousers. *"P'farr,"* the soldier swore again, momentarily distracted by the mess.

That moment was all Septos needed. He snapped into action, his palms bracing himself against the floor, his spine arching backwards as his legs curled up and wrapped themselves around the his enemy's neck. Then Septos straightened his entire body, throwing the guard backwards. *Now,* he thought, *quickly, while I still have the advantage of surprise.* He disengaged his legs from around the guard and jumped to his feet. He wanted to attack at once, but the sudden movement proved too much for him, and a wave of dizziness caught him off guard. He tottered unsteadily while his opponent, now flat on his back on the floor, raised his disruptor. Septos's eyes widened in alarm; panic gave him the strength he needed and he kicked the weapon out of the guard's hand just as he fired. The disruptor went flying and, for an instant, white-hot energy spun like a pinwheel from the weapon, threatening both Septos and the guard. Septos felt the heat of the beam pass within a centimeter from his scalp. Then a deadman's switch shut off the beam, and it dropped harmlessly to the floor.

The guard dove towards his weapon.

Septos dove for the guard.

Septos got there first, reaching underneath the golden helmet to grab the guard's neck between his fingers and squeeze down hard on a certain vital nerve cluster. The guard stiffened, his eyes wide with shock, then dropped face first onto the floor. Exhausted by his exertions, Septos almost collapsed on top of him.

Slowly pulling his hand away from his foe, Septos clambered to his feet, breathing heavily. His ribs still ached where the soldier had kicked them. Using the hem of his merchant's robe, he wiped the blood from his eyes, then employed his fingers to probe the gash on his forehead. To his relief, it felt fairly shallow, although it bled profusely, in the manner of many minor head wounds. *No time to worry about that now,* he thought. Dellas or her subordinates could return at any moment. *I have to get to the command center, alert the others.*

Salvaging the disruptor from the comatose body of the guard, he limped over to the doorway. As expected, Dellas had sealed and locked the exit when she departed. *No matter,* he thought. He wobbled uncertainly upon his feet, feeling slightly lightheaded. *Why does the floor feel so cold? I must be in shock.* He could not grant himself time to recover, though, not with all that was at stake. Fortunately, he knew another way out of the cell, one whose existence Dellas had never even guessed at.

Shivering uncontrollably within his robes, Septos approached the far end of the cell. The wall opposite was bare and unadorned, so as to be conducive to the meditation that had once taken place here, but its appearance, he knew, was deceptive. Certainly neither Dellas or Vithrok had ever guessed at the true nature of this particular room. And why should they have? This quadrant was still a century away from developing genuine holoform technology. "Expose control panel," he croaked, his throat still sore and dry from his captivity.

Concealed holographic projectors complied immediately. The stark white veneer of the wall disappeared, revealing a set of manual controls. Had he chosen, Septos could have converted the walls of the holocell to resemble cloud drifts, waterfalls, flickering firelight, or sparkling meteor showers. Osiris had particularly enjoyed a holographic hunting program that Septos had installed. Septos ignored those options. Instead he activated the emergency transporter system. *Did Dellas really think,* he thought, *that I would seal myself in here with no way out in the event of a fire or earthquake? We value life too much to be that careless.*

The emergency transporter was designed to function independently of the rest of the compound's systems. In theory, it would continue functioning even if all other power supplies were shut down—or if, for instance, the base fell under the control of the Romulan secret police. The emergency system didn't have the interplanetary range of the primary transporters, but it was sufficient to get one safely to the surface—or elsewhere within the complex. *That is all I require,* he resolved. *That and a few minutes at the communications console.*

He keyed in the proper coordinates on the manual control panel, then stepped back as the entire wall faded away, consumed by a swirling cloud of incandescent blue vapors. The billowing azure patterns were strangely hypnotic, especially in his dazed and weakened state. He had to shake his head violently to regain his focus. Taking a deep breath, he raised the stolen disruptor and stepped into the fog.

Just give me a chance, he prayed. *Just a minute or two.*

Chapter Twelve

THE TEMPERATURE inside the installation was almost as hot as the jungle outdoors, although considerably less humid. Set for Romulan standards of comfort, not human. The air was as hot and dry as a Vulcan desert and smelled faintly of orchids. *Must be near the hydroponics lab,* Gary Seven guessed. He recalled that 146 was an avid gardener in his spare time. Too bad his fellow Romulans had invaded his sanctuary.

Once more into the breach, Gary Seven thought as he followed Osiris through the corridors of Deployment Base Alpha. All this covert infiltration reminded him of that time he and Isis had attempted to liberate a former British intelligence agent from the artificial village where he was being held captive as part of an elaborate psychological conditioning experiment. That mission had ended badly, he remembered, primarily because he had underestimated the forces arrayed against them. He hoped he wasn't making the same mistake here.

Twenty-third century Romulans were certainly

more dangerous adversaries than most of the threats he'd dealt with in his own time. Clearly, they had taken 146 by surprise; according to Osiris, neither he nor 146 had known their cover was exposed until they found themselves at the wrong end of several disruptor rifles. Osiris had managed to escape, mauling a few Romulan soldiers in the process, but, unfortunately, the cat had no idea what had occurred within the complex since the Romulans took control. He had not seen 146 since, and feared for the agent's life.

Seven had done his best to reassure the cat. He knew for certain that 146 had survived long enough to send an SOS back across the centuries to Seven's headquarters in Manhattan. *Assuming I've timed this correctly,* he thought, *Septos should be still alive.* Here and there, though, Seven spotted scorch marks and disruptor burns on the solid granite walls of the base, evidence that the Romulan takeover had not been accomplished without some fighting. He just prayed they were in time to rescue his Romulan counterpart—and stop his captors from assassinating Spock in the future.

Part of him wished he could explain to Captain Kirk the full nature of his mission; surely Kirk would be more cooperative if he knew his friend's life was at stake. But then he'd have to explain about Khitomer and Pardek, the Klingon peace initiative, and its long-term impact on Romulan-Vulcan relations, and that was more of the future than Kirk could ever be allowed to know. It was bad enough that the Romulans who had captured the base had apparently learned enough about the future to want to change it. *A little knowledge can indeed be a dangerous thing,* he thought, *especially in the hands of a Romulan.*

The sound of rushing bootsteps, echoing throughout the sturdy stone edifice, interrupted his musings. Osiris's ears perked up and he growled a low warning before turning around and retreating back towards the last corner they had rounded. Seven followed the cat's lead, signalling Kirk with his hand.

Back behind the corner, he flattened himself against the wall so tightly that he could feel the grain of the stone against his cheek, then leaned his head out just enough that he could peer down the corridor they had abandoned. As expected, he saw several Romulan soldiers in full uniform tromping through the intersection at the opposite end of the hall. Joining the hunt for Sulu and Chekov?

Keep going, he urged them mentally. *Don't turn down this way.* He glanced back at Kirk and held up his hand again to indicate that they needed to wait a bit longer. Kirk nodded, his phaser gripped tightly in his hand. Seven admired Kirk's persistence and determination. *Too bad I can't warn him about Soran, either.*

The rhythm of the bootsteps soon died away. Osiris started to hurry forward, but Seven restrained him for a few more seconds. The last thing he wanted to do now was run headfirst into one or more stragglers, not while Kirk was still hanging on to his servo. He counted to ten—slowly—before tapping the big cat on the shoulder. Osiris padded around the corner and was halfway down the next hall when his ears perked up again.

This time the cat and Seven and Kirk barely had time to duck back behind the corner before more guards passed through the intersection ahead of them. *This isn't going to work,* Seven realized. *There's too much activity in this part of the bunker.* He knelt down and whispered into Osiris's ears. "We need to take a detour. Is there an alternative route to the command center?"

The cat growled in reply.

"I don't care if it's the long way around," Seven answered. "We have to take it."

Osiris assented silently, turning around to lead them back the way they'd come. Seven watched the cat's tail flick irritably as he retraced their steps. He couldn't blame the cat for his impatience. He was anxious to get to Septos as well. *This is taking too long,* he thought. Time was running out.

"You seem to have a remarkable rapport with cats, Mr. Seven," Kirk commented, coming up alongside Seven. "I don't suppose you'd care to explain it."

"It's . . . complicated, Captain. Now is not the time."

Kirk sighed theatrically. "Just as well, I suppose. I was always more of a dog person myself."

The guards were not expecting the fog—or the individual inside it. Then again, they never expected that anyone else would obtain access to the transporter controls. Septos fired his disruptor as soon as he was fully materialized, stunning one of the two soldiers Dellas had left standing guard in the command center. The Romulan crashed to the floor, his golden helmet clanging against the stone tiles. The other guard had faster reflexes; he drew his own weapon and fired even as Septos turned his disruptor on him. Septos felt a blast of searing heat and agony strike him above his left hip. Biting down on his lip against the pain, fighting not to let go of his weapon, he clutched this latest injury with his free hand, feeling the cauterized flesh through a newly burned hole in his robes. The exposed skin was still so hot it burned his palm, forcing him to yank his hand away after less than a second. *Ignore it,* he ordered his traumatized nervous system, even though the heat had felt like a hundred *onkians* or more. *Just keep me going for a few more minutes.*

The blue haze disappeared entirely. Despite the pain, he felt a surge of satisfaction as the remaining guard crashed down on top of his companion. He scanned the chamber rapidly, assuring himself that there was no one else. *Good,* he thought. He was in no shape to take on another soldier. *To be honest,* he admitted to himself, *even a mere technician could disarm me at this point.*

The command center occupied the entire bottom level of the base. It was a diamond-shaped chamber dominated by a massive Beta-7 computer terminal built into the northeast wall, its generous display screen stretching all the way to the ceiling. A gliding steel chair rested in front of the terminal, while a tiger-sized couch was shoved up against the southwest wall, beneath the velvety black folds of a hanging tapestry. He saw Romulan tricorders and data padds spread out atop the couch and felt a surprisingly strong sense of violation. How dare these invaders clutter up his office with evidence of their prying? Osiris belonged on that couch, lounging contentedly as he had in the past, not these invasive instruments.

Osiris, he thought. *Where are you now? What are you doing?* He prayed that the cat would not try anything too reckless. *Be careful, old friend. Don't waste your life for me.* The pain in his side burned like a supernova. *There's not enough of me left to worry about. . . .*

He stepped off the transporter pad, located at the southern tip of the diamond, and staggered towards the computer. It was less than a dozen paces away, but the distance stretched before him like a continent. The two stunned guards lay like mountains between him and the computer. He took a long step over them and dizziness nearly overwhelmed him. His vision blurred. He felt foggy, light-headed. The disruptor almost slipped from his grip, but he locked his fingers tightly around its handle. *No,* he thought desperately, blinking his eyes and clutching again at his side, *I can't pass out now!* He stumbled forward on legs that felt far too limp and rubbery. He kept his eyes on the computer. Everything seemed to be growing dimmer, but he could still see the Beta-7 at the end of what looked like a long, dark tunnel. *I have to hurry,* he thought. *Dellas will discover my absence soon. She'll come looking for me.*

He stumbled and fell, his knee smashing against the reinforced steel floor. His weapon escaped his fingers, sliding across the floor away from him. The new pain was almost a relief, distracting him momentarily from the disruptor burn over his hip. Grimacing, he lifted himself up and lurched forward until he was able to grab onto the back of his chair for support. Hovering above the floor on a few microns of compressed air, the chair started to glide out from beneath him, but he locked it in place by pressing the brake controls on the right armrest. He leaned against the back of the chair, letting it support his entire weight for a few moments. *I made it,* he thought, his lungs laboring painfully, his head sagging. *I made it.*

The darkness threatened to overcome him. His eyes closed and, for a heartbeat or two, he was tempted to retreat into the beckoning void. *I can't possibly survive this,* he thought. *I hurt too much to live.* He wanted to shut down his mind and sleep forever.

But he wasn't done yet. He still had to send a warning, stop Dellas. He willed his eyes open and lifted his head up. He stared at the lighted display screen above the computer control panel, trying to make sense of the image on the monitor: some sort of ceremony taking place in a spacious, well-lighted chamber. There were Klingons there, and Vulcans and humans. Septos stared at the frozen image, focusing all his remaining powers of concentration on the task of deciphering the meaning of the scene. *It must be important to Dellas if she keeps it preserved here. What was she up to? What was this all about?*

Although the image was crowded with people, one face dominated the foreground of the image: a dignified Vulcan who looked to be of early middle age. One eyebrow was raised slightly higher than the other in what appeared to be an expression of ironic amusement. The face and the expression seemed familiar to Septos, but also strangely wrong. *I've seen that face before,* he thought. *Who is it? Think!*

It was getting harder and harder to focus. Loss of blood, lack of sleep, shock, physical trauma . . . Septos could diagnose his condition better than he could endure it. He was breathing hard. He felt sick and nauseous. His arms trembled as he clung to the chair. The pain in his side seemed to be screaming at him, sending jolts of agony through him so that every other thought was of the pain. *Ignore it,* his brain screamed back. The gash above his eyes had started bleeding again, sending a trickle of green blood down his face. *Forget it,* he told himself. *The face. Focus on the face.*

The face towered above him, magnified ten times larger than life. That ironic eyebrow arched across the screen like a blackened lightning bolt frozen in time. *I know you,* Septos thought. *Where have I seen you before? Why don't I recognize you?*

Suddenly, as though a box had suddenly sprung open in the pain-ravaged confines of his mind, the name came to him. *Spock.* Septos's eyes widened in recognition. It was Spock, the Vulcan first officer on the *Enterprise,* but looking much older than he had in the last intelligence update Septos had seen. *Time travel,* he remembered. Dellas had mentioned time travel. Was that why the *Enterprise* was in orbit at this very moment? Had Kirk and Spock travelled backwards in time for some reason?

Using Spock as the key, he swiftly identified the other faces in the scene: Kirk, Sulu, Sarek, Azetbur . . . Azetbur? A chill ran through him as his mind pieced the puzzle together. The trick was remembering what was *supposed* to happen. "By the aegis," he whispered in the empty room, "Khitomer!"

The truth sunk in, dulling even the fierce burning in his side. Somehow Dellas had used the Beta-7 to discover what was going to happen at Khitomer over twenty years from now. He had to stop her, even if he was too weak to do so on his own.

Call for help. That was the only answer. It seemed probable that the *Enterprise* was here to stop Dellas as well, but they might just make a bad situation even worse. Time travel was too dangerous for twenty-third century humans to meddle with, especially humans with a personal stake in the future. He needed someone he could truly count on.

If I have to, he decided, *I can activate the self-destruct mechanism, and destroy the entire base.* But someone else had to be informed of the danger, just in case Dellas stopped him before he could accomplish anything else.

He took a deep breath, then unlocked the chair and pulled it away from the computer so that he could drop his weary body onto it. Once more he had to fight the urge to sink back against the support of the chair and let his consciousness slide away. Shaking his head and grimacing, he reached for the control panel, clearing the screen and activating the transwarp transmitter. *Supervisor 194,* he thought. *Code name: Gary Seven.* He was the nearest active agent, spatially *and* chronologically. *Seven is my best and only hope.*

The transmitter needed a few seconds to warm up. He set the power flow at seven-point-five *kolems* and waited for the verification prompt. He tried to calculate how long it would take the message to reach primitive Earth, but adjusting for the time warp made his head spin. His eyelids began to droop once more. He couldn't stop shaking he felt so cold.

Dellas at Khitomer! The very thought enough to freeze his blood.

The ventilation shaft was a tight squeeze, but Gary Seven managed to advance through the narrow tunnel, using his knees and elbows to worm forward. Despite the dark, his eyes could still make out the vague outline of a sinuous green tail bobbing in front of him, only centimeters away from his nose. In the cramped confines of the tubular shaft, Seven could smell the musky odor of Osiris's glossy coat. His own breath seemed to echo off the seamless, smooth metal walls of the tunnel. A cool, air-conditioned breeze blew past him, emanating from the lower levels of the base. "How are you doing, Captain?" he asked in low tones. The shaft was probably soundproofed, but he didn't want to take that chance.

Kirk's voice came from somewhere behind him. "I think I prefer turbolifts," he answered, "but I'm keeping up. Don't worry about me."

Actually, Captain, Seven thought, *I have plenty of other things to worry about:* namely, the present whereabouts and safety of Supervisor 146, and the urgency of destroying the base's transporter capabilities before these mysterious Romulans could successfully alter the future. *If they haven't already done so,* he thought grimly. *How long have the Romulans controlled this base?* Once again, he wished that it had been possible to beam directly from his own base on Earth to this location, but so far 146's transporter pad remained in enemy hands. Hence, here he was, taking the long way around through a maze of interconnecting horizontal and vertical tunnels. Fortunately, Osiris seemed to know the route, leading them onward without hesitation. Running into the cat in the jungle had been a stroke of good fortune, he reflected; he just hoped they still had a little luck left to spare.

Humanoid voices came from up ahead. Osiris issued a warning rumble as they approached a stretch of black metal grillework in the floor of the tunnel. Snatches of conversation drifted up into the shaft through crisscrossing apertures, each one only a sliver wide. Light from below streaked the roof of the tunnel until Osiris passed over the steel lattice quickly, moving remarkably quietly for such a massive animal. Following behind the cat, Seven paused momentarily to peer through the slits beneath him, spying the tops of gleaming golden helmets and the toes of polished military boots.

There were at least two Romulan soldiers below. One of them shifted his position and Seven spotted the muzzle of a disruptor rifle. He strained his ears to make out what they were saying. After over a year on Earth, his Romulan was pretty rusty, but he caught a few words and phrases:

"Federation scum!"

". . . doing here?"

"catch them soon . . ."

I certainly hope they're talking about Ensign Chekov and Lieutenant Sulu, he thought. He did not want to think that the Romulans were aware of any intruders on the premises just yet. Holding his breath, his cautiously made his way over the grille, feeling fairly safe in assuming that Captain Kirk would be equally stealthy in his movements. *Starfleet trains its officers well,* he recalled.

The soldier's voices faded away as Seven and his allies gradually left the lattice behind. They continued to snake through the shadow-dark channel, the wind blowing in their faces. Although Seven prided himself on his peak physical condition, wriggling forward on one's elbows and knees was tiring work. Exertion left a thin layer of sweat between his skin and his borrowed Starfleet uniform. His knees and spine felt cramped and sore; unlike Osiris, he was not accustomed to going about on all fours. *Thank goodness,* he thought, *that claustrophobia was bred out of my ancestors generations ago.*

By Seven's count, they had already descended three levels from the surface. The command center could not be much farther away. *Almost there,* he thought. *At last.*

The tunnel eventually connected with a vertical, tube-shaped shaft similar in diameter to the channel they had just traversed. Warm air blew up from somewhere below. Osiris stopped at the brink of the gap and growled.

Seven listened carefully to the horned cat's description of what was ahead. "This is it?" he asked.

Osiris rumbled his assent. Keeping his voice low, Seven passed the information onto Captain Kirk. "There's a ladder ahead that leads downward to another horizontal shaft that runs above the ceiling of the command center and intersects with the bottom of a turbolift shaft. Assuming there is no turbolift in place, we should be able to open the doors to the command center from within the shaft." Seven watched as Osiris dropped headfirst down the vertical tube in front of them. "Captain, if you will still not return my servo to me, I suggest you have your phaser at hand."

"I'm ready when you are, Mr. Seven," Kirk replied. "Let's get on with it."

My feelings exactly, Seven thought. Despite their differences, he suspected he and Kirk had more in common than might seem obvious. An equal devotion to duty, perhaps, no matter how differently they defined it, and a similar preference for dealing with problems in a hands-on manner. Although he had learned to rely on Isis and Roberta, Seven had never been good at delegating the most dangerous jobs to others. Kirk must feel much the same way. Why else, with a starship full of trained personnel to command, had he beamed down to this planet himself?

Thinking of the ship reminded him of Isis and Roberta, back aboard the *Enterprise*. He hoped they were still alive and well, despite the ongoing threat of Romulan patrols in this sector of space. If nothing else, he was going to need their help when and if he ever completed this mission. *They can take care of themselves,* he reminded himself. *Certainly, this wasn't the first time he had left Roberta in a tight fix, with or without Isis to keep an eye on her. Like the time she had outwitted that power-hungry megalomaniac with the white Persian kitten . . .*

Now was not the time to reminisce, though. Seven crawled over the circular hole in front of him, then backed into the opening so that he could descend feetfirst. Sturdy steel handholds, positioned to accommodate humanoids of conventional height, made the downward climb easier. He heard Kirk scrambling in the tunnel above him, then Kirk's steps on the rungs over his head.

His knees ached in protest when he reached the bottom and crawled into the horizontal tube. *Not much longer,* he promised them. According to Osiris, the opening to the turbolift shift was just ahead—and the command center directly beneath him.

Another ventilation grille, no more than six square centimeters in size, waited a few meters ahead. Light from the control room below cast a checkerboard design on the ceiling of the tunnel. Seven listened carefully as he approached the grille. What was going on underneath him? How many Romulan guards had been stationed in the command center? He needed to assess the situation before they barged in.

To his alarm, he suddenly heard the sizzle of disruptor weapon firings, accompanied by the sounds of bodies hitting the floor and/or groaning in pain. He counted at least three distinct blasts, and smelt the stomach-turning odor of burnt flesh. "Seven!" Kirk whispered urgently from behind him. Clearly, he, too, heard the sounds of warfare. Osiris's tail twitched nervously.

What is happening down there? Who is shooting whom? Seven scurried forward on his elbows and knees until he could see through the slits in the grille. The view was a frustrating one, showing him little of the room below. All he could see was empty floor; a corner of a couch, upholstered in black fabric; and one arm of a Romulan soldier stretched out upon the floor. The arm did not stir. Seven could not tell if its owner was dead or simply stunned.

He heard more groans and ragged breathing. Someone stumbled in the chamber below, smacking into something hard and resistant, then treading with agonizing slowness across the room. *He's limping,* Seven surmised, *whoever he is.* The image of Septos's face, as it had appeared on the Beta-5's monitor back in Manhattan, rushed back into his mind. 146 had been bleeding, he recalled, and obviously injured. . . .

"No," he gasped out loud as the truth sunk in. "Osiris! Kirk! We have to hurry!" *It isn't fair,* he agonized. *I came so close!*

The ventilation tunnel opened up onto a vertical turbolift shaft, several sizes larger than the cramped tubes they had crawled through so far. Osiris growled a report and Seven was relieved to hear that the shaft was currently empty, with no turbolift compartments approaching. The emerald cat pounced onto the floor of the shaft and was quickly joined by both Seven and Kirk. The empty shaft stretched above them for at least four stories, its opposite end lost in murky shadows. It felt good to stand up straight again, but Seven had no time to savor the sensation. Taking no chances, he directed Kirk to use his phaser to fuse the turbolift tracks above their heads, so that no fast-arriving compartment could arrive to squash them flat before they could exit the shaft. The scarlet glow of the phaser beam lit up the interior of the shaft, casting its ruddy radiance over Kirk's face and turning Osiris's green fur the color of mud. The cat's gleaming horn reflected the light as well, shining red as fresh-spilled blood.

Seven approached the sealed door to the command center. Although he listened carefully, he did not hear any more alarming sounds from the other side of the door. Was the struggle already over? Had he arrived too late? *Hang on, 146,* he thought. *Help is on the way.* Aided by the light from Kirk's phaser, he located the manual controls to the turbolift doors. "Get ready!" he whispered to Kirk and Osiris, who stationed themselves in front of the sliding double doors, fully prepared to confront whatever might be waiting for them on the other side. Kirk aimed his phaser at the door and nodded at Seven. *With any luck,* he thought, *we still have the element of surprise on our side.* Seven pulled down the emergency handle, every muscle in his body tensed to spring into action, only nothing happened. The doors stayed shut.

"What in the . . . ?" he gasped, caught by surprise. He tried once more, but the manual controls did not respond. A chance malfunction, he wondered, or deliberate sabotage? He might never know. All that mattered was that time was slipping away. Frustration and impatience raged inside him, but he struggled to remain in control of his feelings. "Kirk!" he barked. "Use your phaser. We have to burn our way in!"

Kirk did not wait for an explanation. Adjusting the setting on his phaser, he directed a high-intensity beam against the sturdy metal doors. Sparks flew and burning steel sizzled as Kirk cut a man-sized rectangle along the outline of one door. *So much,* Seven thought, *for the element of surprise. . . .*

Someone was burning their way in! Glancing back over his shoulder, Septos saw sparks flying, glowing blue and red, from the closed door to the turbolift entrance. *It must be Dellas and her soldiers,* he guessed, *coming to get me.* He had used the Beta-7 to block turbolift passage to this level, and even ordered a complete lockout on the manual controls to the entrance, but obviously that had not been enough to stop Dellas.

He could smell the odor of burning metal, hear the hiss of the energy beams. Already he could see the charred, black outline of the entry the soldiers were cutting into the steel of the door, marring the geometric designs that decorated the door's face.

He was running out of time. His enemies would be through in a matter of seconds. He looked around for his own disruptor and saw it lying on the floor a few meters away. Leaning out of his chair, he reached for the weapon, but it was not close enough to grab onto. He stretched his fingers out as far as he could, but all he could grasp was empty air. The disruptor pistol remained a centimeter or two out of reach, taunting him with its deceptive nearness and accessibility. He tried to lean further, but the effort made his head spin. The pain in his side, where the guard had shot him, was an inferno. He felt close to blacking out.

Never mind, he thought, abandoning the weapon. He was in no shape for a firefight. His thoughts were getting fuzzier with every heartbeat. His limbs trembled. He'd lost too much blood. It was all he could do to stay conscious. Even with the phaser, he couldn't hold them off forever. His only hope now was to alert Supervisor 194 before Dellas and her henchmen burst through the door. There was nothing he could do to stop them, or to prevent them from realizing their foolhardy and wildly destructive plans.

My duty is almost over, he thought, experiencing a singularly Vulcan sense of calm. A line from an ancient human playwright sprung to mind: *"The readiness is all."* Humans were a peculiar species, but some sentiments were universal. Septos was ready to face death as well. It would be up to Gary Seven to stop Dellas now—if only the message got through.

An image gradually formed on the screen of the Beta-7 computer, an image from decades in the past and light-years away: the head and shoulders of a human male on an Earth that had not yet even heard of the Romulan Star Empire. "Yes!" Septos breathed, staring at the screen. Behind him, he could hear the metal door sizzling loudly. They weren't through yet! Maybe he still had a chance to warn the past of the danger Dellas posed to the future. *All I need is a few more seconds.*

Intent on transmitting his warning, he didn't notice the blue haze forming on the transporter pad behind him. The luminescent fog grew thicker and more turbulent. A figure formed inside the haze, gaining shape and solidity. . . .

Kirk switched off his phaser, but kept it aimed in front of him. Lifting his boot, he gave the metal door a heavy kick and a large rectangular sheet of steel fell forward, clanging against the stone floor of the chamber beyond. "Watch the edges," he warned, darting to one side to avoid any possible enemy fire. "They might still be hot."

Light from the command center flooded the shaft, momentarily blinding Seven, whose eyes had grown accustomed to the gloom of the ventilation tubes. Blinking rapidly, he peered through Kirk's improvised doorway into the chamber beyond, half-expecting to see a battalion of Romulan centurions.

Instead, the first thing he saw was his own head and shoulders, projected three times larger than life on a viewscreen that was mounted on the wall across from the turbolift entrance. For a second he feared that his arrival had been detected by some security monitor, then he realized that the Gary Seven upon the screen still wore the conservative white shirt and tie of a professional American male of 1969, the same clothing that he had worn when he first received Supervisor 146's urgent plea for assistance.

That's happening right now, he realized, *just as I feared.* Even though he had anticipated this very paradox, a thrill of *déjà vu* ran through him as he listened to the solitary figure, seated less than five meters away in front of a blinking computer bank, gasp out words that, at least in part, Seven had heard before:

"*146 to 194. Cover exposed by Romulan Intelligence. Capture imminent. Hostiles have seized technology beyond their current capacity, placing all at risk, including the future history of this quadrant. Recommend immediate action. Situation urgent. Must activate emergency self-destruct procedure. Repeat: emergency. I fear there is no escape for me. . . ."*

"Acknowledged," Seven whispered to himself. "194 responding." He stepped forward to assure 146 that help had indeed arrived. Thin tendrils of smoke still rose from the edges of the entrance the phaser had carved.

Intent on his mission, the figure at the computer ignored the sound of the door crashing to the floor. Even from behind, though, Seven recognized Supervisor 146 immediately. His gaze was drawn to a trail of fresh green blood that stretched across the room to where Septos was sitting. Seven wondered how badly his Romulan counterpart had been hurt.

"Watch out!" Kirk cried out from behind him. His arm thrust past Seven's head, his upper finger extended. "Over there!"

Tearing his gaze away from the injured Septos and his own face upon the computer screen, Seven looked where Kirk was pointing and spotted an unidentified Romulan woman emerging from the swirling blue energies of an active transporter platform. The woman wore a Romulan military uniform, circa the twenty-third century or so, and carried a menacing-looking disruptor rifle. Her dark eyes fixed on Septos, who seemed oblivious to her arrival. Utter malice filled her expression.

"No!" Seven cried out, realizing at once what was about to happen. He charged toward the woman, but not fast enough. She raised her rifle with the speed and efficiency of a trained professional and fired a single bright green disruptor bolt at the unsuspecting Septos. The beam burned through the back of the chair and emerged from his chest, right where his heart had been. It was a perfect shot—and a killing one. Septos only had time for a single scream before collapsing onto the floor in front of his chair. The beam continued on to strike the control panel of the computer. Sparks flew from the panel and the oversized image of Seven's face disappeared as the viewscreen went blank.

It's not fair, Seven raged inside, knowing better than most that the universe was seldom fair. He had arrived almost exactly on time, to the very minute, and he had still been too late.

Too late for Supervisor 146, and perhaps for them all.

Chapter Thirteen

ROBERTA FELT LIKE a hijacker, but she didn't know what else to do. The *Enterprise* did not belong to her, yet she couldn't let Doc—no, *Mr.* Spock—take the spaceship back to Earth, not before she could contact Gary Seven and find out what he was planning next. Mr. Spock was right, of course; it was always possible that Seven had finally run out of luck, but if she started thinking that way, what was the point in taking off on ridiculous adventures to the future anyway?

Yes . . . but . . . maybe . . . if . . . All her thoughts and arguments seemed to circle around and bite each other, like a serpent devouring its tail. She felt impossibly conflicted. She wondered if there was any way a space alien like Mr. Spock could possibly understand or sympathize with what she was going through.

Even now, sitting somewhat uncomfortably in Captain Kirk's chair on the bridge of the *Enterprise*, part of her still found it hard to accept that she was actually dealing with a genuine extraterrestrial life-form. Granted, Mr. Spock looked a lot more human than most of the space creatures you saw in the movies, but it was still a trip to be talking to a genuine, living, breathing alien. Okay, so Gary Seven theoretically worked for aliens, and she wasn't quite sure what exactly Isis was (although "demon from hell" was Roberta's best guess), but it was one thing to hold the idea in your head hypothetically, and something else altogether to look a pointy-eared alien in the face while staging a one-woman mutiny on a space ship umpteen-hundred light-years from Earth. *Heck, I'm a New Yorker. I don't even have a driver's license!*

"So, don't you see?" she tried explaining to Mr. Spock once more. "I don't have any choice."

"Sentient beings always have choices, Miss Lincoln. Some are simply more difficult than others." The alien first officer stood calmly a few steps away from her, his hands folded behind his back in a reassuringly unthreatening manner. His stiff and formal posture reminded Roberta of the guards outside Buckingham Palace; boy, had they looked surprised when she and Seven had transported in right behind them!

At least Mr. Spock hadn't tried to have her thrown in the brig or zapped her with his ray gun or anything. *Then again,* she thought, *he can hardly do that while me and my glowing green little friend are in control of the ship.* She turned the crystal cube over and over in her hands, wondering what to do next. She was so stumped she was almost tempted to ask the darn cat for advice. Almost.

Unable to meet Mr. Spock's eyes, she looked around the bridge. She got a good vibe from Dr. McCoy; he was a grouchy old guy, but he seemed to be on her side, although she wasn't at all sure why that should be so, especially after Seven zapped him and the cute Russian guy earlier. The rest of the bridge crew was harder to read, although Uhura seemed to be trying very hard to reach Captain Kirk down on the planet. *I wish there was some way I could help her,* Roberta thought, *but I wouldn't know how to begin.*

"Miss Lincoln, if I can have your full attention."

"Sorry," she said, looking back at Mr. Spock. Forget the palace guards; suddenly he reminded her of her old high school principal. "You were saying something about difficult choices?"

"Indeed," he confirmed. "I have reached just such a decision myself, which may help us to resolve this impasse, but I shall require your cooperation, as well as a considerable degree of trust."

Something about his tone, which struck her as, if anything, even more somber and serious than usual, made her sit up straight. "What kind of trust?" she asked, not bothering to conceal her apprehension.

"There is a procedure known as the Vulcan mind meld," he began.

Isis fumed within her cage. For a few moments there, it had looked like the human female had been about to open the carrier, but then the infuriating creature had changed her mind. She extended her claws in anger and hissed through the bars of the cage.

She had been separated from Gary Seven for too long; she was starting to get fretty. She knew that Seven could take care of himself, wherever he was, but it was that other one who worried her. The female. Isis was still not convinced that keeping her around was a good idea.

Who knew what kind of trouble she could be getting into now?

"Let me get this straight," she said. "You want me to say yes to some sort of Martian ESP thing?" Images from dozens of old Sci-Fi Theater horror flicks raced through Roberta's memory: body snatchers and brain transplants and psychic, mind-controlled zombies. You know, the alien in *The Brain Eaters* even looked a bit like Mr. Spock. . . .

"I do not ask this lightly," he said, "yet it seems to me that much of our conflict is based, as in our previous encounter, on mutual misunderstanding and suspicion. We are each seeing different aspects of the same puzzle and are uncertain as to the other's motives. A mind meld might allow us to overcome the differences that are currently dividing us."

The green cube spun rapidly in her hands as she mulled over Mr. Spock's proposal. He certainly had a point when he talked about the differences between them; they came from different planets *and* centuries. *Talk about a generation gap!* And overcoming differences was supposed to be a good thing; that was a lot of what the whole youth movement of her own time was all about. Still, this was her own brain they were talking about now, and a mind was a terrible thing to waste. . . .

"How do I know you won't use your telepathic powers to, well, brainwash me or something?" she asked.

Mr. Spock did not look offended by her question. "I assure you, Miss Lincoln, that is not my intent. I am proposing a simple exchange of information, conducted on a level so intimate that any deception or miscommunication will be impossible."

"I don't know," she said. "I'm not sure." A mind meld? Simply getting blasted by a laser beam was starting to sound a whole lot better. Ever since she'd hooked up with Gary Seven, she had taken to reading a lot of science fiction, so she thought she had some vague idea of what Mr. Spock was suggesting. Lord knows she'd read enough about strange alien beings with advanced mental abilities. The only problem was, she didn't know what book Seven had dropped her into here. Was this *Stranger in a Strange Land* or *The Puppet Masters*?

Maybe she needed a second opinion, one from another human being. She looked over at Dr. McCoy. The medical officer stood just outside and above the command module, resting his bony elbows on the handrail. "What do you think about all this, Doctor?" she asked. Of all the future people on this spaceship, he seemed the most down-to-earth.

"Personally," he said, "I wouldn't want that green-blooded walking computer within spitting distance of my gray cells, but that's just me." He paused to give the matter further thought. "If you want my professional opinion, though, I have to admit that the Vulcan mind meld is just what he says it is. I've seen Spock meld with people before without inflicting any long-term psychological harm on the other person. To be honest, it usually seems hardest on Spock himself."

"That is supposition, Doctor, and irrelevant," Mr. Spock said curtly. Although the fixed expression on his face did not even flicker, Roberta thought she heard a trace of annoyance in his voice, as though he did not like the doctor's implication of weakness or vulnerability. For the first time, it occurred to her that Mr. Spock might be experiencing some sort of anxiety over this proposed mind meld. Hadn't he said something about a "difficult choice" before? *I must seem just as alien to him as he is to me,* she thought. *Maybe even more so. How would I feel about sharing my brain with a prehistoric caveman?* What sort of sacrifice was Mr. Spock willing to make in order to get through to her?

If he can put his innermost thoughts on the line, can I do any less? "Okay," she said firmly, her decision made. "Let's grok."

Mr. Spock nodded solemnly. He stepped forward and gestured for her to stand up. *What? Right here? Now?* Roberta gulped nervously. Apparently Mr. Spock was not inclined to waste any time. *Probably afraid I'll have second thoughts if we wait any longer,* she thought. *He's probably right.* She rose slowly, relinquishing the captain's chair, then placed the crystal cube gently down on the seat behind her. *It should be safe enough there. After all, I'm not going anywhere . . . I think.*

"Er, what do we do now?" she asked.

"It is not a complicated procedure," he said. He stepped closer so that his face was only inches away from hers. She could see a faint green outline around the whites of his eyes. What had the doctor said before about green blood? The man on the computer screen back home had bled green. . . . "Simply stand where you are," he spoke softly, "and listen to my words."

Mr. Spock raised his hands, his fingers splayed apart, and gently placed them upon her temples. Despite her best intentions, she couldn't help flinching a little when he touched her. She half-expected miniature stingers to emerge from his fingertips and burrow their way into her brain. Instead his touch was surprisingly warm, so much so that she wondered what the body temperature of a Vulcan was supposed to be. *Warm hands, cold heart, I guess.* "Your mind to mine," he intoned. "My thoughts to yours."

So far this was sounding more like a hypnotist's spiel than she liked. Roberta wondered if it was too late to back out, change her mind. What if she had made a terrible mistake? Gary Seven would be lost forever and it would be all her fault, just because she had been naive and trusting and fallen for the oldest alien trick in the book. A harmless mind-merger? Yeah, right!

Then her fears dissolved, along with her identity. . . .

"Your mind to mine." Spock experienced a minor tremor in his resolve as he felt the barriers between their minds beginning to blur. He acknowledged his qualms, analyzed them as he had been trained to do by his father, then placed them aside. Although he was glad to have avoided such an admission, he con-

179

ceded that it was wise to have Dr. McCoy on hand to observe his contact with Miss Lincoln. Like any instance of delicate surgery, every mind meld contained an element of risk; it was only logical to have a trained medical practitioner watching over both participants in the meld.

Not that he truly feared any neurobiological complications; it was the exposure of his own deeply guarded emotions that always daunted him whenever he initiated a mind meld. Unfortunately, such exposure was unavoidable, given the intimate nature of the meld itself. *Let it be so,* he thought. There was too much at risk to let his private apprehensions deter him from a logical course of action.

"My thoughts to yours." Her turbulent feelings lapped over the borders of his own mind like waves upon a beach. He sensed her agitation, her fears and doubts and inner strength. He closed his eyes and saw himself through her perceptions: strange, alien, intimidating. He saw his own face superimposed upon another's. A male, of Vulcan or Romulan descent, blood streaming from a wound in his head. This image was prominent in her thoughts, but he did not understand it yet. He had to press further, deepen their connection, become truly one mind, one spirit, one *katra.*

"My mind to yours."

McCoy watched the meld proceed. Nothing appeared to be happening, just two people standing face-to-face, neither moving a centimeter, but he couldn't take his eyes away. *No matter how many times I see Spock do this,* he thought, *it always makes my skin crawl.* He couldn't help remembering the time another Spock, in a parallel dimension that creepily echoed their own, had ruthlessly raided McCoy's thoughts to learn what the real Jim Kirk was up to. It had been a shocking and humiliating experience that was enough to turn one off Vulcans forever.

And yet, ironically, the genuine Spock seldom looked more human than when he was linked to another, more emotional being. McCoy would never forget the look upon Vulcan's face when he merged with Kollos, the Medusan ambassador; Spock's familiar features had been positively transformed by the other's heartfelt sorrow and pity. It was like seeing an entirely different side of Spock. *Maybe that's what makes this mind meld business so creepy—and so compelling.*

He didn't need to glance around the bridge to know that everyone else was riveted by the same spectacle. Even Uhura seemed to have stopped trying to open hailing frequencies; he heard only a hushed silence behind him.

I hope this works, he thought. *Was it possible that this slip of a girl held the key to Jim's fate?* It seemed unlikely, but she was their last hope. *She's certainly been full of surprises so far.*

Spock and Roberta appeared cut off from the rest of them, isolated in their own private universe. They seemed connected by only the lightest of touches, yet he could sense the energy, the psychic current, flowing between them. Pulling them apart now would be like splitting an atom. There was a vibration, a power, uniting them that took McCoy's breath away. With a momentary start, he suddenly remembered the medical tricorder hanging from his shoulder. He removed the instrument from its case and directed it first at Spock, then Roberta. Their lifesigns looked stable enough, though the tricorder detected a shocking amount of chemical pollutants in Roberta's blood and tissues, even traces of asbestos and nicotine. *That's what living in the past will do to you,* he groused silently. *It was barbaric what people used to put up with.*

Their brain activity seemed to be within their respective safety ranges. Roberta had attained a mental state approximating REM sleep, while Spock's hyper-alert mind seemed to have slowed to a merely human level. The only problem was trying to distinguish her brainwaves from his. The more he monitored the phenomena, the harder it became to tell where Spock ended and Roberta began.

As he looked on, their faces gradually switched expressions. Spock's stern features relaxed conspicuously, losing their rigorously inflexible lines. He looked open and unguarded, almost innocent. Angelic even. "Well, I'll be," McCoy muttered. In contrast, a spooky sort of calm came over Roberta's face. She looked as cold and impervious as the sculpted face on an Egyptian sarcophagus. Like Spock, in other words.

"Brrrr," McCoy whispered to himself. The temperature on the bridge was kept at a level comfortable to most humanoids. Nevertheless, a shudder ran through the doctor as he stared wide-eyed at the union of human and Vulcan.

He's never going to do that to me again, he vowed. *Never in a million years.*

Her mind reeled beneath a flood of memories and sensations: The fierce glare of the Vulcan afternoon, the heat currents rising from the sun-baked desert floor. The rough, scratchy tongue of I-Chaya, her beloved *sehlat,* licking her face. Cold nights atop Mount Seleya, the light from nearby planets shining like moons in the sky, the wind keening through the rocky peaks. The spicy taste of fresh *plomeek* soup, hot from the nutrient processor. Salty, all-too-human tears drying on her cheeks as she ran home from school, unable to face the icy disdain of the real Vulcan children. A hug from her mother, irrational but reassuring . . .

His mind absorbed data faster than he could assimilate it, trying with only partial success to separate the information and impressions from their emotional content: Squatting on a blue shag carpet, watching black-and-white images on TV, Rod Serling intoning dourly against a background of flickering stars, Zorro on horseback, silhouetted against the night sky. More memories flashed across his mind: Swimming in the cool, refreshing waters off Puget Sound, digging for clams on the beach, white foam washing over his toes. Marshmallows toasted over a campfire, sticky and sweet with a slight taste of charcoal. Standing in the rain, damp and cold, waiting for the school bus. All the other kids are bigger than him; why'd he have to skip two grades anyway? Running after his older brothers and sisters, trying to keep up. Looking up "precocious" in the dictionary at Mirror Lake Elementary . . .

Her father looks on in stony silence as she leaves for Starfleet Academy. His mother fights back tears; how can he drop out of high school? She feels her bond with T'Pring, stretching across the light-years between San Francisco and Vulcan. The pained look in Kevin's eyes when he gives him back his ring hurts almost too much to bear. The sudden acceleration of the shuttle, pressing her back into her seat, as it overcomes Earth's gravity. Staring out the window of a Greyhound bus, watching the empty plains roll by on the way to New York. Her first glimpse of the *Enterprise* in spacedock. A want ad in the *Village Voice,* something about "encyclopedia research" . . . ?

Searing pain scorches every inch of her body as the Denevan neural parasites attack her nervous system. He hangs by his fingertips from a window ledge outside the Flatiron Building, dangling fourteen stories above Broadway; how in the world did Seven talk him into this, anyway? She feels her newfound happiness slipping away as the spores disappear from her bloodstream; cold logic reasserts itself. Isis stares at him with baleful yellow eyes, smug and superior as always. The Organians reveal their true form, and she must avert her eyes from the blinding light. He slides down a secret tunnel under the White House, hoping desperately that there's still time to stop Professor

Tepesch from brainwashing JFK and Jackie. Making love to Zarabeth in an ice cave. Sharing a joint with Jimi Hendrix at Woodstock.

Now: The captain is missing. Seven is gone. What should they do? We are in the wrong sector. We are in the wrong time. McCoy wants to wait for Jim. Whatever happened to Isis? The doctor always disagrees with us. Where is that cat anyway? We have to do something. Why are we here? We came through a wormhole. We got a message in the past. Jim wanted to investigate the cloaked planet. Seven said we had to go into the future. The Romulans are up to something. They want to change history. The Romulans are dangerous. Romulans and Vulcans look the same. Vulcans and Romulans are *not* the same. He tried to warn us. They want to kill someone. They're going to kill.

Spock.

Us.

I.

Chapter Fourteen

THE BODY OF the Romulan lay upon the floor of the command center, smoke rising from the gaping hole in his back. *Supervisor 146, I presume,* Kirk thought. Gary Seven appeared transfixed by the sight, frozen in place in the center of the room, between Kirk and the Romulan female who had just shot 146. Kirk still suspected that there was a lot more going on than Seven had admitted to, but he knew when a mission was going badly, and this one seemed to be heading straight to hell.

He was swinging his phaser toward the woman when several hundred kilograms of enraged feline barreled past him, knocking him to one side. Roaring like a thunderstorm, Osiris lunged at the woman who had just killed his—master? companion? partner?—before his eyes. The Romulan's own eyes widened in alarm as she saw the emerald beast hurling at her, its vicious claws extended, its ivory horn spewing venom. Unable to fire her own weapon in time, she dived off the transporter platform toward the couch to her left, shoving the heavy piece of furniture away from the wall.

Osiris crashed into the platform, his claws gouging scratches in the floor where the woman had been standing only heartbeats before. Furious at the escape of his prey, he reared up on his hind legs, standing almost eight meters high, the tip of his mighty horn brushing against the ceiling, and roared at the top of his lungs, his jaws opened wide to expose rows of ivory fangs. His roar reverberated against the walls of the chamber, deafening Kirk and jolting even Gary Seven from his agonized contemplation of the dead Romulan's corpse. His mournful eyes turned toward the towering figure of Osiris.

It was an awe-inspiring display, but tragically short-lived. Recovering from her shock, crouched down between the couch and the wall, with one knee resting on the floor and the heavy tapestry rustling above her, the woman swung up her rifle and fired again. Kirk couldn't hear the sound of the discharged weapon over Osiris's mighty roar, but he saw the energy beam shoot across the room to strike the great cat just below his chin.

She must have adjusted the disruptor's settings, because this bolt did more than simply burn its way through the cat's furry hide. Instead, a burst of deadly radiation, even brighter and more green than Osiris's own coat, suffused the cat from head to toe. For an instant, the glow surrounded Osiris like a halo, and, blinking his eyes, Kirk thought he saw the outline of a humanoid body briefly, almost subliminally, super-imposed over the shape of the great cat, then the radiance faded away, taking Osiris with it. Within seconds, the fearsome creature had been completely disintegrated. Kirk felt an enormous sense of loss, surprised at the depth of the feeling; although he had known Osiris for barely more than an hour, he knew that a rare and noble creature had just been extinguished. He hoped that there were more of Osiris's breed elsewhere in the galaxy, perhaps on this very planet.

In the meantime, there was still the murderer to be dealt with. "Drop your weapon!" Kirk shouted, aiming once more at the woman, but she ducked down behind the back of the couch. *Damn,* Kirk thought. He was severely tempted to set his phaser on kill and burn right through the couch and the woman behind it, but his Starfleet oath stayed his hand. *Only as a last resort,* he vowed, risking a glance at Seven, who was now kneeling beside the dead Romulan, confirming the awful truth. "Are you all right, Mr. Seven?" he called out.

"No," Seven answered brusquely, "but I am still functioning, if that's what you mean." Rising from the side of his murdered colleague, he inspected the damaged control panel. Occasional sparks still flickered across the surface of the panel. "You keep the commander busy, and I'll see if I can activate the self-destruct mechanism."

Easier said than done, Kirk thought, although he found himself reassured that Seven remained coolly intent on his mission, despite the deaths, within minutes of each other, of two of his allies. At least he didn't have to worry about Seven falling apart on him, just keeping one step ahead of a well-armed Romulan warrior. *No problem,* he thought, circling cautiously towards the plush black couch.

A disruptor blast tore through the back of the couch, missing Kirk by mere centimeters. *That was too close for comfort,* he thought, backing away from the couch as quietly as he could so as to not alert the woman to his location. The near miss left his heart pounding, but his mind fell back on his Academy training, carefully assessing his strategic situation: *one armed foe out of my line of sight, with potential reinforcements due at any minute.* Not good.

He glanced quickly at the transporter pad the woman had apparently used to enter the command center. He considered destroying it, but decided against it. He and Seven might need the transporter to escape once Seven engaged the self-destruct system. Better to just keep an eye on the pad, as well as on the turbolift entrance *and* on the woman behind the couch. *Too bad I'm not a Triclopian,* he thought wryly. *I could use three eyes right now.*

Another blast blazed through the couch, this one hissing past him about a meter above his right shoulder. *Every time she fires,* Kirk thought, *she's destroying a piece of her shelter.* Unfortunately, she still had the edge as long as her disruptor was set on kill and his could only stun. He wasn't sure what exactly that couch was made of, but it might be dense enough to blunt a phaser set on stun. *I'm outnumbered and outgunned,* he mused, his finger brushing the setting controls on his phaser. *There may be no way out of this place except through deadly force.* He was hoping it wouldn't come to that, though, especially since, technically, he was the invader on this side of the Neutral Zone. "Seven!" he shouted, then swiftly moved to one side. Sure enough, another disruptor beam shot through the space he had just occupied. The black couch was starting to look like a piece of Swiss cheese, but there was still enough of it to hide his opponent from sight. "How are we doing over there?"

"Patience, Captain," Seven replied. "The commander's disruptor bolt damaged many crucial components. I believe I can compensate by reconfiguring the circuitry, but it may take a few minutes."

"With all deliberate speed, Mr. Seven," Kirk urged, then dropped to his knees as a brilliant green beam incinerated the air above his head. He wondered why the Romulan had not fired at Seven yet. Could it be that she was reluctant to damage the control room equipment any further? According to Seven, this was all about technology, advanced alien technology that Seven wanted to keep out of the hands of the Romulans. *Sounds like a plan to me,* Kirk thought, *if I can just stay alive long enough to give Seven the time he needs.* He felt like he was playing a game of Romulan Roulette; one of these times, the disruptor beam was going to strike home.

For an instant, he thought he glimpsed a piece of gray fabric, the same color as a Romulan uniform, through one of the holes in the couch. He fired his phaser at that tantalizing glimpse of gray, but failed to hear the hoped-for sound of a stunned body hitting the floor. *Tough luck,* he thought, watching carefully for another chance at his foe. *We're both shooting blind, and neither of us is making any lucky shots.*

"Seven?" he called again. Yet another beam sizzled overhead, leaving a meter-long scorch mark across the ceiling.

"Not quite, Captain," Seven answered. "This task is proving more difficult than it first appeared."

Great, Kirk thought. He took a moment to wonder how the *Enterprise* was faring. He hoped that Spock and the others were in a better position than he was at this point.

The tapestry hanging above and behind the disruptor-scarred couch rustled again, indicating movement beneath it. Kirk gave the tapestry a closer look. Gold and silver needlework traced designs like cat's eyes upon the black fabric. An idea occurred to him. . . . Adjusting his phaser to generate heat rather than force, he fired at the tapestry. The velvety fabric burst into flames, then burned free from its hangers, falling down onto his opponent's place of concealment.

An angry scream came from behind the couch, and the woman threw herself into the open as if propelled by an atom-smasher. Smoke rose from her uniform where it had caught fire at over a dozen different locations. She batted at the darting orange and yellow flames with her bare hands, snuffing them out as quickly as she could. Fury contorted her features; beneath the ugly scar on her forehead, her eyes blazed with hatred.

I think I've made an enemy, Kirk thought. The rage on the woman's face looked almost Klingon in its intensity. He prided himself on being a quick judge of character—a vital skill for a ship's captain—and he didn't like what he saw in this particular Romulan's eyes. There was something almost pathological about the fury on display here, he thought, as he watched the Romulan woman battle the flames licking at her clothing.

For better or for worse, her uniform appeared to be at least partially flame-resistant. She quickly extinguished the fires upon her person and seemed more or less unscathed, although Kirk detected the smell of burning hair in the air. "Don't try anything," Kirk said, aiming his phaser directly at the woman. "Let me see your hands."

The Romulan assassin glowered at him, but did as he instructed, raising her empty hands palms up. Her disruptor was nowhere in sight. Kirk glanced quickly at the couch. Fortunately, the burning tapestry had not ignited the adjacent furniture and the blaze already appeared to be dying down. *Good thing the Romulans are so fond of stonework,* he thought. *Less chance of setting this place on fire.*

"You're as resourceful as they say, Captain Kirk," the woman said. Her words were complimentary, but her gaze was anything but. Despite her vulnerable position, she stared at Kirk with undisguised scorn.

"You recognize me?" Kirk kept his phaser on her, discreetly switching it back to stun. "I'm flattered."

"You're historically significant, Kirk." A smirk appeared on her face. "More so than you know."

What does she mean by that? "Nice to hear it," he

replied. "I suppose you intend to make your mark as well?"

For someone facing the wrong end of a phaser, she seemed remarkably confident. "Oh, I'm going to do more than make history, Captain. I'm going to *change* it."

Gary Seven looked up from his efforts at the control panel, visibly disturbed by the woman's words. *How much does he know about her plans?* Kirk wondered. *What isn't he telling me?* He risked a glance at the turbolift entrance. There was still no sign of reinforcements, but he couldn't help feeling that they were pushing their luck. The woman's apparent confidence worried him. "If I were you, I'd hurry," he instructed Seven. "For all we know, I may have set off a silent alarm."

"You did," Seven responded coolly. "I shut it off."

Now he tells me, Kirk thought. He was getting damn tired of being in the dark all the time. He waved the phaser in front of the woman. "Why don't you tell me who you are and what this is all about?"

Seven gave the woman an anxious glance. He seemed more worried about the Romulan revealing her secrets than she was. *There's definitely something he doesn't want me to know,* Kirk deduced. *Maybe several somethings.*

The woman sneered at him. "My name is Commander Dellas of the Romulan Star Empire, and you, Captain James Tiberius Kirk of the Federation Starship *Enterprise,* are far from home, badly outnumbered, and hopelessly out of your depth. You may have had some small success outwitting thick-skulled Klingons over the years, but you cannot begin to grasp the full subtlety of the Romulan mind."

"I haven't done so badly so far," Kirk quipped. "And I've figured out enough to realize that this entire operation is very hush-hush and very important, which makes me extremely curious about what you're planning here. And my associate over there," he cocked his head towards Seven, "has his own stake in stopping whatever you're up to."

Her open hands still poised in the air, Commander Dellas inspected Gary Seven for the first time. The scar above her eyes wrinkled in puzzlement as she examined the stranger at the control panel. Kirk didn't know whether to be pleased or annoyed that Dellas, who obviously knew Kirk's background by heart, clearly did not recognize the time traveller from the twentieth century. *At least that gives us an edge,* he thought, *one we're probably going to need.*

His free hand fingered the slim, metallic servo in his pocket. He wondered if Seven's repairs would go any faster if he gave Seven back his device. Maybe now was the time to trust the man with his weapon again. "Seven," he began, "what if—"

"Captain Kirk," Dellas interrupted loudly. "Under the terms of the Treaty of Algeron, I demand that you surrender to the local authorities, namely myself. Furthermore, we will demand restitution for all damage inflicted upon this installation and its personnel, not to mention your complete cooperation in apprehending any and all Federation nationals currently at large in this sector, which you have illegally and inexcusably invaded will full premeditation and hostile intent. . . ."

Her voice rose as she continued her litany of legalistic objections, seemingly oblivious to the phaser that was even now threatening her at point-blank range. For a second, Kirk wondered if the commander had snapped—there *was* a slightly crazy sheen in her eyes—then the truth hit him. *She's stalling,* he realized, *but what for?* Listening carefully, he became aware of a faint ringing in his ears, an almost inaudible hum that was nearly drowned out by Dellas's breathless rant. It was growing louder, though, gaining strength and urgency not unlike—the comparison occurred to him instantly—a phaser set to overload.

"No!" Kirk gasped. He glanced again at the smoldering couch. *Her disruptor!* "Seven!" he shouted. "Watch out! It's going to blow!"

He never knew if Seven heard his warning. The hum turned into an ear-splitting screech and there was a sudden, overwhelming flash of light and force that picked him up and threw him across the room.

He was unconscious even before he hit the wall.

Chapter Fifteen

"I . . . I," SPOCK MURMURED, obviously shaken. "I, Spock." His hands pulled away from Roberta and explored his own features. His face was pale, without its usual greenish tint. His limbs trembled. He staggered beside the captain's chair, and McCoy rushed forward to assist him. The doctor pulled Spock's arm over his shoulder and wrapped his own arm around the Vulcan's chest, holding him up as best he could.

"Good God, man!" McCoy blurted. "You look like you're in shock! What happened? Are you all right?"

"I . . . am well, Doctor," Spock replied, regaining his composure through sheer force of will. He planted his feet squarely upon the floor of the bridge and let the trembling subside. He regulated his breathing to attain a more focused state of mind. "The experience was more . . . disturbing . . . than I had anticipated, but I believe I will recover."

In fact, the shock of Roberta's revelation—that he

was to be assassinated at some point in the future—had jolted him out of the meld far more abruptly than was advisable. Concerned for Roberta's welfare, he looked for the young woman. She stood a few meters away, blinking rapidly, her face flushed and startled-looking. Her wide eyes locked on Spock's and she gasped out loud, her hands springing to her cheeks.

"Ohmigod, Spock. I should have realized . . . I never thought . . . !" Clearly, Spock deduced, she had underestimated the full extent of a mind meld, as well as the impact of her own memories concerning himself. She stumbled toward him, tripping slightly on the step in front of the captain's chair. "They're going to kill us! I mean, you!"

"What?" McCoy said, confusion written on his face. "Who's going to kill you? What is she talking about?"

"It is a long story, Doctor," Spock stated. With as much dignity as he could muster, he extricated himself from McCoy's grasp and stepped aside. "I require a few moments to process the data myself. Perhaps if you tend to Roberta . . . that is, Miss Lincoln?"

"What?" McCoy said, disoriented. Events appeared to be moving too fast for him, a not uncommon state of affairs, Spock reflected. The doctor's penchant for reacting emotionally to each new event clearly interfered with his ability to immediately comprehend those events. "Yes, of course." McCoy retrieved his tricorder and quickly scanned Roberta's vital signs.

He could not, however, criticize Dr. McCoy too freely in this instance, Spock conceded. He too felt a need to adequately respond to what he had just learned before moving on. It was not purely logical, but it was necessary. His proper functioning required the assimilation of all that the mind meld had revealed.

The Romulans intend to assassinate me several years from now, thereby changing future history. Flatly stated thus, the information lost some of its power to disturb his thought processes. It was fortunate, perhaps, that Roberta knew little more about the incident, except that the assassination was to occur in the year 2293, approximately twenty-four years from the present. This fact was not preordained, though. As temporal theory and his own experience testified, the flow of history could be extremely malleable under the right conditions. Indeed, it was apparently the intent of unknown forces to effect precisely such a change to his own destiny, just as Gary Seven intended to prevent that change.

We are faced then, Spock concluded, *with at least three possible future timelines. One, the future as it will proceed without the interference of either Gary Seven or his antagonists. Two, the future as it will be if hostile forces intervene. And, three, the future that may result if Gary Seven attempts to correct or compensate for whatever changes his enemies succeed in bringing about.*

Three possible futures. From a strictly philosophical perspective, that seemed like more than enough for any mortal being to ask for. Furthermore, it was only logical to assume that all timelines must inevitably lead to his death, the only variable being whether that event would occur sooner or later, therefore it would be irrational to let the revelation of one possible demise interfere with his mission or his reasoning. He admitted to some curiosity about what future action he might take that would be so significant that anyone living today would go to such lengths to avert it, but he could see why Gary Seven would wish to conceal that information. Time travel had its own prime directives, as the Guardian of Forever had once taught them.

"Spock?"

It was McCoy again. Evidently he had assured himself that Roberta had survived the meld in good health, and now wished to do the same for Spock. Without asking for the Vulcan's consent, the doctor scanned Spock with his medical tricorder, his gaze intent on the readout as he swept the device up and down, parallel to the length of Spock's body. "Hmmm," he muttered, mostly to himself, "slightly elevated levels of neurotransmitters, at least by Vulcan standards; heartbeat and blood pressure disgustingly regular; no evidence of biochemical side effects . . ." He lowered the tricorder, then snapped its lid shut, apparently convinced that Spock was not likely to expire momentarily. His weathered face took on a suspicious cast. "Okay, Spock, what's up?"

Spock saw no need to conceal the truth from the doctor. "Apparently, Mr. Seven does indeed have strong reason to believe that unknown parties are attempting to alter the future, a future that somehow requires my death in the year 2293." He explained to McCoy about the message Seven and Roberta had received in the twentieth century.

"And you think the message came from that planet down there, where Jim is?" McCoy asked. Spock noted that Lieutenant Uhura and the rest of the bridge crew were listening intently to their conversation. This was as it should be, he decided; it was good for the crew to be well-informed regarding their situation, although he resolved to say nothing that might serve to lower their morale. He had learned from hard experience, especially during his ill-fated expedition to Taurus II, that it was necessary—regrettable, but nonetheless necessary—to take into account the emotional responses of human beings when occupying a command position over them. Fortunately, Starfleet officers seldom let their emotions get the better of their training. Except, perhaps, for Dr. Leonard McCoy.

"Apparently Gary Seven believes this planet to be the source of the transmission," Spock stated, "and we have no reason to doubt him."

"Of course not!" Roberta exclaimed. Her voice was hoarse with emotion. Her eyes were embarrassingly moist. "How could you possibly doubt any of us, after what you and I just went through?" She grasped Spock's hand and squeezed it. "That was incredible. I *lived* your life, I really did. What a trip! I mean, at first I thought you were just this strange, spooky alien, but now . . . ! You know, we actually have a lot in common. My dad didn't really understand me either, especially when I dropped out of school and hit the road. It was just like you with Sarek. We were both so scared—"

"Thank you, Miss Lincoln," Spock interrupted, gradually extricating his hand from her grip. Roberta's highly emotive response to the aftermath of the meld was becoming uncomfortably personal, particularly in front of McCoy and the others. "I am grateful that you found the experience illuminating. Perhaps now, however, we should concentrate on the matter at hand."

"What?" she said, still slightly disoriented. "Oh yeah." She plopped back down into the captain's chair, then jumped back up again, having forgotten that the crystal cube was still resting where she had just sat. "Oops!" She picked up the cube and raised it in front of her face. The green glow gave her features a curiously Vulcan tint. "Computer, return control of the ship to, um, First Officer Spock."

"And other authorized personnel," Spock suggested.

"Right. And other authorized personnel," she repeated and the cube beeped in response. Stepping away from the captain's chair, she gestured toward the now-empty seat. "All yours."

"Thank you, Miss Lincoln," Spock replied. He

assumed command once more, resting his back against the padding of the chair. Bits and pieces of Roberta's memories continued to spiral across his consciousness, like stray leaves blown about by the wind. *Chocolate mint ice cream. Fireworks on the Fourth of July. A torchlight parade through the streets of Seattle. Central Park in winter. The flare of a machine gun. A yellow submarine* . . . Spock blinked his eyes once, clearing his mind of such psychic residue. There was too much at stake. He could not afford to be distracted by the memorabilia of another's mind, no matter how intriguing. "Lieutenant Rodriguez, what is our status?"

"The helm is responding, sir," Rodriguez said. "I'm awaiting your command."

"So, where were we anyway?" McCoy said sarcastically, placing a hand on the back of Spock's chair. "Oh yes, that's right. You were just about to leave Jim and the others high and dry."

Roberta looked stricken and about to protest, but Spock spoke first. "No longer, Doctor. Our priorities have changed. I have decided, on the basis of the information I received from Miss Lincoln, that the threat to future history is something worth risking the *Enterprise* for. We will remain in this orbit to render whatever assistance Captain Kirk—or Gary Seven—may require to complete their mission."

A misty-eyed Roberta grinned widely and looked like she wanted to hug Spock. To his relief, she refrained from doing so. "I knew it!" she said. "I knew you couldn't go through with it."

McCoy was rendered speechless, if only for a moment. "You mean it? We're not leaving?" Astonishment showed in his baggy eyes. "What the devil changed your mind? Not that I'm complaining, mind you."

"Granted," Spock explained, "the facts of the matter, as relayed to us by Gary Seven, have not changed essentially. But, through my exchange with Miss Lincoln, I have gained a substantially greater faith in Mr. Seven's judgment and reliability. Based on his conduct in other situations, as shared with me by Miss Lincoln, I can only conclude that Gary Seven would not have acted as he has done unless it was absolutely vital to the natural progression of history."

"You're not just saying that," McCoy asked skeptically, "because now you know your own future is on the line?"

Spock felt stung by the suggestion, although he suppressed the response so swiftly that it could hardly have been said to have existed at all. "That would be reasoning unworthy of a Starfleet officer," he responded. "Furthermore, from a standpoint of strict self-interest, it would be highly illogical to risk my existence today to preserve my life some twenty-four years hence."

"If you say so," McCoy said. He looked unconvinced, but Spock perceived no need to further justify his decision to the doctor. There were better uses for his time.

"Mr. Spock," Lt. Uhura spoke up. "Should I call for Security?" she asked, looking pointedly at Roberta. There was, after all, the not-insignificant matter of her illegal takeover of the *Enterprise.*

"That will not be necessary, Lieutenant," Spock declared, seeing no advantage to confining Roberta to the brig. "Miss Lincoln's insights may prove valuable as this mission proceeds." He pointed towards the science station he usually manned. "Miss Lincoln, perhaps you would care to occupy that seat?"

"Got it," she assented. Cube in hand, she scurried across the bridge to take a place at the science station. Her eyes widened as she inspected an impressive array of displays, switches, and knobs. "Wow, I know what all this stuff is now! This is the command functions slave panel, that's the computer audio output control, those are the sensor display input logs . . ."

Spock was faintly alarmed at the speed with which Roberta had assimilated his technical knowledge. Uhura merely looked bemused, until she suddenly stiffened in her chair and held her earpiece closer to her head. "Mr. Spock! It's *Gladiator*. She's coming around again, and heading straight for the planet."

"Confirmed," Ensign Gates reported from her station at navigation. "Sensors indicate that *Gladiator* is approaching us at one-quarter impulse."

Spock was not surprised to hear that the Romulan battle cruiser was still in pursuit of the *Enterprise*. He doubted that Commander Motak would give up easily. "Is there any indication," he asked, "that they are aware of our location?"

"Negative," Uhura stated, shaking her head. "They're still searching for some sign of us, and demanding our surrender at regular intervals."

"Romulans are known for their punctuality," Spock observed, "as well as their persistence." He considered going to red alert, but decided he needed more data first. "What is their weapons status?" he asked automatically—and was surprised to hear Roberta answer him.

"Er, their shields are up," she announced, staring at the long-range sensor display. She fiddled with the controls to the high-resolution EM scanner. "Their disruptors are fully charged, but not targeted." She shrugged her shoulders. "At least that's what these doohickeys say."

"Lord help us all," McCoy exclaimed, openly dumbfounded by Roberta's performance. "Now I've seen everything. Next we'll be putting the blasted cat at the helm . . . !"

The cat, Spock thought. There was something in Roberta's memories, an oddness regarding the cat, that he had not fully addressed just yet. What was Isis indeed? Merely a pet or something far more significant? The mystery nagged at the back of his mind, as though it ought to be more important than it seemed, but there was no time to think about the cat now, nor to share Dr. McCoy's fascination with Roberta's newfound proficiency with starship technology. *Gladiator* posed the immediate threat. All other concerns were secondary.

He had to assume that Commander Motak had not yet detected the presence of the cloaked world. It appeared, though, as if he was about to do so, at which point he would also pose a threat to Captain Kirk, Gary Seven, and the rest of the landing party, not to mention their chances of completing their mission successfully and preventing any alteration to future history. That was an outcome even less desirable than the total destruction of the *Enterprise* and all aboard her. *We are expendable,* he thought. *Gary Seven is not.*

If nothing else, no one will be able to assassinate me in the future if I die in battle today. I can only hope that Seven will be able to repair any damage to the timeline caused by my premature demise.

"They're getting closer," Ensign Gates announced. Under stress, her voice betrayed a slight Brooklyn accent. *"Gladiator* is only minutes away from intercepting the perimeter of the cloaking field."

Spock briefly wondered if it would be possible to lure Motak into crashing *Gladiator* into the planet itself, but quickly rejected the notion. The obliteration of an entire battle cruiser would result in a tremendous and inexcusable loss of life among the Romulans. He reminded himself that Motak was merely defending his home against a suspicious intruder. It would be dishonorable to condemn his entire crew to death simply for performing their duty. However innocent of hostile intent, the *Enterprise* was the ship on the wrong side of the Neutral Zone, and a legitimate target for the Romulans.

Furthermore, it occurred to him, the crash of a battle cruiser into a thriving, class-M planet would be comparable to the catastrophic impact of the asteroid that destroyed Earth's prehistoric dinosaurs. The potential for massive ecological damage, including mass extinctions, was too grievous to even consider inflicting on a living world.

We must protect the planet from Gladiator *and* Gladiator *from the planet, all without endangering Captain Kirk as well.* He saw only one way to achieve that aim. "Lieutenant Rodriguez, take us out of the cloaking field."

"What?" McCoy blurted. "Spock, what are you doing?"

"We must lure *Gladiator* away from the planet," he explained. "The best way to do so is by giving it something to chase."

"Like us, for instance?"

"Precisely."

"Here we go," Rodriguez said, directing the impulse engines by means of the control panel at his fingertips. The *Enterprise* shot out from its orbit around the cloaked world, leaving both the planet's atmosphere and its protective shield of invisibility behind. On the main viewer, an image of the planet's upper hemisphere dropped out of sight, giving way to the starry backdrop of outer space. Distant suns glittered like diamonds against the endless blackness, and a Romulan battle cruiser, its warp nacelles gleaming on opposite sides of the kilometers-long, daggerlike structure that connected its engines to its prow, came rushing towards them, undaunted and seemingly unavoidable.

"So, Spock," McCoy drawled, as the enemy ship grew ever larger on the screen before them, "I suppose that, now that you know how crucial you are to the future of the galaxy, you're going to be even more impossible to live with?"

"Possibly," Spock replied, "but unless we can devise a means of outwitting Commander Motak in the next few moments, you will not have to worry about that very much longer."

Chapter Sixteen

THE LAST THING Kirk remembered was a flash like a supernova. Emerging from a dreamless sleep, he awoke to find himself surrounded by over a half-dozen Romulan soldiers. *I suppose it's too much to hope that this is just a bad dream,* he thought, *like that one where I keep finding myself back at Starfleet Academy with Finnegan. . . .*

He glanced around, swiftly taking in the situation, which looked far from advantageous. The command center was filled with Romulans, all in full military uniforms and bearing weapons, except for an older-looking Romulan wearing a white lab coat and apparently preoccupied with repairing the damage to the control panel caused by the Romulan Commander's disruptor beam. Kirk prayed that damage was beyond the balding scientist's ability to undo, although he could hardly count on such a convenient solution to the crisis. *That would be too easy,* he thought.

"Are you well, Captain?" Gary Seven asked. He occupied a sitting position on the floor a few meters away, and looked as though he had regained consciousness only a few minutes before. His face had been reddened by the heat of the blast, inspiring Kirk to raise a hand to his own face. The skin felt dry and itchy, like a bad case of sunburn. *Could be worse,* Kirk decided; at least he had retained his vision. *Blind and surrounded, now that would have been a tight fix!*

"Well enough," he answered before the nearest guard jabbed the muzzle of a disruptor between Kirk's eyes, ordering him to silence and prodding Kirk hard enough to make his eyes water. Kirk had to fight the temptation to jump up and feed the Romulan his own disruptor, but that, he realized, was probably not the best long-range strategy, no matter how satisfying it might be in the short term. Instead he looked around for his phaser, only to see it resting in the grip of another Romulan soldier who was examining the foreign weapon with great interest. Kirk guessed that he was not likely to get the phaser back anytime soon. Checking his pocket, he was not surprised to find Seven's servo missing too.

A groan caught his attention and he turned to observe the Romulan Commander—Dellas, he recalled—being helped to her feet by two of her underlings. Kirk assumed that she had taken the brunt of the blast since she had been the closest to her discarded disruptor when it overloaded, a sacrifice she had evidently been willing to make in order to render Kirk and Seven defenseless as well. *A bold but effective ploy,* he conceded reluctantly, resolving never to underestimate this particular foe.

He inspected Commander Dellas more closely. The disruptor burst had darkened her face and seared away her eyebrows, which looked even odder on a Romulan than it would on human. Her uniform was torn and burnt in numerous places, confirming Kirk's suspicions that not too much time had passed since the overload knocked out everyone in the room. He didn't recognize the ebony cloak over her right shoulder nor the insignia upon her collar; then again, there was a lot Starfleet still didn't know about the Romulan military.

The commander's personality asserted itself quickly. Shrugging off the aftereffects of the blast, she angrily yanked her arms free from the grip of the solicitous guards, preferring to stand on her own. "Enough," she barked. "You should be watching over our prisoners, not me." The soldiers backed away, exchanging glances nervously and looking more than a little bit frightened of their own commander.

Everything he saw just confirmed Kirk's original assessment of Dellas. He may not have known much about Romulans, but he knew a killer when he saw one. There was a homicidal gleam in this woman's eyes that went beyond the usual Romulan suspicion of outsiders. The Romulan commanders he had encountered in the past, including Motak, had displayed no excessive malice; they had been honorable antagonists, simply doing their duty as they saw it. But this woman was different, he could tell just by looking in her eyes. She reminded him less of the dignified Romulan starship commander he had defeated in the Neutral Zone two years ago and more like such unscrupulous sociopaths as the late Colonel Green, the pseudo-Nazis of Ekos, or even his own crew's machiavellian counterparts in the Mirror Universe. *No wonder Gary Seven doesn't want her using his technology,* Kirk thought. *Looks like he was telling the truth so far.*

"Doctor Vithrok," she demanded briskly, glancing over at the older Romulan scientist. "What is the status of the transporter controls?"

Gary Seven eyed Vithrok intently. He appeared even more keen to hear the scientist's response than Dellas herself. *Of course,* Kirk realized, *the transporter is the time machine. That's how she's planning to change the future—but change it how?* He couldn't begin to guess when and where she intended to tinker with history, but it seemed safe to assume that what was good for Commander Dellas and the Romulan Star Empire would be bad for the rest of the galaxy.

Watching the scientist and assessing his potential as an adversary, Kirk spotted the tip of Seven's servo emerging from a pocket on Vithrok's lab jacket. *So that's where it went,* he thought. He guessed that Seven had spied his weapon as well. Too bad neither of them was in a position to reclaim it.

"I think it's fixed," Vithrok announced, stepping away from the control panel. "The damage was fairly serious, but it appears as if someone else had already repaired the major components." He contemplated Dellas with a quizzical expression on his face. "Commander, I don't suppose that . . . that is, can I ask whether you made any changes to—"

Kirk wondered if Dellas would admit to accidentally blasting the panel herself while liquidating the unfortunate Supervisor 146. Probably not, he guessed; he doubted that one rose far in the Romulan command without shrewder political instincts than that.

"The equipment was injured during my apprehension of these intruders," she said obliquely. "This one"—she nodded toward Seven—"was attempting to repair the transporter for his own corrupt purposes when I set my disruptor to explode."

Kirk briefly considered dispelling Dellas's evasions with the truth, but he couldn't see any obvious advantage to it. Dellas seemed to have her subordinates too cowed to contradict her, regardless of the facts. Instead he decided to try to coax out whatever information he could from his captors. "On behalf of the United Federation of Planets, I protest our treatment here and demand to be put in touch with the proper diplomatic authorities."

Dellas laughed out loud. "This must be that celebrated human sense of humor you seem so proud of. As you must be aware, you can hardly demand anything, legally or otherwise. You were captured in a blatant attempt to infiltrate and sabotage this installation."

"But this isn't a Romulan military installation, is it?" Kirk challenged.

"It is now," she replied, "although you are right that it does not appear anywhere in our computers. Not even the Praetor knows this planet exists, nor about this operation." She smiled coldly. *"I* am the highest authority here, and well within my rights to have you executed on the spot."

"Oh, I doubt that you're likely to do that," Kirk said. "A Starfleet captain, especially one who has eluded the Empire twice before, is too valuable a prize to consign to an unmarked grave on a nonexistent world. That's true no matter how well-connected you think you are."

Dellas regarded him thoughtfully, a scowl upon her radiation-baked, hairless face, and Kirk wondered for a moment if he'd pushed his luck too far. *Better too far than not enough,* he thought, and hoped that he hadn't just devised his own ideal epitaph.

"Perhaps," she said finally, then turned to face a centurion standing to one side. "Is the *Enterprise* still in orbit above us?"

"Yes, Commander," the soldier replied. He had removed his helmet, which he held against his chest. "They have repeatedly attempted to hail their captain, but we continue to jam their transmissions."

"Good," she said tersely. "And the force field?"

"Still at full strength," he reported. "They have fired none of their weapons against it."

Kirk was stunned to hear that the *Enterprise* was still orbiting the planet, but he was careful not to let his surprise show upon his face. *What are you waiting for, Spock? Me?* He would have preferred to hear that his ship was safely away from here, although, from a more selfish point of view, it was good to know that the landing party still had a way off this planet, assuming he could just find a way to disable that force field. Judging from what he had heard so far, it sounded like Chekov and Sulu had successfully eluded the Romulan patrols. They must be hiding out in the jungle, waiting for further word from their captain. He didn't intend to let them down. *We're not dead yet,* he thought. *All I need is a chance.*

"I see," Dellas said, appropriating a fresh disruptor from the centurion. She casually set it on kill. "Very well. You and your men may leave us now. Continue to monitor the Federation vessel and alert me if there is any change."

"Are you sure, Commander?" The centurion gave Vithrok a scornful look; clearly he did not consider the scientist adequate protection for Dellas. "Perhaps I should stay."

"This is not for your ears, centurion, nor for any of your men's." She raised the disruptor confidently. "I can defend myself if necessary." She took Kirk's phaser from another soldier and placed it on a counter next to the computer controls. "Now, go."

Dellas waited until all of the soldiers had left the control room, leaving her alone with Vithrok and the two prisoners, before giving Kirk further consideration. She eyed him suspiciously as she paced slowly around him and Seven. "What I most want to know," she stated, "is why are you here? How much do you know about our purpose here?" An ugly sneer appeared on her burnt face. "I refuse to accept that your presence on this world is a mere coincidence."

"Er, Commander," Vithrok interrupted. "Now that the soldiers have departed, I want to show you this." He lifted the servo from his pocket, rolling the silver cylinder nervously between his fingers. "The centurion found it on Captain Kirk, but it's not Starfleet issue. Citizen Septos had something similar before we confiscated it, as I'm sure you must recall," he appended swiftly.

"I do indeed," she stated, taking the servo from

Vithrok. "An admirably compact and lethal device, at least when employed effectively." She dangled the servo before Kirk's eyes, the light from the overhead lamps glinting off the argentine sheen of Seven's weapon. "Now why would a Starfleet captain be carrying a piece of alien technology identical to one we captured from the former occupant of this base? Curiouser and curiouser, as I believe one of your native fairy tales goes."

You're talking to the wrong person, Kirk thought, sneaking a sideways glance at Seven. The enigmatic time traveller remained silent, paying close attention to Vithrok's activities at the computer station. So far, Commander Dellas had not paid much attention to Seven, perhaps misled by his borrowed Starfleet uniform. *She doesn't realize Seven is the one who made all the travel arrangements for this little jaunt.* He didn't see any reason to fill her in on the real story.

"Why don't you tell me what you're up to instead," Kirk said defiantly. "We both know that you don't belong here."

Dellas laughed, a sound that was anything but infectious. She tucked the servo into one of her boots. "I suppose such displays of bravado impress Klingons, but a Romulan commander is less easily swayed." Swinging the muzzle of her disruptor back and forth between Kirk and Seven, she faced the Starfleet captain. "I'm very familiar with your record, Kirk, and not just your past. I know you have a long history with the Klingons. Tell me, have you ever experienced their mind-sifter?"

"You know, I don't like the looks of this," Dr. McCoy said, shocking no one with this revelation, least of all Spock. To his mind, the nature of the threat hardly required explication.

Gladiator hung in the blackness, a emerald dagger poised to stab at the heart of the *Enterprise* as soon as it came within firing range, which Spock estimated would occur within approximately 2.5 seconds. "Lieutenant Rodriguez, prepare to execute evasive maneuvers," he instructed. "Take us out of this solar system." A moment later, the first disruptor blast shook the *Enterprise*. Spock felt the vibration all the way through to his bones. He clenched his jaws to avoid biting down on his tongue by accident. All around the bridge, red alert lights dimmed momentarily before coming back on again.

"Boy," Roberta Lincoln exclaimed from her perch at the science station once the shaking stopped. She brushed her disheveled blonde bangs away from her eyes. "Those Romulan guys aren't kidding!"

"Apparently not," Spock agreed, briefly wondering why humans always seemed to require assurance that a situation is not intended as humorous. Were practical jokes that pervasive an aspect of their culture? "Evidently Commander Motak does not intend to waste his time with further rhetoric or threats." He established an intercom link with engineering. "Mr. Scott, what is the status of our defenses?"

"After the pounding we got before," Scotty replied, "it's a miracle that we have any screens at all." Spock heard the sounds of vigorous activity in the background of Scotty's transmission; it seemed that extensive work was being performed even as he conversed with the chief engineer. "We're doing what we can down here, but the screens aren't going to hold out for long, I can promise you that!"

"Deflectors down to forty-one percent," Roberta confirmed, "which sounds like pretty bad news to me."

"Less commentary, please, Miss Lincoln," Spock requested as, despite the helmsman's best efforts, another salvo jolted the bridge, provoking a flurry of profanity from Dr. McCoy and a startled gasp from Lt. Uhura. The red alert signals went out entirely this time, and did not light up again. Scanning the ring of duty stations that circled the bridge, Spock saw warning lights and damage alerts blinking on at almost every station, from environmental to engineering. As unnecessary as Roberta's remarks seemed, he could not fault her evaluation of their situation; the *Enterprise* was growing increasing vulnerable, while *Gladiator* had yet to receive any damage. Their only chance was to attempt to balance the equation. "Return fire, Ensign Gates."

"Yes, sir," Ensign Gates acknowledged, her hands manipulating the phaser controls. A beam of scarlet energy flashed across the void to strike against the Romulan warship's deflector shields. Spock spotted the distinctive blue flash of discharged Cerenkov radiation as the shields absorbed the phaser burst, dissipating the destructive energies back into the vacuum of space. Gates fired again and shimmering fire outlined the portside nacelle of the battle cruiser.

Gladiator flickered like a mirage, then disappeared entirely. "Yikes, you disintegrated it!" Roberta exclaimed, sounding both relieved and appalled. "Just like that!"

"I wish," McCoy muttered darkly. He held on tightly to the painted red handrail around the command module, standing directly behind the captain's chair.

"That is far from the case," Spock stated, fully aware that Motak's ship had simply activated their cloaking device, rendering *Gladiator* invisible to all their sensors. The only consolation, he knew, was that the battle cruiser could employ neither its weapons nor its shields while cloaked, guaranteeing the *Enterprise* at least a momentary respite. He doubted it would endure for long.

"Shall I keep firing, sir?" Gates asked. Caught up in the heat of the battle, she seemed eager to strike back at the Romulan cruiser.

"Fire where, Ensign?" Spock said, contemplating

the empty starscape on the viewer. The battle cruiser was nowhere in evidence. "We cannot afford to waste our remaining energy shooting blindly."

"I hope you have a better idea," McCoy commented, lowering his voice so that only Spock could hear him.

The doctor was free to hope, Spock thought, not that it was likely to do much good. Strategically, Motak had the advantage. Not only did the commander have fresh shields and a cloaking device to hide behind, but he could count on reinforcements eventually. Even if both vessels were ultimately incapacitated, left drifting helplessly in space, it was only a matter of time before the Romulans sent more warships to apprehend the *Enterprise*. A temporary stalemate would eventually provide Commander Motak with final victory.

"Uh-oh," Roberta blurted, working the ship's sensor array. "They're back . . . behind us!"

Seconds later, a violent shudder rattled the floor beneath their feet, dramatically confirming Roberta's report. The image on the main viewer shifted as the rear sensors automatically switched the perspective, but Spock caught only a fleeting glimpse of *Gladiator* before it faded from sight once more. Gates released another phaser blast in retaliation. The beam pierced the darkness, continuing on in a straight line that apparently encountered no resistance. "Missed him!" Gates cried out, smacking her fist against her knee in frustration.

Sparks flew from the ceiling as a wounded *Enterprise* suffered the effects of this latest blow. A burning ember landed on the back of Spock's hand. He brushed it away methodically, his mind examining the battle just as he would approach a game of tridimensional chess. The cloaking device was the key, he realized. If he could eliminate that advantage, the *Enterprise*'s own firepower could be brought to bear. Regrettably, however, Starfleet military research had yet to discover an effective counteragent to the cloaking device he and Captain Kirk had removed from the Romulans on an earlier mission. Spock himself had not previously applied himself to the problem, but it was unrealistic to assume that he could provide a technological breakthrough in the midst of battle.

Or was it? His gaze fell upon the green crystal cube Roberta had used to usurp control of the *Enterprise*. "Miss Lincoln," he called out, "is it possible that your computer interface device might be of use in this situation?"

"My what?" Roberta asked. "Oh, you mean this thingie." She held the cube out at roughly eye level. "What the heck do you have in mind?"

Spock recalled that Seven claimed a thorough mastery of cloaking technology on the part of his anonymous sponsors. "If given access to the *Enterprise*'s sensor array, might not your computer be able to penetrate our adversary's cloaking field?"

"Huh?" McCoy said. His confusion was evident. "But you can't detect a cloaked ship, Spock. That's the whole point."

Spock would not be deterred by the doctor's dour attitude. "Just because we lack the knowledge to do something, that does not mean it cannot be done, perhaps even with the tools at hand." He braced himself as *Gladiator* materialized once more out of the ether. "Miss Lincoln, establish the link immediately. Ensign Gates, arm photon torpedoes, but hold your fire until our foe resumes a cloaked state."

In a simple shooting match, Spock knew, *Gladiator*'s shields would outlast the *Enterprise*. Logically, their only hope was to accomplish the impossible, striking against the battle cruiser while its deflectors were rendered inoperative by the cloaking effect. The only variable was, would the *Enterprise* hold together long enough to give Roberta a chance to apply Gary Seven's alien technology to the task of locating a cloaked ship? Spock started to calculate the odds of their survival, then, on an impulse, abandoned the effort.

As Captain Kirk had repeatedly demonstrated, the odds weren't everything.

The casualties had begun streaming into sickbay, just as Christine Chapel had feared. Three already, one from Deck Sixteen and two from the shuttle landing bay. They came in carried and/or assisted by their fellow crew members, whom she immediately set to work loading hyposprays and sterilizing wounds. Fortunately, none of the injuries were life-threatening yet—just fractures and second-degree burns—but the battle appeared far from over. The yellow alert lights had been replaced by flashing red warnings. Doctor McCoy must be on his way, she assumed, unless he had encountered another medical emergency en route—or worse. That was the worst part of holding down the fort like this; she never knew when the doctor himself might be carried into sickbay, wounded or dying, leaving her on her own to cope with the inevitable victims of war.

The floor suddenly dropped out from beneath her feet as a devastating force slammed into the ship. The entire sickbay lurched downward and Chapel stumbled forward, smacking sideways into one of the biobeds. One of her conscripted "orderlies" lost hold of a tray full of medical instruments, which crashed to the floor with a ringing metallic clang. Surgical scalpels, heartbeat readers, med scanners, and anabolic protoplasers rolled across the floor as desperate crew members scurried after them.

Out of the corner of her eye, Chapel saw a specimen cage slide off its shelf and smash onto the floor. *Oh, no,* she thought, *the poor cat!* But there was nothing she could do about that now. "Strap the wounded to the beds!" she ordered, to protect them from any future jolts. "And watch out for yourselves." Part of her wished she knew how the battle was faring, whether the *Enterprise* was giving as good as she was getting, but, in a way, that had nothing to do with her. Let Mr. Spock and the others fight for the ship. Her job was to care for the injured for as long as she was able.

The door to the corridor whished open and two more casualties staggered in. Radiations burns and a head wound, she diagnosed on the run. Performing triage automatically, she handed off the burn victim to an ensign for first aid while she scanned the head injury with her medical tricorder, looking for signs of serious cerebral trauma and praying she wouldn't find any.

She didn't even notice a sleek black shape slip out through the open door.

Chapter Seventeen

DISRUPTORS BLAZED amidst the silence of space. Spock saw an incandescent flash an instant before he felt the impact. McCoy gasped behind him, thrown against the very handrail he had depended on to keep himself upright. For a second it felt like the *Enterprise* was going to flip end over end, but the ship's artificial gravity kept everyone more or less in place. Electrical fires sparked all around the bridge, suffusing the room with smoke. When the automatic fire suppression system failed to activate, Uhura sprung to action immediately, retrieving an emergency fire extinguisher from a shelf beneath the communications console and dashing around the bridge, putting out the blazes wherever they flared up. "Don't worry, Mr. Spock," she called out, coughing loudly and waving away the haze with her free hand, "I think I have things under control."

Spock took her at her word. Uhura was a logical choice to assume this duty; Commander Motak seemed to have no interest in sending transmissions to the *Enterprise*. Spock peered at Roberta through the white trails of smoke. Her translucent cube blinked rapidly atop the ship sensor controls. "Are you making any progress, Miss Lincoln?" he asked.

"I think so," she shouted over the crackling fires and minor explosions that broke out almost as fast as Lt. Uhura could contain them. "It thinks your sensor gadgets are awfully primitive, but it might be able to work with them."

"Let us hope so," Spock answered, finding it intriguing and more than a little remarkable that the fate of the *Enterprise*—and perhaps that of future history—depended on the unlikely abilities of a twentieth century Earth woman and a mechanism of unknown origin. Captain Kirk was prone to "gambling on long shots," as he called it. Spock could not help wondering what the captain would think of this particular gamble.

"Here they come again!" Ensign Gates warned as another flash of energy lit up the forward viewer and the subsequent shock wave tilted the entire bridge starboard, sending them all lurching to one side. Knocked from its setting, the bronze plaque mounted to the left of the turbolift doors crashed to the floor, producing a ringing metallic clang. The hull remained intact, though, Spock noted; the shields were still holding, if just barely. The intercom whistled at his side and he heard Chief Engineer Scott reading off damage reports through a cacophony of static and electronic distortion. He did not need to identify every word to understand that circumstances were dire in the extreme. *We do not have much more time,* he concluded.

Suddenly, the floor buckled only a few meters away, spraying Rodriguez with shards of metal and released plasma. The helmsman let out a single frantic scream before being flung from his seat, landing hard at the base of the main viewscreen. "Good Lord," McCoy whispered hoarsely and hurried forward. He had his

219

medical scanner out and ready even before he reached
the injured man's side. "Talk to me, Arturo," he
urged his patient, using a spray applicator to treat
Rodriguez's visible burns and lacerations. "Don't die
on me, man!"

Throwing an empty fire extinguisher onto the
floor, Uhura rushed back to the communications
station and hurriedly inserted her receiver into her
ear. "Uhura to sickbay. Dr. McCoy requires assistance on the bridge . . . well, send whomever you
can!" She turned toward Spock. "Nurse Chapel
reports more casualties coming into sickbay. No
fatalities yet, but they're running out of room for the
wounded."

Ensign Gates rose to assist the doctor, but Spock
restrained him with a sharp command. "Maintain
your post, Ms. Gates." Although Rodriguez's injuries were apparently severe, he could not concern
himself with the fate of a single crewman; that was in
Dr. McCoy's able hands now. Tapping the vital
functions override panel on his port console, he
transferred helm control to the navigation station,
knowing all the while that simply maintaining their
present course was not enough. They had to go on
the offensive, force *Gladiator* to go to cloaked mode
at least one more time before Commander Motak
came in for the kill. "Hold the torpedoes, but fire
phasers at will."

Gates stared at her wounded comrade for one
more heartbeat, then dropped back into her seat and
depressed the firing controls with a vengeance. A
volley of phaser beams, one after another, detonated
against *Gladiator*'s shields, sending cascades of rip-
pling blue energy around the outline of the warship.
Spock watched the enemy vessel with keen interest.
Would Motak respond in kind or take the better part
of valor, going to cloak before attacking the *Enterprise* again? Much depended on what next tran-
spired.

Spock's eyes widened almost imperceptibly as the image of the battle cruiser rippled like a reflection upon the water before vanishing entirely. *Now is the time,* he thought. *We will not have a better opportunity.* "Miss Lincoln, can you identify the location of the hostile vessel?"

"Almost . . . sort of . . . Got it!" she rejoiced, staring at the sensor displays. Looking across the bridge, Spock did not recognize any of the patterns he could discern. The cube atop the instruments maintained a steady chartreuse glow. "He's standing out like a sore thumb!"

What a curious simile, Spock thought. "Transfer the coordinates to the targeting mechanisms at once," he said, hoping that Roberta had absorbed enough of his technical skills to accomplish this rather elementary task. If not, precious seconds could be lost.

"No problem," she replied, a grim expression on her face. Ensign Gates's jaw dropped as the necessary data was instantaneously fed into the weapons controls. "Sock it to them!"

"Sir?" Gates asked, looking back over her shoulder. She looked more apprehensive than hopeful.

"You heard Miss Lincoln," Spock said. "Fire torpedoes."

Each wrapped in a polished metallic casing, five gleaming projectiles hurled across the vacuum in search of the concealed battle cruiser. Concentrating intently on the scene upon the viewer, Spock waited for the inevitable explosions that would occur when the photon torpedoes found their target. He hoped that *Gladiator* was not so close to the *Enterprise* that their ship would incur further damage from the resulting shock waves, although, in the ship's present state, that was hardly the greatest of their concerns.

As expected, the torpedoes converged on a single location. The sheen of their dark surfaces captured the far-off starlight an instant before all five projectiles were consumed in a savage matter-antimatter reaction, yielding a blinding white light that lasted for only a fraction of a nanosecond. Spock's inner eyelids dropped briefly into place to protect him from the brilliant flash; even still, the explosion left faint blue spots in his vision that lingered for several seconds. He noted automatically that Gates, Roberta, and Uhura were blinking, too. Only McCoy, engrossed in his efforts to preserve Lt. Rodriguez's life, seemed oblivious to the torpedoes's highly visible demise. As the rest of the bridge crew held their breaths, Spock heard the hiss of the doctor's hypospray at work.

Behind Spock, the turbolift doors slid open and two medical personnel ran onto the bridge. They appeared taken aback by the smoke and debris, but only for a moment, quickly joining McCoy at the unconscious Rodriguez's side. The doctor barked orders at both medics while continuing to treat the helmsman's burns. "We need to stabilize him now," he instructed them, "before we get him to sickbay. You, Greenburg, administer aught-point-six-five cc's of cordrazine, stat. Clark, apply the EMR neutralizer. We have to deGauss those metal fragments . . . !"

Confident that the medical situation was under control, Spock scrutinized the screen in front of him for some evidence of *Gladiator*'s status. He hoped that the massive battle cruiser had not been completely destroyed by the devastating impact of the torpedoes, but was merely incapacitated. To his surprise, however, the starlit void upon the screen held neither a wrecked Romulan vessel nor any visible traces of debris. Surely, he reasoned, without shields, the cruiser's cloaking machinery could not have survived an attack of such severity and remained in working order?

The obvious conclusion was inescapable: The photon torpedoes had merely destroyed each other, not

Gladiator. "We appear to have missed our target," he announced.

Gates and Uhura both turned their eyes toward Roberta, who looked both indignant and embarrassed. She draped one hand protectively over the luminescent cube. "That's impossible!" she insisted. "I know I had that sucker in my sights."

Spock considered all the possibilities before replying. "The time delay," he deduced within seconds. "Despite the speed with which we proceeded, there was nevertheless too great an interval between the time Miss Lincoln identified the exact location of the cloaked vessel and the moment when the torpedoes arrived at their preprogrammed destination. During that interval, however brief, *Gladiator* had sufficient time to vary its speed and/or its trajectory, thus evading our torpedoes."

"Oh." Roberta gave her cube a dubious look. Spock believed she grasped his explanation. "So what do we do now?"

He had already anticipated her query. "The most effective solution would be to use your technology to enhance the onboard sensors of the torpedoes themselves." He inspected Roberta's face carefully, making certain that she understood completely what he was proposing. "That would necessitate placing your device within the scanning mechanism of an individual torpedo."

Her voice quavered slightly as she replied. "But, umm, wouldn't that mean blowing it up when the bomb goes off?"

He was relieved that she fully comprehended his intention. "That is precisely the sacrifice I am asking of you, Miss Lincoln. It may be our only chance to escape defeat."

Roberta winced at the very thought, squinching her features together tightly. She lifted the cube from its resting place atop the scanner controls and held it close against her chest. Spock realized that he had asked her to give up what might well be her only link to Gary Seven. "Miss Lincoln . . . Roberta, we do not have much time."

"Ohhh, okay!" she said decisively. She held out the cube to Spock. "Where does it have to go?"

"I can run it down to the forward torpedo bay, Mr. Spock," Uhura volunteered. Spock swiftly surveyed the bridge; everyone else was injured or occupied, except Roberta, who could hardly be expected to know the shortest route to the torpedo launchers.

"Very well," he addressed Uhura. "Refrain from using the turbolifts. They may have been damaged by the hostilities."

"I can manage," she assured him with a confident grin. "Didn't you know I won the Jovian Triathalon back in '59? I'll be back before the Romulans have a chance to sneeze."

Roberta reluctantly handed over the cube to the other woman. "Be good," she whispered to the gently glowing crystal. "Do as you're told." Spock found her willingness to anthropomorphize an advanced cybernetic instrument animistic and rather shockingly primitive; then again, he reminded himself, she *was* from the twentieth century, and a human at that. Uhura snatched the cube from her hands and raced for the emergency exit to the left of the main viewer. Spock heard her steps ring on the gangway to the lower levels of the *Enterprise*. He estimated it would take her approximately 6.3 minutes to arrive at the forward torpedo bays, six decks below, and another 0.8 minutes to explain to the weapons engineers what had to be done. It was probably just as well that Chief Engineer Scott was presently at work in the Engine Rooms; he imagined that the proud and outspoken human engineer would not approve of placing the safety of the ship on an unknown and untested piece of alien technology.

But would *Gladiator* give them time to implement their plan? "Monitor the surrounding space carefully," he directed Roberta, one small portion of his consciousness continually intrigued at the ease with which their anachronistic visitor had adapted to the rhythms of the bridge. "I wish to know the minute the enemy vessel uncloaks."

"Aye, aye, Mr. Spock," she agreed, recovering from the loss of her cube with admirable haste. "I'll keep my eyes peeled."

Under Dr. McCoy's direction, the two medics cautiously lifted Lieutenant Rodriguez's supine body from the floor. A portable stasis field generator kept their patient rigid and immobile, forestalling further injuries. "He'll recover," McCoy informed Spock, following behind Clarke and Greenburg, "if he gets half a chance. God only knows what's waiting for me in sickbay . . . !"

"I shall endeavor to ensure that you arrive there safely, Doctor," Spock said as McCoy passed by him on the way to the turbolift entrance. The medical team apparently wanted to at least give the turbolift a try before taking the long way around.

"See that you do," the doctor drawled, then looked back at him with concerned, compassionate eyes, "and, Spock, good luck."

Luck was not what he required, the Vulcan thought, *only time.* Why had *Gladiator* not yet attacked once more? Perhaps, he speculated, Commander Motak remained puzzled by the *Enterprise*'s near miss with the photon torpedoes. It seemed logical to assume that, given that unexpected development, Motak might be maintaining a wary distance from the Starfleet vessel while he attempted to discern to what extent his battle cruiser's cloaking effect had been compromised. *In that case,* Spock reasoned, *I must give the commander more to think about.*

"Ensign Gates," he ordered. "Fire phasers at maximum possible dispersion. A full 360 degree sweep from every angle of orientation."

"But, sir," Gates protested, "we haven't got much phaser power left to begin with. If we spread the beam that thin, it won't have any punch at all."

"I am aware of that, Ensign," Spock replied. "Knowing that, do you find my command puzzling?"

"A bit, sir," she admitted.

"Excellent. That is exactly the effect I intend." He leaned back against his chair. "Fire as instructed."

Shrugging her shoulders, as if resigned to the fact that the ship's commanding officer had gone insane, Gates pressed down on the firing controls. At once a wave of crimson energy spread out from the *Enterprise* on all sides, briefly encasing the Federation starship at the center of an expanding sphere of phaser light that grew to four times the volume of the ship itself before fading away into the surrounding blackness. Aboard the bridge, the starfield on the forward viewer took on a pinkish tint for only a heartbeat, then reverted to ebony and silver. Once again, Spock detected no sign of a wounded *Gladiator,* but this time he had not expected to. Although visually impressive, the phaser burst had been so diffuse that it was scarcely more dangerous than ordinary background radiation. Even an unshielded vessel, such as the cloaked battle cruiser, could have withstood the discharge; its duranium hull alone would have protected the ship from any phaser damage.

But Spock had never intended to inflict significant harm on *Gladiator* with the showy-but-ineffectual blast. His only target had been Commander Motak's peace of mind. If all went as planned, Motak would waste precious moments attempting to decipher his adversary's seemingly senseless tactic, especially in the context of *Gladiator's* close call with the photon torpedoes only minutes before. It struck Spock that a short period of contemplation and reevaluation would be a plausible response for Motak to take under the circumstances; unfortunately, he remembered, Romulans did not always behave as logically—or as predictably—as their Vulcan cousins.

"Mr. Spock!" Roberta called out. She jerked to attention at the science station. "They're back—behind us!"

"Onscreen," he ordered. "Fire rear torpedoes."

"Yes, sir!" Gates said with enthusiasm. Spock was grateful that his command could not interfere with whatever operations Uhura was now supervising in the forward torpedo bay. He consulted the chronometer located behind the astrogator. By his calculations, the lieutenant should have almost completed her task.

The image on the viewer flipped to show *Gladiator* bearing down on them from behind, swooping through space like one of the birds of prey the Romulans both admired and emulated, its disruptor beam outpacing the cruiser to strike like lightning against the lower hull of the *Enterprise,* whose weakened shields flickered like fireflies beneath the onslaught. Spock felt the force of the attack all the way up in the forward saucer section. Warning lights blinked and sirens screamed. Above the science station, a decorative illustration of the Milky Way galaxy melted and bubbled away. "We've lost the shuttlecraft hanger doors," Roberta reported, then wrinkled her brow. "What exactly is a shuttlecraft anyway?"

Apparently the mind meld was not one hundred percent effective, Spock noted. He experienced a distinct sensation of relief.

Two black photon torpedoes rocketed away from the *Enterprise* to intercept the flight path of *Gladiator.* They exploded upon contact with the Romulan vessel's deflectors, flooding the prow of the cruiser with light but failing to even scratch its shining green hull. Uncloaked, *Gladiator's* shields appeared formidable.

The intercom whistled loudly. Spock pressed a switch on his armrest. "Spock here," he said.

Uhura's voice emerged from the speaker. "The cube has been installed in a torpedo, sir. We're ready when you are."

"Good work, Lieutenant," Spock answered. "Hold until my command." There was no point in firing the augmented torpedo until their enemy was once more cloaked and unshielded. He had to put Commander Motak back on the defensive. "Return fire, Ensign Gates. Rear torpedoes only."

Motak's disruptors struck before Gates could carry out Spock's orders. The entire bridge rattled and dipped sharply to starboard. Spock heard Roberta use a colorful metaphor of a scatological nature, then Ensign Gates was thrown from her seat, tumbling over the astrogator and landing flat on her back near the torn and twisted remains of the helm controls. Electrical sparks sputtered perilously close to her hair and limbs. Gates rolled over, away from the exposed circuitry and tried to drag her way back to the navigation station, but she could barely manage more than a few centimeters at a time. *Gladiator* would cut the *Enterprise* to pieces, Spock realized, before the battered crewman made it back to her post.

He shot out of the captain's chair, lunging for the weapons controls only a few meters away. His right shoulder collided with Roberta, who must have had the same idea. "Sorry 'bout that," she blurted, backing away. "After you." Spock fired the rear torpedoes.

Gladiator dropped out of sight.

Now was the moment he had been waiting for. He dropped back in the captain's chair. "Lieutenant

Uhura," he shouted into the intercom, "release the torpedo."

The first two torpedoes, fired automatically from the rear torpedo launchers, zeroed in on *Gladiator*'s former location, then exploded uselessly against each other. Operating the command functions panel, Spock instructed the viewer to track the third torpedo, the one Uhura and the weapons engineers had fired manually from the forward torpedo bay, the one containing an inexplicable bit of crystalline technology that surpassed even the considerable scientific resources of the United Federation of Planets, the one that held their last, best chance at survival.

"C'mon!" Roberta urged the screen as the gleaming projectile accelerated against the backdrop of—apparently—empty space. "You can do it! Show-'em what a good, old-fashioned Beta-5 can do!"

Less vocally, but with equal concentration, Spock focused on the torpedo's path. At first it seemed completely random, then it reversed course and jetted towards a completely different patch of vacant space. A moment later, the glare of a matter/antimatter reaction exposed nothing less than the sight of a Romulan battle cruiser spinning out of control. Ensign Gates expelled a very human sigh of relief.

Spock preferred to take no chances. "Direct our remaining phaser power against *Gladiator*. Target warp nacelles only."

Gates nodded and took aim at the floundering spacecraft. With seconds, a crimson beam of energized light struck with surgical precision at first one, then the other nacelle at the stern of the battle cruiser. The beam sliced away at the warp engines without encountering even a single blue spark of resistance. *Gladiator*'s shields were down completely. "Miss Lincoln," Spock asked after the phasers had done their work, "what is the status of their warp capacity?"

She inspected the impressive assortment of gauges and displays at her disposal, tweaked a knob or two, then looked over at Spock with a wide grin upon her face. "As nearly as I can tell, they're dead in the water!"

"That is quite satisfactory." With Uhura away from the bridge, Spock activated the communications system himself from the vital function override panel at the captain's chair. He hailed the disabled vessel on the screen. "Commander Motak, this is First Officer Spock of the U.S.S. *Enterprise*. We are prepared to accept your surrender. Do you require assistance?"

In the past, the commanders of Romulan warships had been known to destroy their own vessels to avoid capture. Spock sincerely hoped that Commander Motak would not feel compelled to do so within the safety of his own borders. That would be a tremendous waste of life and materials.

His misgivings grew as *Gladiator* failed to respond. Was Motak determined to commit suicide or had their communications equipment simply been rendered inoperative by the destructive effects of the photon torpedo? "Repeat: This is the *Enterprise*. Do you surrender?"

Scanning various known frequencies, including those employed by *Gladiator* earlier, he detected a return signal containing both visual and audio components. He immediately transferred the reply to the primary viewscreen.

Commander Motak glared at Spock from the bridge of his crippled warship. His dark hair was in wild disarray and there was an ugly olive bruise upon his forehead. A trickle of watery green blood leaked from the corner of his mouth. Behind his head and shoulders, wisps of smoke and bits of broken machinery drifted through what was left of the cabin. Although the life-support systems appeared to function at an acceptable level, it was obvious that the ship's artificial gravity had been knocked out of commission by the *Enterprise's* attacks. As Spock looked on, part of a melted circuit board floated between Motak and the source of the transmission. The Romulan commander batted it away with an angry swipe of his hand.

"Where is Kirk?" he demanded, looking less like a serene, unemotional Vulcan and more like an enraged Klingon warrior. "Does he consider me no longer worthy to speak with him directly?"

"No offense is intended," Spock stated calmly. "The captain is otherwise occupied."

"I hope that means he is dead," Motak snarled, spitting out a piece of a broken tooth. Spock did not correct him. If Motak preferred to think that Captain Kirk was dead, rather than isolated and vulnerable on a nearby world, then Spock was certainly not inclined to dissuade him.

"The captain is unavailable," he repeated. "Do you surrender?"

"Hah!" Motak laughed. "Do you think you've won just because you've defeated me? You're hundreds of light-years from the Federation, First Officer Spock. I have already transmitted a report of your presence here to the Imperial High Command. More warships are warping toward this sector at this very moment. A veritable fleet of some of the finest ships and commanders in the Empire." He wiped a dab of blood from his chin. Spock noted that Motak's hand was wrapped in fresh white bandages. A burn, most likely, he speculated, or perhaps a deep cut. The pain could not be helping to improve the commander's disposition.

"I don't know what ingenious Vulcan trick you played to see past my cloaking field," he continued, "but it won't be enough to save you from the full wrath of the Romulan Empire. You might as well face the truth, First Officer Spock, neither you nor your ship will ever see the Federation again."

"In that case," Spock replied, "I trust you will remember the mercy we have shown your own vessel and crew. *Enterprise* out." He flicked a switch and Motak's vengeful face disappeared from the viewer, replaced by the sight of *Gladiator* still tumbling through space, now a victim of its own unregulated momentum. "Miss Lincoln, what is the status of the Romulan vessel's life-support mechanisms?"

"Good idea!" Roberta carefully examined the sensor displays. "Um, lifesigns appear to be stable. No indications of environmental degradation aboard the ship."

Spock judged that *Gladiator* was in no immediate danger. Now that they had lured the Romulan vessel away from the solar system containing the cloaked world, the nearest sun or planetary body was hundreds of millions of kilometers away. The ship could afford to drift helplessly through the vast emptiness of interstellar space. He had learned what he needed to know: Motak's battle cruiser had been removed as a threat for the time being.

Spock canceled the red alert throughout the ship, reducing their emergency status to yellow alert. He had no doubt that the commander had been telling the truth when he warned that additional Romulan warships had already set course to intercept the *Enterprise*. That was only logical. Fortunately, the utter immensity of the universe would grant him some time before this further threat required immediate action. Even at warp speed, the Romulan military could not instantly traverse the immense distances that all space travel entailed; Spock recalled the many occasions within the Federation when the *Enterprise* had been the only starship within range of a developing crisis. He did not expect that the Romulans could provide reinforcements any faster than Starfleet could. "More foes may be en route," he said aloud, for the benefit of Roberta and Ensign Gates, "but they are not here yet. Our first priority must be to see to the safety of Captain Kirk and the remainder of the landing party." He cocked his head toward Roberta. "I suspect Mr. Seven is expecting you as well."

The turbolift doors whished open behind him and Lt. Uhura hurried back onto the bridge, accompanied by a repair team and a few more replacement crew members who fanned out to take their positions around the cabin. Assistant Engineer Schultz, recently transferred from Deep Space Five, set to work repairing the sundered helm controls. It looked like it might take him a considerable period of time.

Regrettably, they could not wait until all repairs were completed before returning to seek out Captain Kirk. "Ensign Gates, set course for our previous coordinates. Maximum speed."

Chief Engineer Scott would not be pleased, but that could not be helped.

Chapter Eighteen

IN FACT, Kirk had always managed to avoid any Klingon mind-sifters up to now, although Spock had been forced to endure the device's invasive effects on their mission to Organia two years ago. His first officer had been typically discreet and unemotional when describing the experience, but Kirk had some idea of the kind of ordeal Spock had suffered. He wasn't looking forward to trying it out for himself.

He didn't see anything resembling a mind-sifter at hand in the control room, but he doubted that Commander Dellas was just blowing hot air when she threatened to use one on him. At the moment, unfortunately, Dellas held all the cards; she had no reason to bluff.

"Well?" she demanded. "Are you going to tell me what I want to hear?" She kept her disruptor pistol raised and ready. "Why are you here? How much do you know?"

I wish I knew, Kirk realized. Dellas would probably be relieved to learn how little Gary Seven had told him about the Romulan commander's ultimate ambitions, but there was no reason to let her on that little detail. "I know you're planning to change the future," he said, hoping to rattle her.

He succeeded, to a degree. He thought he spotted a flicker of doubt and trepidation in her crazed, sociopathic eyes. She definitely scowled at him, visibly displeased by his words. *I hit a nerve,* he thought. His mind raced, searching for a way to take advantage of this minor victory. *She didn't even want her own soldiers to hear this interrogation,* he recalled. There had to be some way to exploit her apparent mania for secrecy.

"How did you learn that?" she barked. "Who is the source of your information?"

Kirk took care not to even glance in Seven's direction. Let her think that Seven, in the uniform he stole from Chekov, was just another Starfleet ensign. "There's an old Earth expression you may have heard of," he said. "That's for me to know and for you to find out."

"Oh, I will," Dellas vowed, every syllable infused with sadistic promise, "you can be sure of that." She stepped away from the prisoners and called out to the aged scientist working upon the control panel to the late Supervisor 146's computer. "Vithrok, how are your repairs proceeding? I may want to speed up our timetable. We appear to have a security problem."

Vithrok turned away from the machinery. His face was flushed and he was slightly out of breath. Kirk didn't recognize the instruments in his hands; some sort of high-precision Romulan tools, he guessed, suitable for working on delicate circuitry. "I think it's fixed, Commander," he reported, huffing between each word. "I can't promise every function has been restored, but I believe that the transporter controls are now operational."

Damn, Kirk thought. That's the last thing Dellas

needs to have up and running again, not if the transporter could still do double duty as a time machine. Too bad she couldn't have done a better job of blasting it earlier.

"Excellent work, Doctor," she said. "Program the proper coordinates into the computer. There is too much at stake to take chances now. If the *Enterprise* stages another assault, I want to be able to leave on my mission immediately."

This is sounding worse and worse, Kirk mused. A horrible thought occurred to him: what if, by attempting to stop Dellas and failing, he and Seven had only provoked her into setting her mysterious plan in motion even earlier than she had previously intended. They might well have initiated the very disaster—*whatever it was*—that Seven had travelled so far to prevent! He peered at his fellow prisoner, wondering if the same ghastly reasoning was going through Seven's head. It was impossible to tell from Seven's stoic expression, but he certainly looked grim and intense enough. *If you're planning to do something, Mr. Seven,* Kirk thought silently, *you better do it soon.*

"Actually," Vithrok replied somewhat sheepishly, stroking his beard with his free hand, "I can't claim all the credit. This other human," he said, gesturing toward Gary Seven, "did a remarkable job before I got here." The Romulan scientist shuffled away from his work and approached Seven, a look of genuine curiosity on his face. "Where did you learn to do all that? Some of your . . . improvisations . . . were quite original. Revolutionary, even."

"Is that so?" Dellas said. She no longer had eyebrows to raise but Kirk knew that she was intrigued. *I have to distract her from Seven,* he thought. She had already learned too much from 146; he dreaded to imagine what sort of information she could extract from Gary Seven.

"I'm shocked at your lack of expertise," he announced loudly. "Ensign Lincoln is just an ordinary technician. Is Romulan science that far behind Starfleet?"

"There was nothing ordinary about what this man did!" Vithrok protested, obviously offended. It looked odd to see such an unmistakable and petty display of emotion on a Vulcanlike face, even though Kirk knew intellectually that Romulans were unlike Vulcans in very many respects. "This technology is centuries ahead of both Federation and Romulan science. It's taken me months just to learn the basics, and I have been honored by the Praetor himself for my scientific accomplishments. Twice."

"Enough, Doctor," Dellas instructed him. To his distress, Kirk saw that she had not been fooled by his ruse. "You should not let the captain bait you so easily." She scrutinized Gary Seven carefully. "It seems I underestimated you, Ensign Lincoln, if that's really your name. I'd thought you merely another Starfleet foot soldier, a minor pawn in this game, but apparently I was mistaken." She crouched in front of him and thrust the muzzle of her disruptor beneath his chin. "Tell me who you are and what you know about this technology."

At first, Seven said nothing. He simply gazed back at the Romulan commander with an even expression, showing no sign of fear. Kirk was impressed; Seven had almost as good a poker face as Spock.

"Tell me!" Dellas ordered, pushing Seven's chin up with her disruptor.

Seven emitted a sigh of resignation, looking at Dellas in a distinctly condescending manner. "All I can say is that you are poised to make a terrible mistake. You are tampering with historical forces you cannot begin to comprehend."

"I understand enough," Dellas replied. "History is determined by those with the will and the strength to shape it to their own design." She grinned smugly. "All I needed was knowledge of the future—and the ability to go there."

Seven shook his head, acting more like a weary teacher than a prisoner of war. "You have not looked far enough ahead. In the long run, reunification is in the best interests of both the Vulcan and the Romulans, not to mention this entire quadrant of the galaxy."

Reunification, Kirk thought. Was that what this was all about? It was hard to even imagine such an event, Romulan and Vulcan culture had diverged so much over the course of the last millennia. Was it even possible? He would have to ask Spock what he thought, assuming they both got back to the Federation in one piece.

Dellas sneered at Seven. "You are human," she said. "It is you who cannot begin to understand. The Vulcans have learned some interesting things over the years, tricks of the mind and such, but they lack the passion and the courage that makes any race great. The only way Vulcan will ever join the Empire will be as one of our conquests."

"Conquest. What a ridiculous concept," Seven said. "I wish I could have left that behind in the twentieth century." His voice and manner grew more intense and urgent. "Is there any way I can convince you that you're making a mistake? You weren't *meant* to have this technology yet. You're like a child playing with fireworks."

Kirk found Seven's analogy a bit insulting, not to mention depressingly familiar. *Does every more advanced civilization have to compare us to children?* he thought. Bad enough to hear it from the Organians or the Metrons, but from Gary Seven, too?

Commander Dellas evidently took offense as well. "And I thought the captain was insolent," she remarked acidly, her blast-darkened face growing even darker. She pressed her weapon much harder against

Seven's throat, sinking the muzzle of her weapon into his flesh. "Perhaps I should remind you who is holding the gun."

Kirk wondered for a second if Seven had deliberately provoked Dellas, perhaps to trick her into rendering him dead or unconscious or otherwise incapable of being interrogated. Then Seven surprised him by moving faster than Kirk's eyes could follow, grabbing the commander by the wrist and yanking the point of the weapon away from his throat. "What?" Dellas snarled as they grappled for control of the disruptor, dragging each other up onto their feet only a few meters away from Kirk.

He saw his opportunity and seized it, springing to his feet and racing for the phaser resting near the control panel. Vithrok, surprised and flustered by the sudden violence, made a feeble try to block Kirk, but the Starfleet officer easily shoved the old scientist aside. Vithrok staggered backwards, almost falling through the hole Kirk had cut in the turbolift doors. "Commander!" he shouted frantically, grabbing onto the seared edges of the doors with both hands to keep from landing flat on his back. "Commander! You have to stop him!"

Now only the hover-chair stood between Kirk and his phaser. He grabbed onto the back of the chair and moved to push it out of the way, but the damn thing refused to budge. *Someone left the brakes on,* he realized. He didn't waste any time fumbling with the controls; instead he darted around the chair and reached out for the phaser which was only a few centimeters away. *Got it,* he thought.

A beam of red-hot energy struck the phaser first, melting it to slag before his eyes. Yanking his fingers away just in time, Kirk spun around to see Commander Dellas aiming her disruptor with one hand. Her other hand was squeezing Seven at the juncture of his neck and his shoulder in an all too familiar gesture. *A nerve pinch,* Kirk recognized instantly. Seven's eyes rolled upwards until only the whites could be seen. She released her grip and he dropped onto the floor like a marionette whose strings had been cut. "Please step away from the transporter controls, Captain," Dellas insisted, turning her weapon toward him. "We do not want to undo all of Doctor Vithrok's hard work." She nudged Seven's prone body with the toe of her boot. The visitor from old Earth did not react at all, not even with a groan. Kirk stared helplessly at Gary Seven's insensate form. The whole thing had only taken a few moments.

"Perhaps your associate had a point after all," Dellas commented, flexing the fingers of her free hand. "There is a thing or two we can learn from our Vulcan kinsmen." She smiled, gazing triumphantly at the transporter pad. "Now let us see what we can teach them. . . ."

Gary Seven lay sprawled upon the floor of the control room, seemingly dead to the world. *I can't believe it,* Kirk mused again. *I don't believe it.*

He distinctly recalled what had happened, back in the twentieth century, when Spock applied his signature nerve pinch to Gary Seven: absolutely nothing. He wasn't sure who was most surprised, he or Spock, but Seven had proven completely immune to an attack that had immobilized just about every humanoid specimen Spock had ever had occasion to try it out on. Kirk still couldn't figure out why this should be so, especially after McCoy pronounced Seven thoroughly human in all respects, but he had seen with his own eyes Seven shake off the effect of the nerve pinch as though it did nothing more than tickle him. It wasn't something he was ever likely to forget.

He's faking it, Kirk concluded. *He has to be.* Kirk refused to accept that Commander Dellas, who wasn't even a true Vulcan, could deliver a more effective pinch than Spock, not that he intended to share that opinion with her anytime soon. "That man is a Federation citizen," he lied, finding it easy to summon up the appropriate indignation. "If you've killed him, your whole damn Empire is going to pay!"

Dellas acted unworried by his posturings. "He's not dead yet," she stated, keeping her disruptor pistol aimed squarely at Kirk. He backed away from the control panel with his hands above his head. "No one ever dies before I have learned all their secrets, as I trust you will discover in time." She walked around Seven's apparently unconscious body and took Kirk's place by the controls. "Unfortunately, that will have to wait until I have completed my current project. A matter of priorities, you understand."

With her free hand she pressed a button on the control panel and a slot opened on the adjacent wall, revealing a small storage compartment. Reaching inside, she drew out a bundle of folded gray fabric. "Doctor Vithrok, are the coordinates for the time travel set?"

"Yes, Commander," the scientist replied, more confidently than Kirk would have liked. He scurried around Kirk to join Dellas at the controls. *Everything is happening too fast,* Kirk thought. Whatever Dellas was intending, whatever Seven had journeyed so far to prevent, appeared on the verge of happening. Kirk wished he had a better idea of just how worried he ought to be. *Worried enough, I bet.*

Dellas handed off the disruptor to Vithrok, who, rather anxiously, kept Kirk in his sights. The pudgy, balding scientist swallowed repeatedly and stroked his beard. He didn't look like much of a killer, Kirk thought, but he hardly needed to be an expert marksman to fell a human target at such close range. Sometimes a nervous finger on a trigger could be deadlier than the coolest assassin. "Don't move," Vithrok said. It sounded more like a plea than a warning. "There's nothing you can do to stop her . . . I mean, us. You shouldn't have come here. It was useless to try. . . ."

His commander ignored Vithrok's babbling. Moving swiftly and efficiently, she unfolded her bundle, which turned out to be a full-length gray robe of a style Kirk was unfamiliar with. She shook out the garment, draped it over the back of the chair, then removed her communicator from her belt and placed it on the counter near the transporter controls. Unconcerned with propriety, she removed the outer layer of her singed and rumpled uniform, then drew the robe over herself. *Some sort of disguise,* Kirk guessed, *but what was she pretending to be? Where—and when—was her ultimate destination?* The robe stretched all the way to the floor and was pleated heavily from head to toe. An attached hood hung empty behind her head. Dellas tugged on the sleeves to make sure the garment fit, then looked up at Kirk.

"Not very eye-catching, is it?" she remarked. "Trust me, it will be the height of diplomatic fashion several decades from now, at least among the next generation of Romulans." She ran her fingers lightly over her brow, feeling the faint remains of her eyebrows. A slight scowl darkened her expression. "This is a nuisance, but I suppose it will have to do." She pulled the hood over her head, shrouding her hairless forehead in shadow. "Where I'm going, no one is going to be looking at me—until it's too late."

Kirk was getting tired of being the only person in the room, conscious or otherwise, who didn't know the full score. *Enough cryptic hints,* he thought. *Maybe Dellas was more talkative than Gary Seven.* "Perhaps I'd be more impressed," he said, "if you let me know exactly what you have in mind. Or are you afraid to tell me?"

She shook her head inside the heavy gray hood. "I acquire secrets. I seldom share them. Besides, I thought you already knew . . . ?" Bending over, she lifted the hem of her robe to check on the contents of one boot. Kirk saw a glint of silver as she lifted Seven's servo from the boot, then replaced it. "I was intending to use a concealed disruptor to accomplish my aims, but perhaps it would be more ironic to use your sleeping friend's intriguing little device. It's small, discreet, and easily set to kill. Perfect for my purposes."

"Tell me more," Kirk said, flashing his most ingratiating smile. "Maybe I can find the flaw in your plan."

Dellas easily resisted his charm. She straightened and let the hem of the robe fall over her boots. "What was that Terran expression you quoted to me earlier? Oh yes, that's for me to know and for you to find out." She turned a knob on the control panel and Kirk heard a hum commence behind him. Looking back over his shoulder, he saw the transporter pad at the opposite end of the room come to life. A faint blue mist began to form above the pad; it looked distressingly like the haze Dellas had unexpectedly emerged from to kill Seven's fellow agent. "Do not deviate from the plan, Doctor," she informed Vithrok. "After I have departed, adjust the transporter to return me to this time from a point sixty minutes after my arrival in the future. That should be all the time I require to complete my mission."

"I understand, Commander," the scientist answered. "I will begin the procedure as soon as the initial transport is completed." He nodded toward Kirk. "What shall I do with this one? Perhaps I should summon a centurion?"

"That won't be necessary," she insisted. "The fewer who witness this operation, the better." Dellas obviously wasn't the trusting type, Kirk noted. "Captain Kirk is not going anywhere. Let him watch as I transform the future of the galaxy forever." She smirked beneath her hood, her eyes hidden within its umbra, and began walking toward the transporter. "If all goes as scheduled, I will be back in this chamber in a matter of moments."

The original wisps of glowing blue mist had swollen to a dense column of fog that coiled about itself atop the transporter platform. Kirk desperately wanted to know what was waiting on the other side of that fog, but how could he find out while Vithrok's disruptor was pointed at him? He resisted the temptation to sneak a peek at Gary Seven, still presumedly playing possum on the tile floor. If the man was waiting for the right moment to intervene, it would have to be soon.

Over on the counter, Dellas's discarded communicator emitted a harsh buzz. She paused in her path, appearing unsure how to proceed. Her head swung from the communicator to the glowing mist and back again. Would she ignore the incoming message and get on with her mysterious mission, Kirk wondered, or would she be more anxious to receive news from her subordinates? Given that Chekov and Sulu were still unaccounted for, he knew what he'd do if he were Dellas: get as much information as possible.

Kirk pegged it exactly. With an impatient snarl, Dellas spun around and stalked back to the control panel. "What is it?" she demanded, snatching up the communicator and throwing back her hood. Her short black hair was charred around the edges. Disturbed by the movement of the hood, bits of burnt hair flaked off and fell upon her shoulders.

"Commander," a voice emerged from the communicator. Kirk strained his ears to catch every word. "The Federation starship has returned. Sensors confirm it is the *Enterprise*. And, Commander," the voice added, "they're hailing us."

Dellas squinted at Kirk as though he held the key to this new development. In fact, he was even more surprised than the Romulan commander, although he endeavored not to show it. What was Spock doing back here? Kirk had specifically ordered him to get the *Enterprise* to safety if he lost contact with the landing party for over an hour, which surely must have passed by now. *Spock must have a very good reason for disobeying my orders,* he guessed. *He usually does.*

"Put them through," she said decisively. "Use an encrypted mode. I don't want anyone listening to this, including yourself."

"Acknowledged," the voice reported. An instant later, Spock's face appeared on the large screen above the control panel. Kirk noted that the image was an unusually tight close-up, blocking out any view of the ship's interior. *That has to be deliberate,* he deduced; *there must be something on the bridge he doesn't want the Romulans to see, assuming that he was even transmitting from the bridge.* Kirk mulled over the possibilities, frustrated by his lack of clear knowledge of what Spock was up to. *What the devil is happening up on my ship?*

Spock's eyes widened slightly at the sight of Dellas in her robes. "This is the U.S.S. *Enterprise.* Can I assume that you are in control on the installation on the planet's surface?"

"You needn't be so formal, Mr. Spock," Dellas replied. "I know your life story even better than you do, although I confess I am more than a little curious as to what brings you here at this particular time and place."

Spock raised a quizzical eyebrow. "Is this not where and when you intend to launch your attempt to assassinate me in the year 2293?"

Kirk could not conceal his shock at Spock's words. Was that what this was all about? A plot to murder Spock? He threw an anguished look at Seven's inert form. *Why didn't you tell me?*

He knew why, of course. The sanctity of the time line and the inherent dangers in learning one's own destiny, but it still came as a shock. He felt an icy chill run through his entire body.

245

Dellas appeared just as dumbfounded by Spock's casual revelation. She leaned toward the screen, her fists squeezed tightly at her sides. *"How . . . do . . . you . . . know . . . that?"* she demanded, her voice quivering with fury. Taken aback by his superior's wild-eyed intensity, Vithrok backed a few steps away from her.

"That is irrelevant," Spock stated. "The fact remains that Starfleet is familiar with the particulars of your scheme and cannot allow you to succeed."

His implacable manner only served to enrage Dellas further. "Irrelevant!" she snapped. "Everything is irrelevant to you Vulcan eunuchs. Strength. Passion. The courage to survive, the will to conquer." She stepped back from the screen, her chin held high. "My father was like you, a devotee to the heretical teachings of Surak. They did not shield him from the harsh realities of the world; they only made him weaker and unable to protect himself and his family." She raised a clenched fist to the screen. "Your fanatical worship of soulless logic disgusts me. I will have you killed a hundred times if that is what is needed to keep your pallid, pacifistic ways from contaminating the Empire."

"Logic is not a shield," Spock replied, "but a means of discovering the truth. Nor does it necessarily impair one's potential for self-defense." He eyed Dellas dispassionately. "Your father's fate may have been beyond his control, or perhaps there were other factors to consider. Contrary to what you profess to believe, weakness is not synonymous with reason."

"We shall see, Vulcan," she declared. "You cannot threaten me with your starship. This outpost's shields are more than enough to withstand your phasers and transporter beams." Without asking, she seized the disruptor pistol from Vithrok's hand and advanced toward Kirk. "Can you see your captain, Mr. Spock? Do you know what I can do with him?" She grabbed Kirk by the arm and dragged him closer to the monitor, then stepped behind him and pressed the muzzle of the disruptor against his temple. "I want to know who informed you of my plans and I want to know now. Tell who your source is, or I will reduce your captain's brains to ionized particles."

Roberta, Kirk realized. Gary Seven's young companion had to have filled Spock in on the true nature of his mission, not that this answer was likely to satisfy Commander Dellas, even if Spock felt inclined to share that information, which Kirk sincerely doubted. That would only serve to expose and further endanger Seven. Kirk assumed Seven was listening to all this as well; no doubt he was equally curious to find out how much Spock had learned.

By the counter, Vithrok looked on with a distinctly queasy expression. He was probably more at home puttering around in a lab, Kirk guessed, than watching the interrogation and execution of hostages. *It's up to me,* he thought. He knew he was only heartbeats away from dying.

For the moment, though, Dellas was focused on Spock's unreadable features. Taking advantage of her distraction, he suddenly, savagely jabbed his elbow into her midsection, then threw himself to one side. He tore away from Dellas's grasp and felt his elbow connect with solid flesh beneath the voluminous robe. Dellas gasped explosively and fired her weapon, but the beam missed its target, instead etching another scar on the turbolift doors. She did not release the weapon, however, and swung the disruptor in search of Kirk. Hunched over in order to make a smaller target, he scrambled toward the control panel, hoping that Dellas would be reluctant to fire wildly in the direction of Supervisor 146's advanced equipment. Beyond that his plans were fairly sketchy; he was saving his life one second at a time. *If I can just figure out how to bring down the shields . . . !*

"Captain, look out!" Spock shouted from the screen.

"Commander, behind you!" Vithrok yelled. He slammed his palm down on an alarm button and a blaring siren filled the room. *Great,* Kirk thought. *We're going to have company.*

Dellas froze, but it was too late. Moving faster than Kirk would have thought possible, Gary Seven rose to his feet and barrelled into the Romulan commander from behind. Her disruptor flew from her hand and skidded across the floor toward the lift entrance. Vithrok ran for the weapon, but Kirk tackled him before he got too far. The scientist hit the ground hard, his flabby bulk cushioning Kirk's own fall. Vithrok's breath smelled slightly of Romulan ale. *Tsk tsk, Doctor,* Kirk thought. *Drinking on the job?* Vithrok attempted to roll over and strike back at Kirk, yet, even with the benefit of a Romulan's greater than human strength, the reputedly brilliant researcher was no match for a trained Starfleet officer. Kirk smashed his fist into Vithrok's bearded chin. The scientist's eyes snapped shut and his head dropped backwards onto the floor tiles. Kirk massaged his aching knuckles; he'd forgotten how hard Romulan skulls could be.

An angry cry drew his attention to the back of the control room. Kirk looked up to see Dellas wrestling with Gary Seven in front of the transporter pad. The luminescent fog continued to billow above the platform as, with another ferocious snarl, the would-be assassin shoved Seven away from her. She glanced quickly at Kirk and Seven, at the unclaimed disruptor lying on the floor out of reach and at the defeated lump of her chief scientist. Then she made her decision, spun around, and leaped headlong into the mist.

"Stop!" Seven shouted, reaching for her, but his hand closed on nothing but a bright blue haze. Ribbons of glowing vapor slipped between his fingers.

She was gone.

Seven's shoulders slumped for a moment, then he took a deep breath and turned around to face Kirk. "I have to go after her, Captain. It's the only way."

Kirk nodded and stood up beside Vithrok's sleeping body. The scientist's white lab jacket covered him like a morgue blanket. "Understood," Kirk said. "I don't suppose you want me to come along."

"It's your future, Captain. Think about it."

I am, Kirk thought solemnly. How could he not? Part of him was acutely interested in knowing what the galaxy would be like twenty, thirty years from today. What would become of James T. Kirk in the decades to come. Another five-year mission? An admiralty? Marriage and a family? *My son David will be a grown man. What will he think of his father then?* Then again, how did he even know that he was still going to be alive ten minutes from now, let alone twenty-some years from now? After all, Dellas had offered no cryptic hints as to his long-term fate, only Spock's, and Kirk could all too easily imagine himself reenacting Ebenezer Scrooge's ultimate nightmare: staring at a weathered gravestone with his own name on it.

"Maybe it's better if you go after all," he told Seven.

Spock's oversized image towered above them on the viewscreen. "Captain, are you quite all right?" he asked.

Kirk looked around. The emergency siren shrieked on, hurting his ears, but he did not yet hear the bootsteps of approaching Romulan guards. Hopefully, the fused tracks in the turbolift shaft would slow any reinforcements down for at least a few more minutes. Would that be enough time to do what had to be done?

Seven crossed over to the control panel and rapidly manipulated the buttons and switches beneath the viewer. The blaring alarm ceased immediately, much to Kirk's relief. "Activate Self-Destruct Program

Omega-Prime," he addressed the computer. He glanced back at the transporter platform where the swirling blue fog awaited him. His brow furrowed in concentration. "Commence program in twenty standard minutes."

"Affirmative," the computer replied. Kirk wondered why the Romulans had never used voice commands to control 146's apparatus. Perhaps, he speculated, they had disabled the system's artificial intelligence to prevent it from interfering with their unauthorized takeover of the base. *Twenty minutes,* Kirk thought. *That's not a lot of time to get out of here before everything blows up.*

Seven retrieved the fallen disruptor from the floor where it had landed. He set it on stun and tossed it to Kirk, who caught it easily. He checked the weapon's weight and balance. It was slightly heavier than a type-2 phaser pistol. "You'll have to hold off any Romulan soldiers until I get back," Seven informed him. "We can't permit them to disable the self-destruct sequence."

"What about the shields?" Kirk asked. If they could just lower the shields protecting the installation, then Spock could beam one or both of them to safety at the last minute.

Seven shook his head grimly. "I can't lower them from here. Those functions were damaged by Commander Dellas's initial disruptor blast and there isn't time to repair them." He gave Kirk a probing look. "I understand exactly what I'm asking of you, Captain."

He wants me to hold down the fort until the whole place goes up in flames, Kirk translated. It was a sobering thought; he had never expected to go down fighting in the sub-basement of an alien stronghold in the middle of the Romulan Empire. "Spock," he said, addressing the screen. "Are there any other options?"

"None I can see, Captain," he answered. "The shields are quite formidable." *But not formidable enough,* Kirk thought, *to stop Commander Dellas from beaming to the future.* Time travel, apparently, followed its own rules. "We can send down a rescue party on a shuttle," Spock suggested.

"No," Kirk said. The base was too well-guarded. There was no point risking further lives. He hefted the disruptor in his grip and looked at Gary Seven. He cocked his head toward the luminescent fog. "Go," he told Seven.

"Thank you, Captain." The turbulent azure mist was beginning to fade. Kirk examined the churning, energized mass of vapor, struck by how different it looked from the transporter effect he was familiar with. Dellas was on the other side of that mist somewhere, intent on ending the life of a man whom at this very moment commanded the starship in orbit above this very planet. Had she already succeeded? There was no way to know until Spock lived or died over two decades from now. Would he ever know if Gary Seven put an end to her murderous ambitions? The human mind, he felt convinced, was never designed to cope with the tortured causality of temporal paradoxes. By contrast, the menace of hostile Romulan soldiers was reassuringly concrete. *Bring on the troopers,* he thought. *Let Seven worry about tomorrow's tomorrows.*

Without a backwards glance, Seven launched himself into the mist. Kirk saw him receding into the fog for a second, glimpsed the man's back as the glowing vapors enveloped him. Then the mist dissolved into nothingness, taking Seven with it. Kirk found himself alone in the now-silent control room, aside from the dormant body of Doctor Vithrok. Somewhere above him, he heard the hiss of disruptors cutting through solid steel. Dellas's guards were burning their way to him, summoned by the alarm Seven had extinguished. Kirk positioned himself in front of the turbolift entrance, disruptor in hand. *Just like the Alamo,* he thought. Too bad Spock had a front row seat. It had to be hard on him, standing by helplessly while Kirk defended a ticking bomb.

"Fifteen minutes to self-destruct," the computer announced.

Chapter Nineteen

Camp Khitomer, Khitomer Outpost
United Federation of Planets
Stardate 9521.6
A.D. 2293

THE TRAITOR'S BLOOD still pooled on the tile floor.

Gary Seven gave little attention to the momentous drama unfolding around the podium where Kirk, Spock, and the others conferred with Azetbur, the Klingon chancellor, only minutes after the attempted assassination of the president of the Federation. These incarnations of the *Enterprise* crew, so many years older than the individuals he had just left behind in 2269, were perfectly capable of coping with the aftermath of that near tragedy. He was there to stop an even greater disaster from occurring—if he could.

The air was cooler here than on the cloaked planet, the gravity a degree stronger. After spending a little over a year in the relatively provincial environment of twentieth century Earth, it felt odd to be surrounded by such a wide variety of alien races. Edging along the rear of the crowd, beneath hanging pennants of various hues and designs, Seven desperately scanned the vast assembly hall for any sign of Dellas in her nondescript robe. His own borrowed Starfleet uniform was a couple decades out of date, he realized, but there was no time to try to appropriate something more contemporary. He would have to hope that, with everyone transfixed by the dramatic tableau at the other end of the hall, no one would notice his fashion lapse.

A pair of willowy Xela diplomats, their faces concealed behind veils of golden webbing, shifted to the left, obscuring his view of the several rows of seats. Seven clenched his teeth in frustration, then began to work his way up one of the aisles dividing one wing of spectators from another. His gaze swept back and forth over the densely populated chamber, hoping to catch a glimpse of the murderous Romulan from the past. Intent upon his search, he accidentally stepped on the hoof of a snout-faced Tellarite, who snorted at him indignantly before returning his attention to Kirk and his valiant compatriots.

Where was she? Seven's anxiety grew by the second. Dellas was here, he knew, with his own stolen weapon, no less. He tried not to visualize what the servo could do to Spock at its maximum setting.

Kirk said something up front, and the entire assembly rose to its feet, making it even harder to see across the entire hall. Seven arched his feet to peer over and around the tawny mane of a regal Klingon delegate. Something about the Klingon's profile was strangely familiar. *Oh, right,* he realized, *Colonel Worf.* The roar of the applause was deafening, but it was not loud enough to drown out the insistent question that clamored within Seven's mind.

Where is she?

"You've restored my father's faith," Dellas heard the Klingon leader say. The ridges on Azetbur's brow were less pronounced than those of many of her warriors. Dellas wondered briefly if the chancellor had a trace of human blood in her. That would certainly explain her distressing adherence to her father's doctrine of peace between the Federation and the Klingons. *As if the Klingons could ever be trusted . . . !*

Wrapped in her all-concealing robe, the brim of her hood pulled down to hide the disruptor burns upon her face, she crept through the packed assemblage to get a better shot at Spock. The troublesome Vulcan, his somber face creased with age and concern, kept a watchful eye on a Vulcan woman, much younger than he, whose expression held only defeat. *Fear not, Valeris,* Dellas thought. *Your failure shall be avenged within moments.*

It was possible, she realized, that she might never return to her own time, now that Kirk and his unknown ally had taken possession of the control room back in another time and place. There was always a chance that her centurion might reclaim that battlefield, thus providing Vithrok with an opportunity to call her back from the future, but she could not count on that. She stared at the revered Starfleet captain conversing with Azetbur, so very different and yet so very much the same as the youthful human she had dueled with only hours before. She had learned from that experience that Kirk was nothing if not unpredictable. He might yet manage to strand her in this era permanently.

Worse yet, either Kirk or his enigmatic ally might try to use the alien time travel apparatus to undo what she was about to do, in which case she might have to travel through time yet again to kill Spock once more, and so on *ad infinitum.* Or else she would simply have to kill the accursed Vulcan at some later point in his life. Certainly, she had time; Spock would not devote his efforts to reunification until some seventy-five years from this date. One way or another, Spock would die.

It doesn't matter what Kirk tries, she affirmed. All she could do now was complete her mission and hope for the best. Spock would never meet Pardek. The

Greg Cox

cause of Romulan-Vulcan reunification would die in
its cradle, consigned forever to the realm of unre-
alized possibilities. She felt the weight of the intruder's alien weapon lodged securely against her calf.

"And you've restored my son's," Kirk said softly. In
one of the outer pews, a middle-aged human diplomat
wearing a green sash began to clap slowly. Soon the
entire room emulated his lead, rising up like a surging
wave to join in a standing ovation for the heroic crews
of the *Enterprise* and the *Excelsior*. Even the ranks of
the Klingon soldiers, their scarlet sashes stretched
tightly across their dark leather armor, applauded
Kirk and the others. Dellas shook her head in amazement; no matter how many times she had witnessed
this scene on Citizen Septos's monitor, she still
couldn't believe it. Klingons cheering for Kirk? Astounding.

She refused to let herself be distracted by the
spectacle, however. Clapping herself, to avoid notice,
she gently elbowed her way through the mob of
delegates until only a single row of applauding dignitaries stood between her and the platform occupied
by honored Starfleet heroes. Ironically, she found
herself standing just behind Sarek of Vulcan, her
target's distinguished father, and a certain young
Romulan delegate. *Pardek,* Dellas thought with scorn.
Was her knowledge of the future coloring her perceptions, or was the senator-to-be already contemplating
Spock with a treacherous expression on his face?

She glanced to the left and right to see if anyone was
watching her, but, no, all present remained fixated on
Kirk and Spock and their fellows as they humbly
accepted the assembly's display of respect and affec-
tion. *Excellent,* she thought. There would never be a
better opportunity. Pausing in her applause, she bent
down to slide one hand within her boot and drew out
a slender silver cylinder. The compact weapon felt
cool in her hand.

Spock stood not more than seven meters away from
Dellas, a few steps to the left of his captain. His calm,

256

impassive face offered no clue to his feelings at this moment. *Odd,* she thought, she had never realized before how much the older Spock resembled her father. To her surprise, she felt a pang of regret at what she had come to do.

She raised the silver instrument and pointed it at Spock. Her thumb caressed the minute firing mechanism set into the device's gleaming surface. An instant's pressure and the deed would be done. *Now,* she thought.

Suddenly a hand fell over her own. A voice spoke through the hood covering her ears. "We don't want to disturb any of these important people. They're making the future."

He gave the silver device a precise twist just as Dellas pressed down on the button.

The beam fired, but the target evaporated. So did the entire assembly hall. The blue fog swallowed them up instantly, and Dellas's death-ray disappeared into a chaotic void outside time and space. She let out a cry of frustration.

That was close, Seven thought. Good to know the servo's automatic recall function was still working. It had saved him several times in the past, although never quite in this manner. He struggled to restrain the hooded figure in his grasp, holding on tightly to both her wrists. Thanks, too, for that all-concealing hood; that was how he had spotted her in the end. Most of the dignitaries at this event, including all of the Romulans, had not seen it necessary to cover their heads indoors. Only Dellas, compelled to conceal the injuries she'd received from the overloaded disruptor, had hidden beneath the shadow of a hood.

He wrenched the servo from her clutch even as the blue haze began to thin. Seven reclaimed the device with more than a little satisfaction; it struck him as quite appropriate that, in the end, Dellas's insane scheme was undone by the very technology she had twisted to her own purposes. Poetic justice, of a sort. He hoped that Supervisor 146 would have approved. And the faithful Osiris as well.

Through the fading mist, he glimpsed the control room he and Dellas had left behind not long ago. The sound of disruptor blasts rang in his ears. *Out of the frying pan into the fire,* he thought.

We've saved Spock's future. I only pray I haven't doomed Kirk's present.

Chapter Twenty

Romulan Star Empire
Stardate 6021.6
A.D. 2269

"FIVE MINUTES to self-destruct."

Thanks for the update, Kirk thought wryly.

It wasn't the first time he'd raced a time bomb, but it looked like he might be around for the final tick of the clock this time. Outside the control room, an undetermined number of Romulan soldiers were crowded into the turbolift shaft, eager to charge into the chamber and vaporize the upstart human who had penetrated the nerve center of their new base. So far, Kirk had managed to keep them back with the frequent application of some well-placed disruptor bolts.

Another shining helmet poked cautiously from behind what was left of the turbolift doors. A blast of corrosive energy from Kirk's disruptor sent the helmet ducking back into the dimly lit shaft. Kirk leaned forward on the edge of the hover-chair's seat and waited for the next brave soul to dare the doorway. At least he didn't have to worry about pulse grenades; he could just imagine what Commander Dellas would do

Greg Cox

to any of her subordinates who even risked destroying the precious equipment in the control room. He didn't blame them for being cautious.

"Four minutes to self-destruct."

The base had to be destroyed, he knew. Its advanced technology, now exposed within Romulan borders, was a threat to the Federation—and the future itself. If he had to go up in flames with it . . . well, that was only his duty. *At least, Spock is here to witness my last stand.* The Vulcan's face, looking far more grimmer than normal, watched him from the monitor. *Funny,* Kirk mused, *I always thought I'd die alone.* He fired another shot at the entrance just to keep the Romulans on their toes.

"Three minutes to self-destruct."

He sneaked a peek at the transporter platform. No Romulan sneak attack beaming in, but no sign of Gary Seven either. "Spock," he began, suddenly feeling strangely tongue-tied. How did you say good-bye forever to your best friend? "It's beginning to look like I've finally used up all my nine lives."

On the screen, Spock's arched brows shot upward like old solid fuel rockets. "Captain!" he said hoarsely, his voice choked with uncharacteristic emotion. "The cat!"

Chief Engineer Scott was in the primary transporter room, waiting anxiously for the shields on the planet below to falter for just a moment so he could beam the captain to safety, when Isis arrived. His eyes widened in confusion as the door slid open a crack and the cat slipped inside. "Say there!" he exclaimed. "What the devil are you doing here?"

His expression grew even more astounded when, before his very eyes, the black cat vanished and *she* materialized instead. "Saints preserve us!" he gasped.

She was a humanoid female of striking appearance, clad in a revealing two-piece outfit that contrasted shimmering black silk against pale, alabaster flesh.

Equally black was the lustrous dark hair that fell below her shoulders. Two velvet hairpieces, shaped like the ears of a cat, decorated the top of her scalp, while a strangely familiar silver collar sparkled around her throat. Golden eyes, dwelling beneath long black lashes, considered Scotty with a mixture of amusement and curiosity. She waved a languid arm toward the transporter controls. "May I?" she purred.

He staggered backwards, taken aback by the unexpected transformation and profoundly grateful that there was nothing wrong with his heart. His eyes, though . . . now, that was another thing altogether. Keeping his sights on the seductive figure, and unable to do otherwise, he reached out and activated the intercom unit on the wall. "Mr. Spock," he exclaimed, "you're not going to believe this, but Mr. Seven's wee kit is here, and she's just changed into a full-sized lassie!" The exotic cat-woman stepped forward, rustling the sheer black fabric of her skirt, and inspected the transporter controls. "And, Mr. Spock, I think she wants to use the transporter."

To his surprise, Spock took his startling news in stride. "Understood, Mr. Scott. Please allow your visitor to proceed."

Scotty couldn't believe his ears. "Are you quite certain, Mr. Spock?"

"This individual may be the captain's last hope," Spock stated emphatically. "And time is of the essence."

"If you say so, Mr. Spock." Scotty remained dubious. He could only hope that someone would explain it all to him eventually. He nodded at the lady in question. "All right, lassie. It's all yours."

Costumed more appropriately for a night spot on Argelius Two than for the primary transporter room of the starship *Enterprise,* the woman confidently took her place behind the podium containing the transporter controls. Her hands deftly worked the equipment, adjusting this, realigning that. Scotty tried to keep track of what she was doing, but she moved too quickly for his eyes to follow and, besides, what he did see didn't seem to make sense. "Whoa there," he blurted at one point. "You can't do that. The Heisenberg compensation ratio is all wrong. You're going to bollix the quantum spin regulators. . . ."

The woman ignored him. *Just like a cat,* Scotty thought. She continued to wreak havoc on the transporter's carefully maintained settings and parameters. The chief engineer felt like an expert driver stuck in the back seat while a lunatic sat behind the wheel. What was Mr. Spock thinking? Why put the captain's life in the hands of a bloody pussycat?

Or whatever this baffling creature was.

"Two minutes to self-destruct."

The Romulans were growing more desperate to recapture the control room. No doubt they could hear the countdown as well, Kirk realized, especially with those keen Vulcanlike ears. He was impressed by their discipline and determination; lesser forces would have already evacuated the installation in anticipation of the devastation to come. *They're not going to stop,* he thought, *until all of us are dead.*

A ferocious hail of disruptor fire came from the phaser-carved doorway into the turbolift shaft, forcing him to abandon his comfortable seat to take a more defensive posture behind the overturned couch. To avoid an accidental fatality, he had already shoved Dr. Vithrok's insensate form up against the wall adjacent to the doorway, out of the line of fire. Keeping his head low, Kirk shot directly into the barrage and was rewarded with the sound of a Romulan body striking the floor. The assault barely slackened, though. Beams of destructive energy zipped above his head, so close that he could feel the heat of the disruptor rays. He had no illusions that they were set on stun.

His own disruptor was running low on power, but that hardly mattered. Whatever form of conflagration destroyed the compound would end the standoff long before either side ran out of ammo.

"One minute to self-destruct."

This is it, he thought. *I just hope the* Enterprise *makes it back home in one piece.*

He released another blast at the gaping breach in the turbolift doors, then was jolted by the sound of the transporter pad humming back to life. His gaze darted quickly from the control room entrance to the transporter platform, where he saw that same incandescent haze taking form once more. *This is bad,* he thought. There was no way he could hold off incursions from two directions.

Was there any way the Romulans could halt the countdown at this point? Kirk vowed not to give them a chance, no matter what it took.

He did his best to maintain a close watch over both fronts of the battle. Lethal energy bolts scorched the bare stone wall behind him while two humanoid outlines gradually formed within the churning blue fog. Kirk fired at the door again, just to keep the Romulan troops occupied, then swung his weapon around to target the new arrivals. His finger tightened on the trigger.

"Don't shoot, Captain," Gary Seven called out, and Kirk pointed the disruptor toward the ceiling. The time traveller emerged from the haze, pushing a cloaked figure ahead of him. Kirk recognized Commander Dellas at once. She glared at him from beneath her hood with baleful, unforgiving eyes. "Fire!" she shouted at her troops. "Kill him! Kill them both!"

Seven used the commander as a human shield, while Kirk covered Seven and his prisoner with a blistering cascade of disruptor beams until they were safely beside him behind the couch. He cast an urgent look at Seven. "Spock?"

"The future is as it should be," Seven assured him. He kept his servo pointed straight at Commander Dellas. She started to open her mouth again, but Seven flicked a switch on the silver device and she drooped onto the floor. Even tranquilized, the look on her face was bitter and angry.

"Ten seconds to self-destruct," the computer announced. Seven looked to Kirk for confirmation.

"You called it a bit close," Kirk acknowledged. He glanced at the transporter pad. Disruptor fire from the doorway struck home against the platform, dispelling the luminescent mist and causing showers of sparks to erupt from the base of the platform. "Maybe too close."

"I see," Seven said quietly. At the control panel across the room, blue electric fire crackled across the array of lighted buttons and exacting gauges as Supervisor 146's futuristic computer prepared to consume itself. On the imposing screen above the controls, Spock's alert visage flickered, then disappeared as the monitor went blank. Kirk thought he heard Spock mention Scotty's name just before he was cut off.

"Five seconds to self-destruct, four, three, two . . ."

Kirk closed his eyes instinctively and braced for the inferno to come. Would he feel the shock wave, he wondered, or simply a single second of all-consuming heat and agony? Every nerve ending of his body anticipated the searing pain. Instead, he felt an unmistakable tingle rush through him from head to toe. He was being beamed out! *But how?* he wondered. *The shields . . . ?*

He opened his eyes to find himself crouching on a transporter pad aboard the *Enterprise*. Dellas and Gary Seven and Doctor Vithrok had also materialized, although both Romulans lay unconscious upon the floor of the transporter.

With a sigh of relief, followed by a deep breath of the *Enterprise*'s pressurized atmosphere, Kirk rose to his feet and saw Scotty standing several meters away from the transporter controls. The chief engineer had one hand on the intercom and an absolutely flabbergasted expression on his face. "Mr. Scott?"

Apparently quite speechless at the moment, Scotty nodded at the transporter controls. Kirk followed the engineer's gaze until he spotted the sleek black cat sitting atop the controls, casually scratching one ear. Purring loudly, the cat leaped from the podium to Gary Seven's waiting arms.

"Good girl, Isis," he cooed at the animal, tucking her against his chest and affectionately stroking her head. "That's a good girl."

Chapter Twenty-one

THE PLANET DUWAMISH hung in space upon the main viewer. Judging from the heavy amount of cloud cover encircling the world, Kirk wasn't surprised that they were having trouble with flooding. He couldn't even see the southern continent, where most of the colonists lived, through all the turbulence in the atmosphere. "Begin transporting emergency medical supplies immediately," he spoke into the intercom receiver on his starboard armrest. "Contact the leaders of each settlement and determine what their most pressing needs are."

He inspected the chronometer located behind the astrogator between Sulu and Chekov. He shook his head in wonder.

"I still can't believe you got us here," Kirk said to Gary Seven, "let alone two hours ahead of our scheduled arrival time." Seven and Roberta Lincoln stood to the port side of the command module. Both had changed back into their garb from the twentieth century, which Kirk found distinctly reassuring; he had never truly been comfortable with the sight of Gary Seven in a Starfleet uniform, regardless of the circumstances. Roberta stared in open amazement at the vapor-swathed orb upon the screen. The cat, Isis, whose name Kirk was now never likely to forget, was cradled, as usual, within Seven's arms. She looked merely decorative, and deceptively harmless.

"I don't suppose," Kirk asked, "that you'd care to explain exactly how that wormhole trick works, not to mention how your furry little friend there managed to beam us out through the Romulans' shields?"

Seven gave his cat a gentle pat on the head. "I'm afraid I can't tell you that, Captain. Trust me, your culture is not ready for those technological break-throughs yet, which is why I took care to remove all records of the procedures from your ship's computer banks. Just be thankful that Isis was able to make do with the equipment at hand to beam the four of us to safety, as well as the remaining Romulan soldiers." Seven permitted himself a faint smile. "I suppose I could mention, without going into any of the details, that warp technology and transporter science are not as unrelated as you might think. Both involve an artificially induced translocation within the space-time matrix itself. . . ."

Seated at the engineering station, Scotty leaned forward avidly. Isis let out an outraged squawk.

"There, there, girl," Seven murmured to the animal, smoothing down the ruffled fur along the cat's spine. "I was being careful. I wasn't going to spill all the beans."

Just our luck, Kirk thought. *The cat subscribes to the Prime Directive.*

"I still say it's bloody impossible, all of it!" Scotty fumed. Once he got over the shock of the cat/woman's miraculous intervention, the chief engineer had been acting personally offended that both Seven and Isis could make his beloved *Enterprise* do things he'd never even dreamed of. "There's some manner of trickery afoot, you can be sure of it."

Seven tactfully changed the subject. "Captain, if I might ask, what do you intend to do with our prisoners?"

Commander Dellas and Dr. Vithrok remained confined in the brig, pending the proper disposition of their cases. Although Kirk had been content to leave the other Romulans stranded on the jungle planet until a rescue ship stumbled onto them, which probably wouldn't be long now that the planet's cloaking device had been destroyed, Dellas and Vithrok presented a trickier problem, especially with all they knew of what was yet to come. The ruthless commander, in particular, was too dangerous to let run around loose.

"I'm not sure," Kirk admitted. "Once our relief mission here is completed, I expect I will turn them over to Starfleet Intelligence, at which point they will undoubtedly end up as a bargaining chips in our ongoing dealings with the Romulan Empire. I wouldn't be surprised if one or both of them were eventually returned to the Romulans as part of a prisoner exchange, although not until Starfleet thinks they've wrung every last piece of valuable info from her or him."

"I thought as much," Seven stated, all business once again. "There may be more we can do to avoid a replay of this near disaster." He turned his head toward Spock. "Mr. Spock, correct me if I'm wrong, but I believe that most Vulcans possess the ability to delete specific memories from a subject's mind via a telepathic mind touch?"

Spock's eyes found Kirk, then looked away quickly. "That is true," he admitted. "I have done so myself . . . under special circumstances."

Kirk wasn't sure exactly what Spock was referring to, but he had to concede that Seven's suggestion had some merit. There was something inherently disturbing about the idea of tampering with anyone's mind like that, but something had to be done about these Romulans's frighteningly prophetic knowledge of the future. Certainly it was a far more humane solution than any the commander herself would have conceived. "Don't worry, Mr. Seven," he said. "I'll see to it that they can't try this again. Is that an acceptable option to you, Mr. Spock?"

"Yes, Captain," the Vulcan said solemnly. More than anyone else, he had the most to lose if Commander Dellas or Dr. Vithrok retained their unnatural understanding of Spock's possible destiny. *He's taken this all even better than anyone had a right to expect, even from him,* Kirk thought, *although, when you think about it, we don't know a whole lot more than we did before. I always knew Spock was a singularly unique individual, with a lot to offer the universe. Commander Dellas's bizarre assassination scheme only confirms that.*

"Any more loose ends you're worried about, Mr. Seven?" Kirk asked. He left his chair to join Seven and Roberta by the railing.

"Not that I can think of, Captain," Seven said thoughtfully. "I regret the deaths of both Septos and Osiris, but unfortunately their fates fell within the natural progression of the time line. They were apparently meant to die now, in their own time, unlike the anomalous threat Dellas posed to Mr. Spock in your own future. I'm afraid I must content myself with the knowledge that our time travel technology has been kept out of the hands of the unready."

"You know," Kirk said, "I could point out that you seem to have little or no qualms about using your own time machine."

"That's different, Captain," Seven stated without a trace of humor. "I know what I'm doing."

Some things never change, Kirk thought, *and Gary Seven's maddening self-assurance seems to be one of those things. No wonder he's so fond of that cat. They both were accustomed to acting superior to everyone around them.*

"Well, Miss Lincoln," he said, "I hope you enjoyed your trip to the twenty-third century."

Roberta threw up her hands in the air. "It hasn't been the most mellow trip I've ever taken, but, boy, has it been a mind-blowing experience!" She gazed again at the alien world on the viewer. "Are there really human-type people living there?"

"7,323,501," Spock confirmed.

"Give or take a newborn baby or two," McCoy added. "Maternity wards seldom take time off for floods."

Isis meowed loudly and Gary Seven nodded in agreement. "If you no longer have need of our assistance, Captain, we should return to our own era."

"Can't we stay and look around a little longer?" Roberta asked in a beseeching tone. "I still haven't figured out what a tribble is."

Isis licked her lips.

"Maybe another time," Seven said simply. "Captain?"

Kirk shook Seven's hand, then did the same with Roberta. "Mr. Chekov, if you would please escort our guests to the nearest transporter room."

The young Russian eyed the man, woman, and cat suspiciously. Evidently, he had not forgotten the way Seven had waylaid him with a tranquilizer beam earlier. "After you," he said sullenly, patting the phaser on his hip and gesturing toward the turbolift.

Kirk watched as the three time travellers, along with their reluctant chaperone, disappeared within the turbolift. He strolled back to his chair and slowly settled in. There was still much to do to aid the hard-pressed settlers on Duwamish, and he was anxious to get to work.

And yet . . .

"I have to admit, gentlemen," he said to Spock and McCoy, "that I'm a trifle uneasy about letting a self-righteous wild card like Gary Seven run around through history." He rested his chin on his palm. "Do you think it was wise just to let him go like that?"

Spock rose from his science station and approached the command module. "I'm afraid we had no choice, Captain. I have continued to probe the historical records for evidence of both Gary Seven's and Roberta Lincoln's activities in the past. Aside from the instances I discussed with you earlier, I have uncovered yet another episode that provides a most compelling reason for allowing our recent guests to fulfill their destinies."

"Which is?" Kirk asked.

"Yes, cough it up, Spock," McCoy said impatiently. "Don't leave us hanging."

If Kirk didn't know better, he would have sworn that Spock paused for nothing more than dramatic effect. *How very human,* he thought.

"It seems," Spock said finally, "that, almost three decades after the time they have just returned to, Mr. Seven and Miss Lincoln, as well as their remarkable feline ally, will be instrumental in the eventual defeat and overthrow of one Khan Noonien Singh."

Even McCoy was impressed. "Well, I'll be," he muttered.

Khan, Kirk thought gravely, remembering the indomitable warlord who had tried to extend his conquests to include the twenty-third century, *and at the height of his power.* The trio had quite a task ahead of them. *Better them than us, I guess.* One clash with Khan was enough for a lifetime.

Greg Cox

"That's a fascinating bit of historical trivia, Mr. Spock," he said. Captain Kirk turned his attention back to the tempestuous atmosphere of the planet upon the screen. "Now then, I believe we have a flood to handle. . . ."

272

Chapter Twenty-two

811 East 68th Street, Apt. 12-B
New York City, United States of America
Planet Earth
A.D. 20 July 1969

THEY GOT BACK in time to watch the moon landing on
TV, or rather on the circular monitor of Gary Seven's
Beta-5 computer. Roberta was surprised at how indis-
tinct and scratchy the black-and-white images were,
especially compared to all the high-tech scanners on
the U.S.S. *Enterprise.* She hoped she hadn't been
spoiled forever by the conveniences of the next, next,
next century.

"One small step for man . . . a giant step for mankind," Neil Armstrong intoned, no doubt uncomfortably aware of the millions and millions of ears back
on Earth listening in on this megahistoric moment.
Does he have any idea, she wondered, *where that big
step is going to lead?* She sure did, and it gave her
renewed hope for the future of that struggling, feud-
ing, fussing species known as the human race. *A
United Federation of Planets,* she marvelled. *Imagine!*

"Do you ever think we'll run into Spock and Kirk
and that bunch again?" she asked. She was stretched
out on the couch watching the footage from Apollo

Eleven. Gary Seven sat behind his desk, jotting down some notes on their completed mission; later, she knew, he would dictate a fuller report to the automatic typewriter in the next room. Isis was curled up on the plush orange jar opposite the couch. She alone seemed profoundly disinterested in humanity's first walk on the moon, preferring to devote all her attention to cleaning her paws.

"Who knows?" Seven replied. "I am certain that the aegis will assign a new operative to that era eventually, but the obligation to preserve and nurture civilization, as you have surely noted, can lead one down the most unexpected paths. Certainly, the crew of the *Enterprise,* and those that follow them, will frequently find themselves at the cutting edge of history."

"So what happens to them anyway?" Roberta asked. "Do you know?"

"The same thing that happens to all of us, Miss Lincoln, if we're lucky. A mixture of tragedy and triumph that eventually passes into the realm of memory." He lowered his pen to the desktop and loosened his tie. "So, are you still interested in attending the motion picture you mentioned earlier?"

Roberta heard a hissing sound from the overstuffed orange chair. Glancing across the office, she was surprised—but not *too* surprised—to see an exotic, dark-haired woman looking back at her with an aloof, almost haughty expression on her elegant features. Roberta blinked involuntarily, and when she opened her eyes again, the woman had vanished, as usual. Isis the cat turned her back on Roberta and coiled up into a ball of shining black fur.

Not again, Roberta thought. She'd lost track of how many times this had happened to her over the past twelve months or so, and never when Seven was looking! *Fine,* she decided, *big deal.* After jumping three hundred years in the future, and piloting a starship, it was going to take more than a smug, sneaky cat-lady to rattle her. "A movie sounds great," she enthused, giving Isis her best this'll-show-you look. "But how 'bout we hit *Funny Girl* instead of *2001?* After the trip we just took, I'm afraid it won't live up to the real thing!"

Epilogue

THE TRAITOR'S BLOOD had been washed away at last.

Spock considered the busy assembly hall. Now that the stain of death had been efficiently disposed of, and Valeris and her fellow conspirators escorted away by the president's personal security team, there was little evidence of the violence that had briefly marred the proceedings, except for, paradoxically, a more receptive and convivial atmosphere among the gathered ambassadors, ministers, and delegates. It seemed odd to conclude that attempted murder and subterfuge could increase the probability of peace, but that appeared to be precisely the case. *Fascinating,* he thought.

He walked past the podium and, for a moment, felt a peculiar chill along his spine, almost as if, to use a typically colorful human expression, someone had "walked on his grave." Then the moment passed and Spock went on his way, barely missing a step. Although it looked as though the reception might endure for hours, he did not intend to linger further.

There was much work to be done; among other duties, he needed to provide Starfleet officials with a complete report on the events of the past few hours before returning to the *Enterprise*.

His father, as grave and imposing as always, stood a few meters away, conversing with a Vulcanoid individual whom Spock did not recognize, although he deduced from the man's attire that he was some manner of Romulan official, perhaps a senator or consul. Sarek observed Spock's approach and beckoned him over with a minute motion of his hand. The gesture was so subtle and controlled that it was unlikely that anyone who was not born of Vulcan would have even been aware of the summons. Even Spock thought that, at times such as this, his father resembled a marble statue more than a living entity; nevertheless, he dutifully joined Sarek and the other man in one of the aisles leading to the back of the hall.

"My son," Sarek spoke, "I should like to introduce you to an individual with whom you may find much to discuss." The other man, whose prominent jowls suggested a dignified visage just beginning to succumb to age, appraised Spock with his eyes. He had an alert and confident manner with just a hint of calculation; more like a statesman, Spock judged, than a starship commander. "Let me present Senator Pardek, of the Krocton Segment of Romulus."

Spock raised his hand in the traditional Vulcan greeting. "Live long and prosper, Pardek of Romulus."

"And you as well," the senator replied. "You would be surprised at how long I have been looking forward to this meeting."

STAR TREK ®
THE NEXT GENERATION ™
THE
CONTINUING
MISSION

A TENTH ANNIVERSARY TRIBUTE

♦The definitive commemorative album for
one of Star Trek's most beloved shows.

♦Featuring more than 750 photos
and illustrations.

JUDITH AND GARFIELD REEVES-STEVENS
INTRODUCTION BY RICK BERMAN
AFTERWORD BY ROBERT JUSTMAN

Available in Hardcover
From Pocket Books

POCKET
BOOKS

1413-01

JAYME WAS RIGHT—no one paid any attention to three orange-clad workers opening the access port in the alleyway. Kids were running past, women were hanging clothes out overhead, and antigrav carts laden with warehouse goods or fresh produce trundled by on both sides.

Closing the portal overhead, they stood in a rounded dirt-floor chamber similar to the one shown on the media broadcasts—where Data's head was found. Titus felt a sinking feeling, wondering if all the caverns had been reconditioned by the workforces over the years.

"This way," he ordered, keeping his worries to himself. At the rear of the chamber was a long ladder leading down. Here the walls were more jagged and the black pit was too deep to be illuminated by their hand lights. Titus began to feel a little better. "Down we go!"

"Wait," Jayme said, unslinging her pack. "We have to put these on."

She held out the white jet-boots issued by Starfleet.

Titus took one look and groaned. "We don't need those!"

"I'm not going without safety gear," Jayme insisted. "And I'm not going to let you two go, either. This is supposed to be fun, not life-threatening." She glanced down into the shaft. "And those rungs look slimy."

Bobbie Ray checked the two pairs she set out for them. "You brought my size!"

Jayme slipped her white boots on and tightened the straps. With a little puff of dust, she activated the jets and lifted a few inches off the ground. "Good for thirty hours use."

Bobbie Ray buckled his boots on and was soon lifting himself up to the ceiling. "Maybe we should skip the ladder and go down this way."

"Maybe you want to give up now and go back to the Quad!" Titus retorted. "What's the use of exploring if you might as well be in a holodeck?"

Both of them hovered silently, staring down at him. After a few moments, Titus flung up his hands. "Have it your way, then! But we only use the boots in an emergency or I'm quitting right now."

Jayme sank back down to the ground. "That's why I brought the jet-boots. For emergencies."

Titus waited until Bobbie Ray also slowly floated down before jerking on his jet-boots and tightening them in place. "*I* think if you can't manage to hang on to a ladder, then you get what you deserve."

Bobbie Ray laughed. "Then you go first, fearless leader."

Titus had the satisfaction of hearing the Rex's laughter abruptly end as they started down the ladder. For most humanoids, any sort of vertical drop offered a test of nerves. Especially when you couldn't see the bottom.

The light at the opening dwindled as they descended. He skipped the side tunnel that went in the direction of the Presidio and Starfleet Academy, choosing to go as deep as they could. The fracture widened at the bottom, becoming more rugged and raw. They went through a steeply inclined crack, into an underground canyon that stretched as far across as the Assembly Hall. A stream had eroded the bottom into a gorge, and they had to edge along the wall, brushing their hands against the slippery, calcified coating on the rocks. Titus could imagine the tremendous force of earthquakes breaking open the crust around the San Andreas Fault, leaving behind a network of caverns and crushed rock.

Titus took them up a high talus mound and into the next cavern, where flowstone coated the cave fill, narrowing the volume of the void. This cavern was filled with fallen ceiling blocks and the stalactites had been broken off short by earth tremors. Additional seepage gave them an unusually fat, short appearance.

They retreated to the shaft. Though the ladder left off, the shaft continued down. Titus uncoiled the rope he had brought and hooked them into it. The other two followed him without a word of complaint.

It wasn't far to the bottom, where another inclined tunnel led them east again, following the path of the caverns overhead. Water coated the walls, and after tramping carefully through the tunnel, Titus noticed a fissure overhead only because he was looking for it. Just as he suspected, once they had muscled their way up to the top of the shaft, they were in another large cavern, in line with the other two they had passed through.

"It was cut off from the last cavern by the talus mound," Titus said nonchalantly, pleased that he had guessed correctly.

They had to go through a jog in the shaft to get into the cavern, and they were slightly elevated above the floor. Jumping down, Titus felt the loose rock shift and slip under his feet. Jayme actually went down on her hands and knees, unable to keep her balance, while Bobbie Ray hung on to the stone lip they had just jumped over, staring up open-mouthed at the dramatic long, hanging ceiling that dripped continuously, the fat drops sparkling like rainbow stars under their hand lights.

"Look up here!" Jayme called, halfway up the gentle slope of the talus incline. "I think the ceiling fell in back here."

"It looks like the roof sank until it ran into the ground," Bobbie Ray agreed, swatting at the elusive, fat drops that bombed them from above.

They climbed the shifting slope to the point where the ground and ceiling met. Rounded debris constantly moved under their hands and knees. Titus examined some of the bits and was surprised to see elongated pieces as well as the more traditional "pearls."

"Why aren't there any stalactites in this cavern?" Jayme asked, standing in the last possible space at the upper end. A dense curtain of drops speckled the air in front of them.

"If there's too much water, there's no time for the sediment to form between each drop," Titus explained.

"That's what makes the cave pearls—the sediment forms as they're polished and agitated by the water."

"I think they're beautiful," Jayme said, gathering a few in her hand.

Titus squatted down next to her in a relatively drip-free zone. He aimed his tricorder at one of the elongated pearls. "This is bone! Human bone!"

Bobbie Ray immediately dropped his pearls, absently rubbing his hands on his coveralls as he looked at the tricorder readings. "You're right. They're ancient!"

Jayme was also hanging over his arm, trying to see. "Give me a second," he ordered, keying in the commands. "Somewhere between twelve and fifteen thousand years old!"

"That's when humans first moved onto this continent," Jayme breathed, gently cupping her pearls in her palms. "They must have used these caves as shelter or storage. This is amazing!"

Titus hardly had a chance to savor their find before Bobbie Ray muttered, "Uh-oh! I think we've got trouble."

The Rex was staring back at the hole they had climbed up. Water was welling up and pouring over the low lip that held back the piles of cave pearls. It made a rushing sound as it disappeared into the ground.

"What's happening?!" Bobbie Ray cried in true panic. "How are we going to get out?"

Jayme dipped her fingers in the water and stuck them in her mouth. "Salty. That's what I was afraid of. The tide must be rising."

They both turned to look at Titus, mutely demanding that he do something. He knew he probably looked as panicked as Bobbie Ray. "The tide?"

"Yes, the tide's coming in," Jayme repeated, frantically scrambling through the cave pearls to the wall, examining it with her hand light. "I don't see a high-water mark anywhere. Could it . . . Is it possible . . ."

"You mean this whole cave gets filled with water?" Bobbie Ray asked in a high voice.

Titus could only shake his head. "I don't know! We don't have oceans on Antaranan!"

"What!" Jayme shrieked. "You brought us in here and you didn't know what you were doing?"

"I'm going in," Titus said, suddenly feeling much calmer, knowing that he had to take control. He'd gotten them into this mess.

"You'll drown!" Jayme cried out. "That tunnel we came down—it's lower than this cave. It must be filled with water too!"

Titus swallowed, remembering how long the tunnel was. "We may not have oceans on Antaranan, but that doesn't mean we didn't have water. I'm a good swimmer."

"I'm not!" Bobbie Ray wailed, trying to shake the water from the fur on his hands. He was shivering and wet through.

"Get up to the top," Titus ordered. "I'll be back with help."

The other two cadets reluctantly retreated as he flung gear from his pouch—water flask, extra rope—leaving only the necessities with enough room left to wedge his jet-boots in.

Standing hip deep in the hole, wincing from the biting cold water, he glanced back up at the cadets. "Hang tight!"

They didn't look reassured.

Taking a deep breath, he ducked under the water. Immediately he knew it wouldn't work. The surge of water welling up carried him back to the surface.

As he broke into the air again, he was saying, "All right! It's all right! I've got an idea."

He quickly removed the jet-boots from his pouch and strapped them on. Water was nearing his waist now. He didn't care if it killed him, he wasn't going to give up this time.

Diving down headfirst, he turned on the boots. The jets churned the water and almost drove him into the rock wall, but he eased off the power and used his hands to guide him around the jag in the tunnel. Underwater, even with the hand light he could hardly see, so he groped his way down, feeling the scrape of rocks against his coveralls as the boots propelled him through the water.

Everything was getting dark and hazy, and his chest seemed ready to burst. Titus wasn't sure he was going to make it to the vertical shaft.

* * *

Jayme felt sorry for Bobbie Ray, huddled next to her at the top of the talus slope. "Maybe it won't reach this far," she offered.

Bobbie Ray was wiping at his fur with the fleshy palm of one hand, smoothing and smoothing it, pressing all the water out. Then he would twitch and shake, making the damp hair stand out again. Then he would pick another patch and begin the whole process over again. It seemed more like a nervous reaction than an effort to dry himself.

"Do you think he drowned yet?" Bobbie Ray asked, unable to meet her eyes.

"Umm," she murmured. "By now, he either drowned or got out alive."

"Are you going to try it?" Bobbie Ray asked.

Jayme wasn't aware that her calculating glances at the hole had been that obvious. "I'll try it before I drown in here."

Bobbie Ray went back to stroking his fur, concentrating on every swipe.

"I'll help you," she assured him.

"That won't do any good. I could barely pass the Starfleet swimming requirements. And you don't know how hard that was for me."

Jayme silently patted his knee. She wasn't sure she could make it, but every bit of her mind and body was focused on that hole, ready to dive through the water and turn on her jet-boots just like Titus. Even if it did kill her. Because that was better than sitting here until the water rose up around her chin.

"I just wish I knew if he made it," she murmured.

"Wait a few more minutes. Maybe he'll come back."

They both stared at the hole.

The shaft was full of water too. Titus desperately revved the boots, aiming straight up, his hand clenched on the control so tightly that even if he drowned he knew he would surface.

When he thought he was passing out, he broke into air. The shower of water that rose with him, and his surge in speed left him gasping and laughing and, when he finally could, crying out in relief. Arrowing up, he raised both arms, trying to pick up more speed, thinking about Jayme and Bobbie Ray back in that death trap.

He was going so fast that the opening approached before he realized it. Braking, he hit the ceiling and bounced down, managing to twist in midair in order to land on the floor of the access entrance.

Still panting and gasping, almost hysterical with his near miss, he rolled over in the dirt, trying to wipe the muddy dust that settled on his face and eyes. When he could finally see, Starsa, Moll Enor and Nev Reoh were several meters away, standing in the access room staring at him.

"What happened to you!" Moll Enor demanded.

"What are you doing here?" Titus said at the same time.

Starsa raised one hand slightly, blinking in amazement at his dramatic appearance. "I listened outside your door the other night, and I heard you planning to come down to the caves without me—"

"You what!" Titus interrupted, wishing he could box her ears. "I should report you—"

"I saw the hole filling with water," Starsa retorted, "and my tricorder said you were down there."

"We beamed over because we were afraid you were in trouble," Moll Enor added.

"We are!" Titus forgot about Starsa's gross invasion of privacy—just one of many—seeing only the heavy packs Nev Reoh was sitting on. "Jayme and Bobbie Ray are trapped in a cavern down below. The tide's coming in and it's filling the tunnels!"

Look for STAR TREK Fiction from Pocket Books

Star Trek®: The Original Series

Star Trek: The Next Generation®

Star Trek: Deep Space Nine®

The Search • Diane Carey
Warped • K. W. Jeter
The Way of the Warrior • Diane Carey
Star Trek: Klingon • Dean W. Smith & Kristine K. Rusch
Trials and Tribble-ations • Diane Carey

#1 *Emissary* • J. M. Dillard
#2 *The Siege* • Peter David
#3 *Bloodletter* • K. W. Jeter
#4 *The Big Game* • Sandy Schofield
#5 *Fallen Heroes* • Dafydd ab Hugh
#6 *Betrayal* • Lois Tilton
#7 *Warchild* • Esther Friesner
#8 *Antimatter* • John Vornholt
#9 *Proud Helios* • Melissa Scott
#10 *Valhalla* • Nathan Archer
#11 *Devil in the Sky* • Greg Cox & John Gregory Betancourt
#12 *The Laertian Gamble* • Robert Sheckley
#13 *Station Rage* • Diane Carey
#14 *The Long Night* • Dean W. Smith & Kristine K. Rusch
#15 *Objective: Bajor* • John Peel
#16 *Invasion #3: Time's Enemy* • L. A. Graf
#17 *The Heart of the Warrior* • John Gregory Betancourt
#18 *Saratoga* • Michael Jan Friedman
#19 *The Tempest* • Susan Wright
#20 *Wrath of the Prophets* • P. David, M. J. Friedman, R. Greenberger
#21 *Trial by Error* • Mark Garland

Star Trek: Voyager®

Flashback • Diane Carey
Mosaic • Jeri Taylor

#1 *Caretaker* • L. A. Graf
#2 *The Escape* • Dean W. Smith & Kristine K. Rusch
#3 *Ragnarok* • Nathan Archer
#4 *Violations* • Susan Wright
#5 *Incident at Arbuk* • John Greggory Betancourt
#6 *The Murdered Sun* • Christie Golden
#7 *Ghost of a Chance* • Mark A. Garland & Charles G. McGraw
#8 *Cybersong* • S. N. Lewitt
#9 *Invasion #4: The Final Fury* • Dafydd ab Hugh
#10 *Bless the Beasts* • Karen Haber
#11 *The Garden* • Melissa Scott
#12 *Chrysalis* • David Niall Wilson
#13 *The Black Shore* • Greg Cox
#14 *Marooned* • Christie Golden
#15 *Echoes* • Dean W. Smith & Kristine K. Rusch

Star Trek®: New Frontier

#1 *House of Cards* • Peter David
#2 *Into the Void* • Peter David
#3 *The Two-Front War* • Peter David
#4 *End Game* • Peter David

Star Trek®: Day of Honor

Book One: *Ancient Blood* • Diane Carey
Book Two: *Armageddon Sky* • L. A. Graf
Book Three: *Her Klingon Soul* • Michael Jan Friedman
Book Four: *Treaty's Law* • Dean W. Smith & Kristine K. Rusch